THE STAR LORD

By
BOYD ELLANBY

I0616784

ARMCHAIR FICTION
PO Box 4369, Medford, Oregon 97504

*For more information about Armchair Books and products, visit our
website at...*

www.armchairfiction.com

Or email us at...

armchairfiction@yahoo.com

THE TITANIC IN OUTER SPACE!

To some passengers the maiden voyage of a starship was nothing more than a pleasure cruise, to others it meant the grand hope for a new life on some far off new world. But for one interstellar tycoon it was the gamble of a lifetime—a gamble that absolutely couldn't be lost. Only the Captain of "The Star Lord" himself knew of the true danger that faced every person on aboard that ill-fated space vessel.

Come join the crew and passengers of The Star Lord. This magnificent starship is about to undertake a white-knuckle adventure that pits man's overt need for survival against his latent desire to do the right thing.

FOR A COMPLETE SECOND NOVEL, TURN TO PAGE 71

CAST OF CHARACTERS

CAPTAIN EVANS

An honorable space veteran, but does he have the experience and backbone to bring his ship and passengers safely to port?

DR. ALAN CHASE

He was looking for a new lease on life and moving to a radiation free planet may be just what the doctor ordered.

BURL JASPERSON

Chairman of the Board of a lavish starship. His blind ambition was to break records and gain fame, no matter what the cost.

WILSON LARRABEE

This trip on the Star Lord was to honor his dead wife, but little did he know the explosive fate that awaited him.

TANYA TAGANOVA

This beautiful female celebrity had a heart of gold, but would she have the courage to make it through a bumpy ride on a starship?

TOM AND DOROTHY HALL

This newlywed couple decided to take their honeymoon on board a starship; destination…unknown.

CHAPTER ONE

THE *Star Lord* waited, poised for her maiden voyage. The gigantic silvery spindle, still cradled in its scaffoldings, towered upwards against the artificial sky of Satellite Y.

The passengers were beginning to come on board before Captain Josiah Evans had finished checking the reports of his responsible officers. The ship was ready for space, now, and there was nothing more he could do until takeoff. With long, deliberate steps he walked to his cabin, closed the door, and in the privacy he had come to regard as the greatest luxury life had to offer him, he sank into his chair and reached for the post-bag which had been delivered by the morning's rocket ferry from earth.

There were no personal letters for him. He rarely received any and never really expected any, for his career had always been more important to him than personalities. Shoving aside the official documents, he picked up the small brown parcel, slit the pliofilm covering with his pocket knife, and inspected the red leather cover with its simple title: *Ley's Rockets and Space Ships*. At the bottom of the cover was a date: May 1, 2421, Volume 456. In the nearly five hundred years since the publication of Volume one, which listed all the earth's rocket ships on half of one page, the annual edition of this book, regularly edited and brought up to date, had become the spaceman's bible.

Captain Evans was annoyed to find that his hands were shaking as he leafed through the pages, and he paused a few seconds, trying to control his excitement. His black hair had begun to turn gray above his ears, and there were a few white hairs in his bushy eyebrows. But a healthy pink glowed under the skin of his well-fleshed cheeks, and the jut of his chin showed the confidence of one used to receiving immediate, unquestioning obedience. When his long fingers had stopped their trembling, he found the entry he had been looking for, and a triumphant smile lighted his heavy features as he settled deeper in his chair and read the first paragraph.

THE STAR LORD

By

Boyd Ellanby

To some passengers a maiden voyage was a
pleasure cruise; to others it meant a hope for
new life. Only the Captain knew of its danger!

"*Star Lord: newest model in space-ships of the famed Star Line.   Vital
Statistics: Construction begun February 2418, on Satellite Y.   Christened,
October 2420.   Maiden voyage to Almazin III scheduled spring, 2421.*"

He looked up at the diagram of the ship, which hung on the

wall at his right, then, glanced at the zodiometer on his desk. May 3, late spring.

"Powered by twenty-four total conversion Piles. Passenger capacity 1250. Crew and maintenance 250. Six life boats, capacity 1500. Captain: Josiah Evans."

His throat swelling, he was almost choked with pride as he read the final Statistic. This, he thought was the climax of his career, the place he had been working towards all his life. It had been a long road from his lonely boyhood in a Kansas orphanage, to Captain of the earth's finest spaceship.

The *Star Lord* was the perfection of modern space craft, the creation of the earth's most skilled designers and builders, the largest ship ever launched. Protected by every safety device the ingenuity of man had been able to contrive, she was a palace to glide among the stars.

His heart beat more rapidly as he read the next section.

"Prediction: her maiden voyage will break all previous speed records, and regain for her backers the coveted Blue Ribbon, lost ten years ago to the Light

Lines."

No question of that, he thought. No faster ship had ever been built. But he frowned as he read the final paragraph:

"*Sidelights: Reviving a long obsolete custom, certain astrologers in London have cast the horoscope of the Star Lord and pronounced the auguries to be unfavorable. This verdict, plus the incident at the christening, has caused some head-shaking among the superstitions fringe, and some twittering about 'cosmic arrogance'. But few of the lords of the earth, we imagine, will therefore feel impelled to cancel their passages on this veritable Lord of the Stars.*"

EVANS remembered that christening. High in the scaffolding he had stood on the platform with the christening party; the Secretary of Interstellar Commerce, the Ambassador from Almazin III, the Governor of Satellite Y, and President and Mrs. Laurier of Earth.

Swaying gently in the still air, the traditional bottle of champagne hung before them, suspended at the end of a long ribbon. Mrs. Laurier's eyes were shining, her cheeks flushed, as she looked at her husband for a signal. At his smile and nod she had said in a high clear voice, "I christen thee *Star Lord!*" and then reached out to grasp the bottle. Before she could touch it, somewhere above them the slender ribbon broke.

The bottle fell like a stone, plummeted straight down and crashed into a million fragments on the floor of the satellite.

An instant's shocked silence, and then a roar of voices surged up from the crowds watching below. Mrs. Laurier had put her hand to her mouth, and shivered.

"What a dreadful thing!" she whispered. "Does that mean bad luck?"

President Laurier had frowned at her, but the Secretary of Interstellar Commerce had laughed.

"Don't be alarmed, Mrs. Laurier. There is no such thing as luck. Even without a bath of champagne, this magnificent vessel will prove that man is certainly master of the universe. She begins her life well and truly named."

The Star Line ought to abandon that silly custom of christening a new ship, thought Captain Evans. It was an archaic ceremony, utterly irrational, a foolish relic of a primitive world in which people had been so uncertain of their machines that they had had to depend on luck, and to beg good fortune of unpredictable gods.

Taking up *Ley's Space Ships* again, he began fondly to reread the page, when there was a knock at the door and a crewman entered.

"Mr. Jasperson to see you, sir."

The Captain stared, a tiny muscle in his cheek quivering.

"You know I'm not to be disturbed until after takeoff, Stacey."

"Yes, sir. But Mr. Jasperson insisted. He says he knows those rules don't apply to *him*."

Evans closed the book, laid it on his desk, and stood up. He leaned forward and spoke softly.

"Tell Mr. Jasperson—"

"Tell him what, Josiah?" boomed a voice from the opening door. "You can tell me yourself now."

Burl Jasperson was a portly little man with legs too short for his bulging body, and clothes that were too tight. His head was bald except for a fringe above the ears, and he might have been a comical figure but for the icy blue eyes that probed from under the dome of his forehead.

"What have you got to tell me? You're quite right not to let the ragtag and bobtail bother you at a time like this, but I know your old friend Burl Jasperson is always welcome."

With scarcely a pause, the Captain extended his hand.

"How are you, Burl? Won't you come in? I hope the Purser has taken care of you properly?"

"I'm comfortable enough, thanks, and I'm looking forward to the trip. It's odd, come to think of it, that though I've been Chairman of the board of directors, and have spent some thirty years managing a fleet of space liners, yet I've never before made a trip myself. I don't like crowds of people, for one thing, and then I've been busy."

"What made you decide to go along on this one?"

REACHING across the table, Jasperson picked up the silver carafe and poured himself a glass of water.

"Ah! Nothing like a drink of cold water! The fact is, I wanted to check up on things, make notes of possible improvements in the Star Line's service, and sample passenger reactions. Then too, I'll have the satisfaction of being present on the trip, which will establish the Line's supremacy, once and for all. This crossing will make history. It means everything to us, Josiah. You know we're counting on you to break the record. We want to win back the Blue Ribbon, and we expect you to manage it for us."

"I shall do my best."

"That's the spirit I like to see. Full speed ahead!"

"Certainly—consistent with safety."

"Consistent with *reasonable* safety, of course. I know you won't let yourself be taken in by all this nonsense about the imaginary dangers of hyperspace."

"What do you mean?"

"All this nonsense about the Thakura Ripples! But then, of course you're a sensible man or we wouldn't have hired you, and I'm sure you agree with me that the *Star Lord* can deal with anything that hyperspace has to offer."

Jasperson adjusted the set of his jacket over his plump stomach while he waited for an answer, and Captain Evans stared at him.

"Is that why you're wearing a pistol?" he said dryly. "To help the ship fight her battles?"

"This?" His face reddened as he patted his bulging pockets. "Oh, it's just a habit. I don't like being without protection; I always wear a gun in one pocket and my recorder in the other."

"You'll scarcely be in any danger on the ship, Burl. Better leave it in your cabin."

"All right. But about the Ripples—you aren't going to take them seriously, are you?"

"I wish you'd be a little more frank, Mr. Chairman. Has the Star Line suddenly lost confidence in me?"

"No, no, nothing of the sort! We've every confidence in you, of course. But I've been hearing rumors, hints that we may have to make a slow crossing, and I've been wondering. But then, I'm sure that a man of your intelligence doesn't take the Ripples any more seriously than I do."

"I don't know what gossip you have been hearing," said the Captain, hesitantly. " 'Ripples' is probably a very inaccurate and inadequate name for the phenomenon. Thakura might equally well have called them rapids, falls, bumps, spaces, holes, or discontinuities."

"Then why did he choose to call them Ripples?"

"Probably because he didn't know exactly what they are. The whole problem is a very complicated, one."

"Complicated nonsense, I call it. Well, we won't quarrel, my dear Josiah, but don't let them hold us back. Remember, we're out to break all records!"

CHAPTER TWO

UNDER the artificial sky, crowds of people streamed into the administration building of Satellite Y. The jumping-off place for all rockets and ships going to and from the stars, Y-port was a world of its own, dedicated to only one purpose, the launching and berthing of ships.

It was a quiet and orderly place as a rule, and its small permanent colony of workmen and officials lived a spartan existence except for their yearly vacations on Earth. But today it seemed as if half the earth's people, friends and relatives of the passengers, had chosen to make the port a holiday spot of their own, to help celebrate the launching of the *Star Lord* on her maiden voyage. The rocket ferry between Y-port and Earth had had to triple its number of runs in the past week, and this morning's rocket had brought in the last of the passengers for Almazin III.

Alan Chase trudged wearily along with the crowd entering the building, trying to close his ears to the hundreds of chattering voices. He was tall and very thin, and his white skin clothed his bones like brittle paper. Walking was an effort, and he tried to move with an even step so he would not have to gasp for breath as he moved slowly forward with the line before the Customs desk. In his weakness, the gaiety around him seemed artificial, and the noise of voices was unendurable.

Just ahead of him in line was a young man in an obviously new suit; the pretty girl holding to his arm still had a few grains of rice shining in her hair.

"That will be all," said the Inspector. "I hope you and Mrs. Hall have a very happy honeymoon. Next!"

He gritted his teeth to stop his trembling as the Inspector

reached for the passport, glanced at a notation, then looked up.

"I'll have to ask you to step in and see Dr. Willoughby, our ship's doctor. It will only take a moment, Dr. Chase."

"But I'm not infectious!"

"But there seems to be some question of fitness. In cases like yours the Star Line likes to have a final check, just to make sure you'll be able to stand the trip. We're responsible, after all. Last door on my right."

Close to exhaustion, Alan walked down the hall to the last door and stepped inside. A healthy, rugged man with prominent black eyes looked at him with a speculative glance.

"And what can I do for you?" Holding out, his passport, Alan sank down into a chair, glad of a chance to rest, while Dr. Willoughby studied the document, then looked up, the routine smile wiped off his face.

"Well! So you're Dr. Alan Chase. I've been much interested in the papers you've been publishing recently. But this is bad news, Dr. Chase. I suppose you had an independent check on the diagnosis?"

"Not even one of our freshmen could have missed it, but I had it confirmed by Simmons and von Kramm."

"Then there's no question. How did you pick it up, doctor? Neosarcoma is still rather a rare disease, and it's not supposed to be very infectious."

Alan tried to speak casually, although just looking at the rugged good health of the man opposite him made him feel weaker.

"No, it's not very infectious. But after medical school, I went into research instead of practice, and I worked on neosarcoma for nearly five years, trying to devise a competitive chemical antagonist. Then, as used to happen so often in the old days, I finally picked it up myself—a lab infection."

THE older man nodded. "Well, you're doing the right thing now in going to Almazin III. I've made some study of the disease myself, as you may know, and I entirely agree with your theory that it is caused by a virus, and kept active by radiation. Since the atomic wars, the increased radioactivity of the earth undoubtedly stimulates mitosis of the malignant cells. It feeds the disease, and kills the man. But on a planet like Almazin III where the radiation index is close to zero, the mitosis of the sarcoma cells stops abruptly, virus or no virus."

"I'm glad to hear that," said Alan. "I've read some of your papers on the subject, and the evidence sounds pretty convincing."

"It's conclusive. If you arrive in time you've nothing to worry about. I've seen men as badly off as you, with malignant growths well advanced, who migrated to Almazin III and recovered within a year. Without radioactivity to maintain it, the disease seems to be arrested immediately, and if the tissue damage has not gone too far, the tumor regresses and eventually disappears. Once you're cured, you can come back to earth and take up your work where you left off. Well, let's check you over."

The examination was brief. Dr. Willoughby initialed the passport, and offered his hand.

"You should stand the trip all right. But I'm glad you didn't put it off any longer than you did. Another two months of earth's emanations, and I'm afraid I couldn't have certified you. It's lucky for you that the *Star Lord* is the fastest ship in space. That's all, Dr. Chase. I'll be seeing you on board."

In the swiftly moving elevator cage Alan ascended the slender pylon to the boarding platform, crowded by a group of quarreling children in charge of an indifferent nursemaid.

The Chief Steward, rustling in starched whites, stepped forward at the port, clicked his heels, and curved his thin lips into a smile.

"How do you do, sir. The Star Line wishes you a happy voyage. Will you be kind enough to choose?"

Following his nod, Alan looked down at the silver tray extended for his inspection, and then stepped back as a heavy perfume assaulted his nostrils.

"What are those?"

"Carnations, sir, for the gentlemen's coats, and rose corsages for the ladies' gowns. Compliments of the Star Line."

"But they're white!"

"Yes, sir. The white flowers, the only kind we are able to grow in Y-port, are symbols of the white light of the stars, we like to think."

"What idiot gave the Star Line that idea?" said Dr. Chase. "You know stars are all colors—white, green, yellow, blue, and even red. But white carnations are a symbol of death."

Steward Davis lowered his tray. "Then you don't care to wear one, sir?"

"Not until I have to," said Alan. "Now please call some one to show me my cabin."

"Band playing in the lounge, sir. Tea is being served in the Moon Room, and the Bar is open until just before takeoff."

"Thanks, but I've been ill. I just want to find my cabin."

"Boy!" called Steward Davis. "Show this gentleman to 31Q."

ALAN followed the pageboy through a complex of corridors, ascending spirals of stairs, down a hall, and to the door of Cabin 31Q. The boy threw open the door and Alan stepped in, then halted in shocked disbelief at sight of a white-haired old man who was just lifting a shirt from an opened suitcase.

"I am Dr. Chase. Isn't this Cabin 31Q?"

The old man beamed, his pink skin breaking into a thousand tiny wrinkles. "That's right. 31Q it is."

"Then what are you doing here?"

"Have you no powers of observation? Unpacking, of course. I was assigned to this cabin."

Staggering over to a bunk, Alan sagged back against the wall. He lifted his tired eyelids and stared at the sprightly old gentleman.

"But I was promised a cabin by myself!"

The old man looked distressed. "I'm very sorry, young man. I, too, hoped to have a cabin to myself. I learned only a few minutes ago that I was to be quartered with another passenger—evidently you. Somebody made a mistake, there's no question of that, but the Purser tells me that every bit of space is occupied, and no other arrangements can be made. Unless you want to postpone your voyage, and follow in a later ship?"

"No," said Alan. His voice had sunk to a whisper. "No, I can't do that."

"Then we'll have to make the best of it, young man," he said, picking up a pile of handkerchiefs and putting them in the drawer he had pulled out from the wall.

"Let me introduce myself. I am Wilson Larrabee—teacher, or

student, according to the point of view. Some years of my life I've spent being a professor of this or that at various universities, and the other years I've spent in travel. Whenever the bank account gets low, I offer my knowledge to the nearest university, and stay there until I pile up enough credits so I can travel again."

"Sounds a lonely sort of life, with no roots anywhere."

"Oh, no! My wife loved traveling as much as I do, and wherever she was, was home." He paused, his hand arrested in the act of hanging up his last necktie, and for a moment his face was somber. Then he finished hanging up the tie, gave it a little pat, and continued cheerfully.

"We saw most of the world, in the fifty years we had together. The last trip she made with me, out to the Moon and back, was in some ways the pleasantest of all. After we returned, we started planning and saving and dreaming of making one last grand tour outside the solar system. And then—well, she was more than seventy, and I try to think that she isn't really dead, that she just started the last tour a little ahead of me. That's why I'm making this jaunt now, the one we planned on the *Star Lord*. Yes…it's certainly lonely, in a way, but she wouldn't have wanted me to give up and just stay at home, just because I had to go on alone."

GLANCING at Alan's bent head, Professor Larrabee abruptly banged shut the lid of his empty suitcase and shoved it into the conveyor port in the wall to shoot it down to Luggage. Then he straightened up and rumpled his white hair.

"That's done, young man. Will you join me in the Bar for a space-cap?"

"Sorry, sir. I'm very tired. I just want to rest and be quiet."

"But a frothed whiskey would help you to relax. Come along, and let me buy you a final drink before we take off for eternity."

Alan noticed with distaste the white carnation in the coat lapel of his companion. "I hardly like to think of this trip as being syn- onymous with eternity," he said. "You sound as though you didn't expect to come back."

"Do I? Perhaps I made an unfortunate choice of words. But do you believe in premonitions, Dr. Chase?"

"No. All premonitions stem from indigestion."

"No doubt you are right. But from the moment of boarding this ship I have been haunted by the memory of an extremely vivid story I once read."

"What kind of a story?"

"Oh, it was a scientific romance, one of those impossible flights of fancy they used to publish in my boyhood, about the marvels of future science. This was in the days before we had got outside the solar system, but I still remember the tale, for it was about a space-ship which was wrecked on its first voyage."

"But there've been hundreds of other such stories! Why should this particular one be bothering you now?"

"Well, you see," said the professor apologetically, "it's because of the name. The coincidence of names. This other ship, the one in the story—it was called the *Star Lord.*"

"I wouldn't let that worry me. Surely it's a logical name for a spaceship?"

Professor Larrabee laughed. "Logical, and perhaps a trifle pre-sumptuous. But I'm sure it's a meaningless coincidence, my boy. Now how about that drink?"

Alan shook his head.

"Come, Dr. Chase. Allow me the liberties of an old man. You're obviously ill, you want to crawl into a hole and pull the hole in after you, and enjoy the deadly luxury of feeling sorry for yourself. But we can't do that sort of thing. Let me prescribe for you."

With an effort, Alan smiled. "All right, Professor. I usually do the prescribing myself, but right now I'm too tired to argue. I'll accept a space-cap with pleasure." He swallowed a panedol tablet to ease his pain, then pulled himself up.

"That's the spirit, my boy! We will drink to the *Star Lord,* that she may have a happier fate than her namesake."

FIVE minutes before takeoff. The first signal had sounded. The Bar was closed by now, the lounges deserted, and in theory the twelve hundred and fifty passengers were secure in their cabins, waiting for the instantaneous jump into hyperspace.

At the port, Chief Steward Davis leaned against the wall with his tray of wilting flowers, while the Second Officer and two crewmen stood by, waiting for the final signal to close the port.

They were startled by a sudden commotion, a flurry of voices, and turned to see the elevator doors open on the loading platform. A group of laughing people surged forward.

"But I'm late again, darlings!" cried a vibrant voice. "You must let me go now! The ship is waiting just for me, I know. Stop holding me!"

"But we don't want to lose you!" called a man.

"You know I'll be back in the fall."

"But the theater can't get along without you!"

"But it won't be forever, darling!"

Still laughing, Tanya Taganova pulled away from her teasing friends. She was a tall woman, very slender; very beautiful, with her burnished auburn hair and warm brown eyes. She walked forward with the swift precision of a dancer, in her flared gown of stiff green satin, whose ruff stood out about her slender neck to frame a regal head. In her arms she carried an enormous sheaf of red roses.

With light steps she entered the port, then turned to wave at her friends and give them a last challenging smile.

The Second Officer asked sharply, "Are you a passenger, Madame? You're rather late."

"And I tried *so* hard to be on time for once in my life! I'm very sorry, lieutenant!"

"Quite all right, Madame. You got here in time, and that's what counts. But you'll have to hurry to get to your cabin before take-off."

"Wait!" said Steward Davis. His long face had come to life as he looked at her admiringly and extended his tray of flowers.

"White roses? For me?" she said.

"Yes, Madame. Compliments of the Star Line."

Turning her head, she moved away. "Thank you; but I'm not ready to wear white roses, yet. It's not that they're not lovely, but—" she raised her arms, burdened with their scented blooms, "you see that I already have so many flowers, and the red rose is still for the living!"

Davis banged his tray to the floor and shoved it aside with his foot.

"All right, Madame. Now we'll have to hurry. We'll have to run!"

A FINAL bell rang, a final, light flashed.

On the floor below the ship, the crowds of relatives and wistful stay-at-homes gazed up at the beautiful metal creation, poised on its slender fins, nose pointed towards the opened dome.

A vibration began, a gentle, barely perceptible shuddering of the ground which increased in frequency. It beat through the floor, into their feet, until their whole bodies quivered with the racing pulse that grew faster, faster, as the twenty-four total conversion Piles in the ship released their power. Then, as the people watched, between one instant and the next, the ship vanished. In the blink of an eyelid she had shifted to hyperspace.

The *Star Lord* had begun her maiden voyage.

CHAPTER THREE

By the second day out, most of the passengers felt completely at home. The ship had become a separate world, and the routines they had left behind them on earth, and the various routines they would take up again some six weeks from now on Almazin III seemed equally remote and, improbable. Life on the *Star Lord* was the only reality.

She moved through the uncharted realms of hyperspace, travelling in one hour's time as measured by earth watches, more than twenty light years distance, if measured in the units of real space. The ship itself was quiet. The vibration of the takeoff had ended in a moment, and now the passengers could hear no noise and hum of motors, could feel no motion against swelling waves, no battering against a barrier of uneven air. The artificial gravity induced a sense of security as absolute as though the ship were resting on living rock.

Although most of the cabins were small, they were cleverly designed to provide the maximum of comfort, even the least expensive of them. For the very wealthy, the rulers of the galaxy's finance, the owners of the galaxy's industries, the makers of the galaxy's entertainment, there were the luxury cabins. The floors glowed with the soft reds of oriental rugs, the lounge chairs were upholstered in fabrics gleaming with gold thread. Cream-colored satin curtains fluttered in an artificial breeze at the simulated windows, and on the walls hung tranquil landscapes in dull gold frames. To those who had engaged them, the ornate cabins seemed only appropriate to their own eminent positions in life.

Delicious meals were served three times a day in the several dining rooms, the softly lighted Bar was never closed, and every day three theaters offered a varied program of stereo-dramas. There was even—the most marvelous, daring, expensive luxury of all—a swimming pool. The pool was small, and was open only to the first cabin passengers, but the fact that a ship travelling to a distant solar system could afford room enough for a pool, and extra weight for the water needed to fill it, seemed evidence that man had achieved a complete conquest of the inconveniences of space travel.

One luxury, however, freely accessible to even the poorest sheep herder on earth, was denied the passengers of the *Star Lord.*

They could not see the stars. They could not see the sky.

The ship had portholes, of course, and observation rooms which could be opened if at any time she cruised in normal space, but the ports and observation windows were closed now, for there was nothing to see. The ship was surrounded by blackness; the impenetrable, unknowable blackness of hyperspace, but this black emptiness did not frighten the passengers because they never bothered to think about it.

But the builders of the ship had designed it so that even the simple pleasure of looking at a friendly sky should not be denied its passengers. An artificial day and night of the appropriate length was maintained by the dimming and brightening of lights, and the main lounges were bounded with special walls, which looked like windows, through which could be glimpsed bright summer days, fleecy clouds drifting over a blue sky, and, in the evenings, soft starlight.

EVERY passenger should have been soothed into contentment by these devices, but by the end of the first week, Burl Jasperson was restless.

He hated to sit still, and the hours and the days seemed endless. His bald head and portly body were a familiar sight as he roamed the ship, inspecting every detail as though it were his personal responsibility. Once a day he called on Captain Evans to check on the progress of the *Star Lord*, once a day he chafed under the cold courtesy of the Captain's manner, and then wandered on. In his jacket he wore his pocket recorder, and he was momentarily cheered whenever he found an excuse for making a memorandum:

"Chairs in lounge should be two centimeters lower. Sell Deutonium shares. How about monogrammed linens for the first cabins? Install gymnasium?"

As he walked, he murmured these thoughts to his recorder, and each night his meek and colorless secretary sat up late to transcribe them into the locked notebook which was his special charge, after Jasperson had taken his sleeping pills and crawled into bed.

On the evening of the eighth night out, Burl Jasperson wandered into the Bar, and drummed his pudgy fingers on the table as he waited to give his order.

"A glass of ice water, and a Moon Fizz. And be sure you make it with genuine absinthe. You fellows seem to think you can get away with making it with '*arak*, and your customers won't know the difference. Well, just remember I'm one customer that does, and I want *real* absinthe."

"Yes, sir, Mr. Jasperson," said the Bar steward.

Turning restlessly in his chair, Burl let his eyes stop on the white-haired old gentleman beside him, happily consuming a brandy and soda. After a moment's inspection, he stuck out his hand confidently.

"My name's Jasperson. Everything all right? Enjoying the trip?"

The pink skin wrinkled in amusement.

"I am Wilson Larrabee. Everything's fine, thank you, except that the ship is almost too luxurious for a man of my background. A professor's salary does not often permit him indulgences of this kind."

"You a professor? Of what?"

"Various things at various times. Philosophy, physics, Elizabethan drama, history of science—"

"Myself, I never could understand why a sensible man would go into that business. No money. No prestige. Never doing anything, just reading and thinking."

"Every man to his taste," said Larrabee.

"Yes, within limits. But the things some of you professors think up! Most of the ideas do more harm than good, scaring people to death, hurting business. You'd think they ought to have more sense of responsibility!"

He tasted his drink, then nodded knowingly at the bartender. "This is something like! *Real* absinthe."

Professor Larrabee studied his companion. "I can hardly suppose, Mr. Jasperson, that you hold professors responsible for all the ills of the world. And yet you seem disturbed. Did you have something in particular in mind?"

"Yes. The Thakura Ripples!"

AMUSEMENT vanished from the professor's eyes. "What about them?"

"Why are people so afraid of them? As far as I can see, they're just a piece of nonsense thought up by a dreamy-eyed physics professor, and he hypnotized people into believing in them. But as I was telling Captain Evans last night, they've never been seen, never been measured, and there's nothing at all to prove that they have any existence outside the mind of a madman. And yet people are afraid of them!"

"And just what are the Thakura Ripples?" said Alan Chase, drawing up a chair. "Waiter, I'll have a space-cap."

"Feeling a little better tonight, Alan?" asked his friend.

"Some, thanks. I just had a checkup from Dr. Willoughby, and he thinks I'm more than holding my own. Now go on about the Ripples. Where are they? What do they do?"

"Suit yourself," Jasperson muttered. "If you want to tell ghost stories, go ahead."

"Thank you. The Thakura Ripples, my boy, are an unexplained phenomenon of hyperspace. We do not know what they are—only that they are dangerous."

"But I thought that space was entirely uniform?"

"Alas, no. Not even normal space can be called uniform. It has been known for a long time that variations exist in the density of the interstellar gases. Just why they occur, what pattern they follow, if any, was for many years one of the major unsolved problems confronting astronomers and physicists. Then they learned that these variations in density of the interstellar gases were directly connected with the development of the successive ice ages on the earth, and eventually a study of the collisions and interactions of the various light forces from the stars in the galaxy made the pattern clear. We know, now, that the variations occur only in a certain band of space. They may occur at any given place within that band, but their position is constantly shifting and unpredictable."

"Now you see it, now you don't?" said Alan.

"Exactly. Now it was Thakura's theory that the Ripples are an analogous band of mysterious forces existing in hyperspace. They may be tangible barriers, they may be force barriers, we do not know. But a ship entering this lane *may*
go through it without damage, and by pure chance take a course which misses all these bumps in space. Or, by going slowly and using his instruments to feel his way, a navigator can often sense them ahead, and if he is skillful he may be able to dodge them. But if, in some terrible moment, he smashes head-on against the Thakura Ripples, the conversion Piles, which power his ship, are immediately affected. They begin to heat, perhaps to heat irreversibly, and if they get out of control, they may vaporize. In the last fifty years at least five ships have vanished in this region, and it was Thakura's belief that they were disintegrated on the Ripples."

"But there isn't any evidence!" Jasperson exploded.

"Isn't a demolished space ship evidence?"

"No! It's evidence that something went wrong, certainly, but it doesn't tell us *what* went wrong. I'm not an unreasonable man, professor, I'm a hardheaded business man, and I like to deal with facts."

"I don't have an intimate knowledge of these matters, of course," said Larrabee, "but it was my impression that in the past fifty years since travel in hyperspace became common, several ships have been unaccountably lost."

"Your first figure was right. Five ships have been lost—that much is fact. Why they were lost is still a question. It's my considered opinion that they were lost by human failure; the crewmen let the Piles get hot, and the ships were helpless. In the early days they had to get along with only one or two Piles, and if they went wrong, the ship was done for. But we've changed all that. That's why the *Star Lord* has twenty-four Piles. No matter what happens it's impossible that *all* of them should go bad at once. She can ditch the dangerous Piles and still always have power enough left to make port. One thing is certain, this ship will never be wrecked on the Ripples of a mad scientist's imagination! A phenomenon like the Ripples, is impossible. If it existed, we'd have had some proof of it many years ago."

"But surely you don't mean to imply that if we don't know a fact, it is therefore impossible?"

"Not at all. But you know yourself, Professor Larrabee—you're an educated man—that by this time our physicists understand the universe completely, from A to Z. There are no unexplained phenomena. Thakura is shut up in a madhouse now. In my opinion, he was already insane when he published his theory."

Larrabee was nodding, thoughtfully. "I wonder what makes you so certain of your theory?"

"What theory? I never deal in theories, I'm talking fact."

"Your theory that we have unveiled all the mystery of the universe; how do you know? Every now and then, of course, man lives through a century of such amazing progress that he concludes that nothing remains to be learned. But how can he ever be certain?"

"But we are certain! Most physicists are in agreement now that there hasn't been one single unexplained physical aberration in the past century!"

"Most physicists except Thakura, you mean?"

"But Thakura is insane! We understand all the physical phenomena of the universe."

"Except the Thakura Ripples?"

Jasperson slammed down his glass and stood up, his face red and puffy. "Steward! More ice water! I'm getting tired of those words, professor. Do you think for one, minute I'd have risked my life to come on this trip if I'd thought there was the slightest danger?"

Alan looked up languidly. "You mean you wouldn't mind sending a crew and passengers into danger—as long as you could take care to be safe yourself?"

"Surely you're not afraid, Mr. Jasperson?" said Larrabee.

"No. What is there to he afraid of?" He gulped down his drink. "Nothing can wreck the *Star Lord*."

CHAPTER FOUR

WHEN Dr. Alan Chase woke up next morning and glanced at his wristwatch, he realized that the breakfast hour was nearly over. Professor Larrabee had already left the cabin.

Alan was not hungry. It had been many months since he had really enjoyed an appetite for food, but he got up and began to dress, so that he could perform the duty of eating. But his clothes, he noticed, were beginning to fit a little more snugly. He fastened his belt at a new and previously unused notch, buttoned his jacket, and then performed the ritual he carried out every morning and every evening.

Touching a facet in the ornamentation of his wristwatch, he walked about, geigering the room. Radiation normal, somewhat less than earth's normal, in fact. The twenty-four Piles were well shielded, and if this continued, he should survive the journey in fair shape.

At the door of the dining room he paused, for the entrance was blocked by Steward Davis and the young couple he had noticed the day they left Y-port.

The tall young man with rumpled black hair was arguing, while the pretty girl clung to his arm and watched his face admiringly, as though he were the only man in the world.

"But Steward," said the young man, "Dorothy and I—that is, Mrs. Hall and I—we felt sure we'd be able to have a table by ourselves. We don't want to be unreasonable, it's only that this is our honeymoon, maybe the only time we'll ever get to spend together, really, and we like to eat alone, together, I mean. That's the reason we chose the *Star Lord*, because the advertisements all talked about how big and roomy it was, and how it didn't have to be so miserly with its space as they did in earlier ships. They said you could have privacy, and not have to crowd all together in one stuffy little cabin, the way they used to."

"I'm sorry" Mr. Hall," said the Steward crisply. "We are all proud of the spaciousness of our ship, but not even the *Star Lord* can provide separate tables for everybody who— Oh, *good* morning, Mr. Jasperson! Glad to see you, sir." Turning his back on Tom, he smiled and bowed to the new arrival. "Everything all right, sir?"

"Good morning, Dr. Chase. No nightmares last night? 'Morning Davis. Tell that waiter of mine to be more particular about giving me plenty of ice water. I like plenty of water, and I like it cold."

"Sorry, sir. I'll speak to him at once." He bowed again as Jasperson strode on.

"Then could we—" Tom began. Davis whirled with an impatient frown. "What? Are you still here? Surely I made it clear that there's nothing I can do, Mr. Hall?"

"But couldn't you at least move us to another table?"

"I regret that you are dissatisfied with our arrangements. All table space was allocated before we took off from Y-port."

"But you've put us with such noisy people!" said Tom stubbornly. "They keep talking about how much money they made in deutonium, and they refer to us, right in front of us, as the babes in the woods. They may be rich, but they haven't the manners of a six-year old. We *can't* stay at that table."

"Mr. Hall, I can't waste any more time with you. If all our passengers were to demand special privileges—" He shrugged his shoulders.

DOROTHY Hall whispered shyly, "Ask him, then, what about that man?" and she nodded her head slightly to the right.

"Yes," said Tom. "You say there isn't enough room, but what about that table over there? It's made to seat two, and there's just that one man who eats alone."

Davis glanced over. "Oh, yes. But that's Mr. Jasperson! He likes to be by himself."

"Who's Mr. Jasperson?"

"A very important man."

"And I'm not?"

Alan broke in. "Excuse me, Mr. Hall. I am Dr. Chase. Won't you join my table? Three of the people assigned places there are Almazanians, a diplomatic mission, I think, and they naturally prefer to have their own cuisine in their own cabins, so we have room for three more."

"How about it, Steward," said Tom. "Any objections?"

Shrugging his shoulders, Davis strolled away.

Tom glared at the retreating back. "That guy has the face of a murderer. He can't be decent to anybody with less than a million credits."

Dorothy laughed. "Never mind, Tom. Someday you'll be the most famous lawyer in the Interstellar courts, and maybe you'll get a chance to prosecute him for arson or treason."

Alan led them to the rear of the dining room, where his two table companions were finishing the last sips of their coffee, and lighting the first cigarette of the morning.

"Miss Taganova, may I present Tom and Dorothy Hall, who would like to share our table."

Tanya lifted her beautiful auburn head and smiled a welcome. Professor Larrabee stood up, his pink cheeks crinkling with pleasure as he shook hands with Tom.

"Young people make the best companions," he said, "especially on long journeys."

Alan sat down and reached for the vitamin dispenser. "These particular young people want privacy. They're on their honeymoon, and would hardly shed a tear if all the rest of the world suddenly ceased to exist."

"It's not quite like that, Dr. Chase," said Tom, his face reddening, "but those people at our other table were just out of our class, one way or another. The men talked all the time about their bank accounts, and the women clawed at each other about which one had the biggest house, and the biggest pearls and diamonds and emeralds, until we began to feel smothered in a blanket of credits and diamonds."

"Credits and diamonds must be very nice things to have," said

Tonya. "I've never managed to collect many of either."

"I've nothing against them in themselves," said Tom, "but right now they don't seem to matter very much. We had to wait five long years to be married, five years for me to finish my law training, and for Dorothy to wear out her family's opposition. They didn't want her to throw herself away on a penniless lawyer."

"As if I were a child who didn't know her own mind," said Dorothy. "Well, I wanted Tom, penniless or not; and anyway, in a few years he's going to be the finest lawyer in the Interstellar Courts."

"I hope you'll always be as happy as you are now, children." The professor's eyes were misty as he stood up. "Come, Miss Tanya. Take a stroll with me, and bring back to an old man a brief illusion of youth."

"But you'll never be old!" she said affectionately. "You're still the most fascinating man on the ship."

Like every other man in the room, Alan watched with envious eyes as Tanya took the professor's arm and sauntered to the door, the heavy taffeta skirts of her pearl-gray gown swishing and rustling as she walked.

WITHIN the sealed hulk of the *Star Lord* the twenty-four Piles silently did their work, out of sight, out of the thoughts of the passengers. Driving the ship through the unknowable infinities of hyperspace, they held her quiet, steady, seemingly without motion. They behaved as they were intended to, their temperatures remained docilely within the normal limits of safety, and the ship sped on.

The technicians and maintenance men, the navigators, the nucleonics men, all kept aloof from the social eddies frothing at the center of the ship. They lived in another world, a world of leashed power, in which the trivial pursuits of the passengers were as irrelevant as the twitterings of birds.

In the central tiers occupied by the passengers, each morning the walls of the lounges and dining rooms resumed their daily routine of simulating the panorama of earth's day. Lights glowed into a clear sunrise, brightened into a sunny sky across which light clouds scudded.

Children played in the nurseries, grownups idled through the hours, eating the delicious food, taking a dip in the priceless pool, attending the stereodrams, and playing games. At the cocktail hour, the orchestra played jaunty tunes, old-fashioned polkas, waltzes, mazurkas; at dinner, it shifted to slower, muted melodies, suitable background for high feminine voices, deep male laughter, and the heavy drone of talk.

In the walls, the sun set, twilight crept in, and the stars came out. After the stars had been advancing for several hours, people finished their dancing and card games, walked out of the theaters, had a final drink at the Bar, paused at the bulletin board which detailed the ship's daily progress, and went to bed.

Dr. Alan Chase followed his own routine. Each, morning and each evening he geigered his cabin and found the radiation still below the earth normal. He was surprised to find that he was holding his own, physically, instead of becoming progressively weaker, as he had expected, and he began to feel hopeful that he might quickly regain his health on the inert atmosphere of Almazin III. He was not strong enough, however, to take part in the active games of the passengers, and had not enough energy to try to make friends, except for the people at his dining table—particularly Tanya.

Of all the lovely women on board, he thought Tanya Taganova the loveliest. He knew he was not alone in this, for the arresting planes of her face, the dramatic color of her rustling taffeta gowns, attracted many followers. He would sit in the lounge at night and watch her dancing, and then realize, suddenly, that she had disappeared, long before the evening was over. She was an elusive creature, as unpredictable as a butterfly.

Wandering listlessly about the ship, one afternoon he stepped through the open door of the Library. In the almost empty room he saw the auburn head of Tanya, bent over so as to hide her face and show him only her glowing hair. She raised her head as he approached.

"Are you looking for a book, Dr. Chase?"

"No, I just wondered what was interesting you so much."

SHE shifted her seat, to let him see a large sheet of rough

drawing paper covered with a chalk sketch of a desolate gray marsh over which green waves swirled from the sea, behind them loomed rose-colored granite hills.

"I'm a scene designer, you know. But at home, somehow, I never have time to myself. People will never believe I'm serious, and when I want to get some real work done, I run away on a trip, by myself. Right now I'm sketching out a set for a new stereodrama we're staging next autumn. This particular one is for a melancholy suicide on Venus. I've several more here." She pointed to a scattered heap of drawings.

The soft chime of the library telephone interrupted them. Tanya rose and moved to the desk.

"Yes? Not now, youngster. I'm working. Yes, maybe tomorrow."

Alan had been examining her drawings. "Is this what you do during the hours when you disappear?"

"Usually. Sometimes I drop into the playroom to chat with the children. They're more interesting than their parents, for the most part, and nobody ever seems to pay much attention to them."

"But do you have to work at night, too? When you disappear in the middle of the evening, everybody misses you. The men all watch for you to come back, their wives sigh with relief, and old man Jasperson toddles around and searches the dance floor and bleats, 'Where's Miss Tanya? She was here just a little while ago, and now I can't find her anywhere!'"

"I know. But one dance an evening with him is about all I can stand. I don't really like the man."

"But why? He's a little stupid, but he seems a harmless sort of duck. In a financial deal, of course, I can see that he'd be sharp and ruthless—that's how men like him become millionaires—but he can't knife anybody on shipboard."

Tanya slashed a heavy black line across her drawing, bearing down so hard that she broke the chalk, and threw the pieces to the floor.

"He's a coward! Haven't you ever noticed the way he bullies the waiters? How he patronizes Professor Larrabee, and ignores the young Halls? And to hear him tell it, you'd think only his advice makes it possible for Captain Evans to run the ship! I'm afraid of men like that. They're cowardly and boastful, and in a crisis they are dangerous!"

"What an outburst over a fat little bald-headed man! Aren't you letting your dramatic sense run away with you?"

Laughing, Tanya picked up her chalk and resumed sketching. "Probably, but after all, I earn my living with my imagination."

"Then you aren't just a rich young woman dabbling in the theater?"

"No indeed. If you could see my bank account! No, I'm going to Almazin III to make authentic sketches of the landscape. We may do a show set in that locale, next year."

"I wish I could see some of the shows you stage."

"When we get home, I'll send you a pass."

He did not answer. Suddenly the melancholy Venusian scene she was creating depressed him, as if it had been a reflection of his own barren life.

"Or don't you like the theater, Dr. Chase?"

"It's not that," he said hastily. "Only—" He shrugged his shoulders. "Something about this ship, I suppose. Home seems so very far away."

"Have you felt that too? I've had the feeling, sometimes, that earth isn't there any more, and that this ship is the only reality."

CHAPTER FIVE

BY the end of the third week out, Burl Jasperson was afflicted by an almost intolerable tension. He prowled the ship like a tiger, nor he could think of nothing more to do. For the moment there were no more improvements to suggest to the Star Line, no more brilliant financial deals to execute, and each empty minute seemed to swell into an endless hour. He tried to relax by viewing the dramas on the stereoscreen, but he was always too uneasy to sit through an entire performance, and would leave in the middle to resume his pacing of the corridors.

At his private table in the dining room he stared at the empty chair across from him, munching his food mechanically, seething with unrest. He could see Tanya's gleaming head across the room, with Alan Chase's beside her, and he tortured himself with imagining the light laughter, the friendly talk, which must be taking place there. Never, before this trip, had he been made to feel so unnecessary, so much an outsider. Wasn't he a lord of finance, a master of industry, the kind of a man to be respected and admired? Of course, less successful men called him ruthless, he realized, but he was not ruthless—only realistic. He was an able man, and if he expected people in general to take orders from him, it was only because he was more intelligent and more capable than the people to whom he gave his orders. Nothing wrong with that.

But these miserable empty days were beginning to frighten him. He felt lost. The ship ran by herself, without needing his help, and there was no doubt at all that she would win the Blue Ribbon. Although he questioned Captain Evans sharply, and checked every day on the minutest data of the voyage, so far he had found nothing to criticize—except the coldness of Josiah Evans' manner.

He ground his teeth through a stalk of celery in a vicious bite. After all, wasn't he Chairman of the board of directors of the Star Line? Wasn't it his right, even his duty, to make sure that everything was going well?

The crowd of diners had grown thin, now, and he could see

clearly the little group at Tanya's table. They were laughing, and he could see the delightful animation, which always disappeared, whenever he tried to talk to her.

Steward Davis sidled up, a deferential smile on his long face.

"Is everything all right, Mr. Jasperson?"

"Um."

"Looks like we'll get the Blue Ribbon this trip, doesn't it, sir?"

"Um."

"If you should ever want any special dishes, sir, any little delicacies not available to everyone, I should be glad to speak to the chef."

Jasperson pushed his plate away. "I'll remember, Davis." Throwing down his napkin he stood up. His waiter came running.

"Dessert, sir?"

WITHOUT answering, he strode across the room, trying to compose his mouth into a smile as he reached his goal.

"Miss Taganova, would you care to join me in the bar for a drink?"

They all looked up at him in astonishment.

"But I've just finished dinner," she said.

He waited, uncertainly. At last Professor Larrabee pointed to the unoccupied chair.

"Perhaps you'd care to join us, instead?"

No one else spoke, and he sat down nervously. Conversation had stopped, and at last he broke out with explosive force.

"I wish Captain Evans would speed up this ship. It feels as if we'd been on the way forever. And still three weeks to go!"

"Do you find three weeks so long a time?" asked the professor.

"It seems like eternity. I wish something would happen. Why can't we have a little excitement?"

"Couldn't you find any more banks to break today?" Alan drawled. "No gambles on the stock exchange?"

The professor broke in soothingly. "Now, there's an idea! You're obviously a gambling man, a man of action. Do you play poker? Why don't you get up a little game among your friends? That ought to provide you with excitement for one evening at least."

"Would you join the game?"

"No, no, my dear Mr. Jasperson! You and I do not move in the same circles. I confess, I enjoy the delightful uncertainties of poker, but I could never afford to play for your stakes."

"Then we'll make the stakes what you can afford. Each raise limited to five credits?"

"In that case, I might consider it."

"You, Dr. Chase?"

"Too exciting for an invalid, I'm afraid."

"You, Mr. Hall?"

Tom squeezed Dorothy's hand under the table. "No, thank you, Mr. Jasperson. My wife and I, we have other plans."

"If it's money, young fellow, I'll stake you, and you can have a year to pay me back."

Tom grinned. "You're very generous. But what makes you so sure you'd be the winner?"

"I always win. Will you join the game, Miss Taganova?"

He accepted her silent headshake without protest.

"Then I'll try to round up two or three others. We don't want a big crowd—too many people make me nervous. Perhaps Willoughby will play, and I'll get Captain Evans. He doesn't like the game, but he'll sit in if I insist. See you in my suite in half an hour."

THE poker game had been in progress for more than an hour when Captain Evans entered the parlor. Frowning, Jasperson looked up.

"You're late, Josiah. I told you we'd begin at nine."

"Sorry, Burl. I was delayed." Jasperson paused in the act of raking in the pot, and looked up sharply.

"Anything wrong?"

"No, all serene."

"Anything you need my advice on?"

"No, just a routine conference with the navigator."

"Then pull up a chair and get in the game."

Nearly half the chips were piled in front of Jasperson, and across from him a modest heap sat before the professor. At his right the baggy-eyed only son of a deutonium millionaire fingered his dwindling pile indifferently, and on his left Dr. Willoughby stared unbelievingly at his few remaining chips, three blues and a couple of whites.

"I'll just watch," said the Captain. "You know I'm not much of a gambler. Chess is my game."

"Oh, come on, Josiah. I insist that you play. Prove that you've got red blood in your veins."

Evans hesitated, but remained standing. "I'd rather just look on."

"Now look here, Captain. Doesn't the Star Line always try to please its passengers? Well, I'm a passenger. Or is it just your native caution that makes you afraid of losing?" His laugh did not entirely disguise the irritation in his voice.

"All right, anything to oblige," said Evans wearily, pulling up a chair. "What stakes are you playing for?"

The Captain lost, slowly and steadily. Mechanically he went through the motions of dealing, discarding, drawing, and betting, but it was obvious that his mind was not on the game. Jasperson rarely lost a hand, if he had stayed at all, while Professor Larrabee's luck was unpredictable, the pile of chips before him fluctuating, growing or diminishing with startling swiftness.

They were interrupted once when a waiter came in with a tray of bottles and glasses. The Captain refused.

"But one drink won't do you any harm," said Jasperson.

"I never drink in space. For one thing, the rules of the Star Line explicitly forbid it, as you should know."

"Yes, I helped make that rule. That means I can release you from it."

But Evans was firm. "I never drink in space," he repeated. "I'll take two cards—no, make it three."

The professor surveyed his hand with his customary sprightly air.

"I'll play these," he said.

Jasperson discarded. "I'll take one."

Captain Evans languidly opened the betting, but after the first round he dropped out, and only Jasperson and the professor remained. Each raised the other persistently, and while Jasperson grew more and more excited, the professor smiled as usual, his eyes glinting with amusement.

"And another five," said Larrabee.

For the first time, Jasperson hesitated. "You sure you mean it, professor? I kind of hate to clean you out, especially because I doubt if you can afford, it."

"Suppose you let me be the judge of what is, after all, a private matter?"

"All right, it's you that will go bankrupt, not me. And another five."

"See you, and raise you five!"

JASPERSON sat back and pondered, his cold eyes calculating. "Now let's review the situation, just among friends. The professor's a smart man, and he isn't rich. He saw me draw one card, so he can make a pretty good guess what I probably hold, if I drew the right card, but he's playing a pat hand, and playing as if he meant it. Well, I've put a lot of credits in that pot, but I never did believe in throwing good money after bad, even in a friendly game. I quit."

"What? You mean you're going to drop out without even seeing me?"

"I know when I'm licked. Five credits is five credits, even to me." He threw down his cards and reached to gather in the deck.

Slowly Professor Larrabee raked in the chips, as Jasperson went on complacently.

"That's the only principle a practical man can work on. Know when you're licked. Get all the facts, analyze all the data, and then act on the logical conclusion, no matter how much you may hate to. It was clear to me that you must have drawn a pat flush that would top my straight, so I simply decided not to waste any more money."

"Thank you, Mr. Jasperson. I appreciate the gift."

"It was no gift. You had me beat."

"Did I? Only if you had all the facts, only if you analyzed all the data, and only if you reached the correct conclusion. Perhaps you ought to see what I held."

Deliberately he turned over his hand and spread the cards.

Jasperson jumped to his feet in a rage. "But that's a handful of junk! Not even a pair! You held a bust, and I had you beat!"

"Certainly. But you didn't know it. Without all the facts, you acted on a faulty conclusion."

Breathing noisily, his plump face flushed, Jasperson smashed his fist into his pile of chips and scattered them to the floor.

"A pure bluff! I hate bluffing!"

"Then you miss a great deal of fun in life," said Larrabee calmly. "I find it dull just to analyze data and then bet on a sure thing. I like a little excitement."

Slowly the financier sank back into his chair. He gulped in a large breath of air and tried to steady himself, a sickly smile around his mouth.

"Excuse me, Professor. But you took me by surprise." Hands trembling, he began to shuffle the deck.

There was a knock at the door, and a crewman entered.

"What is it, Stacey?" said Captain Evans.

"Chief Wyman is waiting to see you in your quarters, sir."

With a sigh of relief, the Captain turned in his few chips. "Time for me to quit, anyway."

His face still red, Jasperson looked up hopefully. "Shall I come with you? Any way I can be of use?"

"No thank you, Burl. I'll leave you to your little game."

IN the Captain's quarters, Chief Wyman was pacing the floor.

"Sir!" he burst out. "This is it! We've hit the Thakura Ripples!"

"Impossible, Wyman! It's too soon. What's happened?"

"You told me to report as soon as we ran across anything suspicious, sir. Well, look what our screen has been picking up."

He handed over a plastic record tape, perforated by minute notches, which outlined an unsystematic, jagged line of peaks and hollows.

"We've been getting this stuff all evening."

"Doesn't seem to mean anything. It doesn't show any sort of pattern."

"No, sir, and it may not mean anything, but it's different from what we've been getting up till now. And then another thing. It's probably not serious, but the number ten Pile has started to heat."

"Begun to heat? What's wrong with Pile Ten? One of your

men been getting careless?"

"I'm positive not, Sir. I have complete confidence in all of them."

Captain Evans studied the record tape, a worried frown on his forehead.

"It's just possible, I suppose, that the Ripples—Is Pile Ten heating fast?"

"No, sir. It's still below the critical level, and of course we're putting in dampers."

"I wish we *knew* something definite about the Thakura Ripples," the Captain burst out, "what they are, what they do, what they look like, and *how* they affect our atomic Piles! If only Thakura were still a sane man, and could finish up his calculations!"

"Maybe Thakura was crazy to start with," said Chief Wyman, "or maybe the Ripples drove him crazy. I don't know. But I do know Pile Ten is heating."

"Well, keep watching it. Double the checks on the other Piles, and let me know of even the slightest rise."

As soon as the door had closed, Evans opened the desk panel and buzzed Operations.

"Pilot Thayer? Captain Evans here. I am about to give you an order. As soon as you have executed it, come at once to my cabin, and bring Navigator Smith with you. Here it comes. Reduce speed immediately, repeat immediately, to one-half, repeat one-half. That's all."

CHAPTER SIX

NOBODY felt the alteration in the progress of the *Star Lord*. Within the metal casing of the ship nothing was changed. The sunny scenes in the walls were just as bright, and the synthetic light of the slowly moving stars at night was just as soothing. For the passengers, the black menace outside the ship did not exist. Because change of speed cannot be felt in hyperspace, they had no way of realizing that the *Star Lord* had slackened her pace and was feeling her way cautiously as a blind man to avoid the ominous barriers of the Thakura Ripples.

On their way to their cabins that night, there were a few people who noticed that the bulletin which detailed the day's run had not been posted on the board, but they wondered only for a moment why it had been omitted, and then forgot the matter.

Going in to breakfast next morning, Burl Jasperson stopped to read the bulletin as usual, to find how many light years distance had been put behind him in this interminable journey, and he clenched his fist at finding a blank board before him.

Abruptly turning his back on the dining room, he proceeded straight to the Captain's quarters, where Stacey stopped him in the anteroom.

"Where's Captain Evans?"

"I'm sorry, Mr. Jasperson. The Captain left orders he was not to be disturbed."

"He'll see *me*. Let him know I'm here."

"I'm sorry, sir. My orders were, nobody was to be admitted. He was very specific."

Stacey did not budge, but the inner door swung open and the Captain's tired face peered out.

"You have a very penetrating voice, Burl. I suppose you might as well come in. It's all right, Stacey. Stand by."

He moved to let Jasperson enter, and closed the door.

About the desk sat Chief Engineer Wyman, Chief Pilot Thayer, and Chief Navigator Smith, all studying a chart laid out before them, and making computations. They looked up at the interruption.

"What's going on here?" said Jasperson. "If you're having a conference of some kind, I should be in on it."

"Just routine work, Burl. What is it you want?"

"Somebody is getting careless. The bulletin of yesterday's run has not been posted. It's little things like that that make all the difference in the reputation of a shipping line. Somebody ought to be reprimanded. What was the day's run, by the way? Well, speak up, Josiah! I'm waiting."

Evans reached for a sheet of paper from the desk and silently handed it across. Jasperson looked at the figures, frowned, and spoke angrily.

"Have your computers broken down, Captain Evans? Or is this a joke? Why, that's only about two-thirds our usual distance. At this rate it will take us from now to eternity to arrive."

"You'd better sit down, Burl." The Captain looked steadily at him. "Those figures explain why I ordered that the bulletin was not to he posted. Not one passenger out of a hundred would have noticed much change in the figures, but I do not want to alarm even that one in a hundred. I have ordered the ship to proceed at half-speed."

"What? Have you lost your mind?"

"We are approaching the Thakura Ripples. It just isn't safe to go any faster."

Expelling a long breath, Jasperson spoke more calmly.

"That means we'll be late in reaching Almazin III?"

"Three or four days, perhaps, not more. Eventually we'll get through this danger zone, and then we can resume speed."

"But we *can't* be late, Captain Evans! Surely you haven't forgotten that we're out after the Blue Ribbon? The Light Line's ships have made it in forty-three days, and we've got to do it in forty-two or less. This trip is a matter of prime importance to the Star Line, and a delay of even three days would keep us from breaking the record. I thought you understood all that?"

SIGHING, the Captain shook his head. "I know all that. But we are in dangerous regions, and I can't risk my ship just for a piece of silk! Last night Pile Ten started heating. It's still hot, and we may have to expel it. I hadn't expected to reach the Ripples so soon, and had even hoped we could avoid them entirely, but evidently the limits of the band haven't been charted very accurately. The only safe thing is to go slow."

"But the Ripples are imaginary! Why do you think we've hit them?"

"There's the number Ten Pile."

"But why should only that one out of the twenty-four be affected? And even if it is heating, that's no good reason for slackening speed."

Captain Evans glared back at the plump little man, then his eyes wavered, and his fingers fiddled uncertainly with the papers on his desk. His chief officers were watching him intently. At last he straightened his shoulders and spoke sternly.

"Mr. Jasperson. Surely it will not be necessary to remind you that I am the Captain of this ship. I am in sole command. Is that correct?"

"Yes, but—"

"Would you seriously advise me to go contrary to my own knowledge, my own instinct? To run this ship into an area of danger, to risk the lives of the passengers, all for a piece of ribbon? Would you want to take the responsibility of giving me such an order, even if I should agree?"

As Jasperson looked around at the watchful faces of the Engineer, the Pilot, and the Navigator, some of the belligerence left his voice.

"Certainly not, Josiah! And anyway, it's not your knowledge I'm quarreling with. If you run the ship according to the facts, you'll do all right. It's when you let your judgment be influenced by your imagination that I object. But by all means, do as you think best. When the Star Line loses confidence in its Captains, they replace them. I'll look in again, if I may, later in the day."

When the door had closed behind him, Pilot Thayer shook his head wonderingly. "You'd think he ruled the universe!"

"He's a man of very limited imagination," said the Captain. "But never forget, he wields a great deal of power. Now, are your orders clear? Smith, you'll continue your charting."

"I'm doing my best, Captain, but what am I charting? Sometimes I wonder if maybe your friend Jasperson isn't right. If the Ripples are imaginary, maybe I'm getting gray hairs trying to make a map of something that isn't there!"

"Chart it anyway! We can't take chances. Wyman, I'm not a bit satisfied with the way Pile Ten is behaving. It should have cooled to normal before now. Watch it. If we have to dump it, we want to act before it gets too hot. Anything else?"

"One other thing, sir," said Engineer Wyman, pointing to the diagram of the ship which hung on the wall. "Pile Ten is located just below Lifeboat C, and the radiation index of Boat C is getting a little high."

"That's bad. Well, keep shoving in the dampers, and keep me posted."

After they had gone, he sat for a while at his desk, studying the data on the papers before him. He paced the room for a few minutes, then paused to pick up the little red volume of *Ley's Space Ships*. He had no need to open it. It fell open of itself at the well-read page, and his eyes rested for one rich moment on the words: *Captain: Josiah Evans.*

What name, he wondered, feeling almost physically sick with uncertainty, what name would be printed in the next edition?

THE orchestra played melodiously at lunch time. The chef had produced delicacies even more delectable than usual, and at each table the waiters poured sparkling white wine into long-stemmed glasses, while murmuring softly, "Compliments of the Captain!"

"Is this a special occasion?" asked Tanya.

"Not that I know of, miss."

"Every meal feels like a special occasion," said Alan, "because I get to talk to you."

"Sh-h! Here come the Halls."

Tom and Dorothy flitted in to the table, hand in hand, still absorbed in the wonder of being together, scarcely aware of the world about them, then left, without finishing their dessert. Alan and Tanya looked after them with affectionate amusement, but Professor Larrabee seemed withdrawn and a little sad, as though they evoked memories of a time now lost to him forever.

"They make me feel so *old!*" said Tanya.

"And lonely?"

"Perhaps, a little. They seem so sure, somehow, that all the rest of their lives will be just as happy as this, always."

"And why not?" said Professor Larrabee.

The orchestra swayed into a final soft chord, and immediately a voice spoke from a loudspeaker in the ceiling.

"Ladies and gentlemen!" Conversation stopped, the room became quiet.

"Ladies and gentlemen. The customary lifeboat drill will be held this afternoon at 1600 hours. The attendance of all passengers is requested."

The voice stopped, the orchestra resumed its playing, and the passengers sipped their coffee.

"I wonder why he said 'customary'?" said Tanya. "We've been out about three weeks, and this will be the first drill we've had. Do you suppose something is wrong?"

"I'm afraid your sense of the dramatic gets the better of you," said Alan. "What could be wrong with the *Star Lord?*"

"Maybe her name," murmured Professor Larrabee, and his eyes looked haunted.

SOLITARY at his table, Burl Jasperson sipped at a glass of ice water as he pondered. For the first time in his life he was not quite sure what course to follow. He wanted that Blue Ribbon for the Star Line, and yet—he did not know what to do. While he listened to the announcement of the lifeboat drill, his lip twisted in contempt. Just like Josiah Evans, he thought, to be over-cautious and run the risk of starting a panic.

Still thinking, he left the dining room and went to the main lounge to study the illuminated map of the ship. The three-dimensional panorama showed the slim and elegant body of the *Star Lord,* tapered like a silver spindle. Six small ships, three on each side of the long axis, each capable of carrying 250 people, were fastened into her hulk. Seemingly a part of the ship itself, their outer walls forming a part of the ship's wall, they were designed to be detached at the touch of a button, and launched into space as free craft.

When the warning bells rang, he joined the crowd of passengers who were assigned to Boat F, peered at the boat through the transparent panel, and listened attentively to the instructions. It was Steward Davis, he noted approvingly, who was in charge.

"Passengers will file in through the usual port and walk to the farthest unoccupied seat, and buckle themselves into place. They have nothing further to do. Crewmen will take care of the mechanics of detaching and launching the boat. You will note that there are no separate cabins, only rows of seats as in the primitive airplanes, but you will find this no real discomfort, since the boat would undoubtedly be picked up after a very short interval by some alerted space liner."

Jasperson raised his voice above the crowd's hum.

"What about provisioning? Are the boats stocked on Y-port?"

"No, Mr. Jasperson, except for food concentrates, and one air tank which is placed there for the greater comfort of the crewmen who must go in to clean or to make minor adjustments. The boats are not fully provisioned until the need arises. After all, we don't want to invite trouble, do we?"

People laughed appreciatively.

"No," he went on, "if there should be an emergency, we have specially trained crewmen whose job it is to stock reserves of air and water. They would go to work as automatically and efficiently as machines. Any other questions?"

Jasperson lingered after the indifferent crowd, to inspect the boat more closely, then slouched away.

ALL that afternoon he prowled the ship, trying to make up his mind. He stopped now and then to question a business acquaintance, ask a journalist his opinion, and he quizzed Larrabee again, more sharply than before, about the hypothetical Ripples. He kept moving, and as he walked he calculated, bringing to bear all the power of a mind which he believed to be logical, and which his financial success had proved to be keen and intelligent. All his life he had trusted his judgment, and it had rarely failed him—barring accidents like that unfair poker game. At last, as the hours went on, his decision crystallized. He had made up his mind.

At dinner he drank champagne in addition to his usual ice

water, and only half heard the scraps of conversation in the dining room. There was to be a special masquerade dance, he gathered. People around him were excitedly planning the improvisation of costumes. He would not get himself up in any silly costume, he decided, but if his plans went well, he might look in later in the evening, on the chance to being allowed to glide over the waxed floor with the lovely Tanya.

After finishing his last drop of coffee he went directly to the cabin of Captain Evans, who had begun to eat his simple dinner.

The Chairman of the board of directors pulled up a chair and sat down, without waiting to be asked.

"Look here, Josiah, I want to talk to you. I've been thinking. I'm afraid I was too brusque this morning. That's a bad habit of mine, and I want to apologize. But after all, we should not be quarreling, for your interests and mine are the same, as you surely realize."

Captain Evans pushed away his tray, lit a cigar, and puffed stolidly. "I realize that I must consider the safety of my passengers, if that's what you mean."

"That's included, of course." Jasperson made his voice warm and persuasive, the voice that had swayed boards of directors, the voice that reassured hesitant bankers.

"Passenger safety is always paramount, of course, and I respect your attitude there. But in this particular case, isn't it possible that you are being too cautious?"

"But Burl! Can the Captain of a ship *ever* be too cautious? Think of his responsibility!"

"His responsibility is very great, and I would never advise you, nor permit you, to shirk yours. But sometimes caution may cease to be a virtue. Think about this caution of yours for a minute. Surely you believe that I would never urge you to do anything against the interests of the ship, or against your own conscience? Now you have an excellent mind—logical, objective, clear. That was one reason we chose you for this place. Try to consider, for a moment, the bare possibility that your decision to reduce speed may not have been justified."

EVANS was silent, and finally Burl asked, "How far did we get today?"

"240 Light years."

"And if you decide to continue at that speed for five or six days, that means we'll be approximately three days behind schedule in touching Almazin III?"

"About that."

"And that means we won't break the record. Now consider the reason for this very unhappy situation. Think about it with an open mind. You have one Pile heating—but has that never happened to a ship before, even in normal space? You and I both know it happens, and that ships have been lost because of a defective Pile. Logically, why shouldn't this be just another such case? You say it is caused by the Ripples, but as man to man, what objective evidence can you bring forward to prove their existence? I'm not trying to browbeat you, you understand, but just to ask you to look at the matter carefully. You said yourself, this morning, that you hadn't expected to be meeting the Ripples at this point— you had thought they occurred in a rather different area of hyperspace. Couldn't that mean that they don't really exist, anywhere?"

Captain Evans wiped his glistening forehead with his handkerchief.

"Yes," he said. "I was surprised. I'll admit I didn't expect them here. But there's so much we don't know about hyperspace!"

"No, there's so much we *do* know! Are you a child, to fancy there are goblins outside just because it's dark? There is a perfectly rational, alternative explanation for the things that worry you. Why can't you accept them?"

Evans got up and began to pace the floor. "I guess I'm following a hunch."

"But would you make us lose the Blue Ribbon for a mere hunch? Don't you trust your own objective judgment?"

Sweating heavily, the Captain tried to stub out his cigar, but his hands were moist and his fingers trembled.

"I don't know!" he shouted. Then he went on, his voice low and tired. "You may be right, Burl. You may be right. We may not have hit the Ripples. The Ripples may not even exist, although some very competent spacemen and some very brilliant physicists are convinced they do. But how can I judge? How can I be sure?"

Jasperson leaned forward, intent as a cat on a bird.

"None of the other Piles have started to heat? There's nothing else to make you suspicious?"

"Nothing except the space record tape, and that makes no sense."

"Exactly. Then why don't you look at this situation as a hard-headed spaceman should, and order full speed ahead?"

"Burl, there are fifteen hundred lives dependent on me. How can I take such a chance?"

"It wouldn't be a chance. And if by the one unlucky chance in ten million there should be trouble, you have ample lifeboat space for everyone. Isn't it worth the gamble?"

"I don't like gambling lives against a piece of blue silk ribbon."

JASPERSON sighed. "Come, Josiah, be reasonable. I would-n't think of giving you an order, or trying to interfere with your decision in any way, but surely I may be allowed to help you to reach the correct decision? How will you feel when the *Star Lord* limps into port four or five days late, and you have to explain to the Board that she was late because you were trying to dodge some non-existent Ripples. You're afraid! Change your frightened point of view, and that will make you change your orders and get us on the way once more, full speed!"

Muttering to himself, wiping his brow, Captain Evans walked around the little room, while Jasperson sat back and watched him with cold, intent eyes. Evans glanced once at the little red book, half covered with papers, and pain contorted his face.

Suddenly he stepped to his desk and called Engineer Wyman.

"What about that space tape, Wyman? Has Smith been able to detect any pattern in the impulses?"

"No, sir. No pattern of any sort we can recognize, anyway."

"And what report on Pile Ten?"

"Pile Ten is doing nicely, sir. Lost half a degree in the last hour. By tomorrow she ought to be back to normal limits."

Clicking the phone, Evans resumed his pacing in the heavy silence. At last he faced Jasperson and spread out his palms, his face gray as parchment.

"All right, Burl. You're probably right. I won't argue any longer."

"Good man! The Star Line will know how to appreciate your decision." He hesitated, and asked, "You'll agree, now, I didn't push you into this? It's your own free decision?"

Calmly, Evans answered. "It is my own responsibility."

He buzzed. Operations.

"Wyman? Captain Evans speaking. Full speed ahead!"

CHAPTER SEVEN

ON the dance floor late that night, a crooner in blue Venusian mask and wig hummed the melody while the orchestra wailed and zinged behind him. The lights had been dimmed to a purple midnight, and shadowy couples flitted about the room, swaying, humming, laughing. Horned devils danced with angels, pirates and Roman senators guided in their arms lovely Cleopatras and sinuous mermaids. Hunched over the little tables, clinking glasses, grotesque silhouettes of Martians, Venusians, and Apollonians whispered intimately.

The walls of the room displayed the evening stars of late summer, and, special event for a gala evening, a fat yellow half moon sailed lazily in the sky.

The *Star Lord* shuddered, briefly. Briefly the crooner's voice wavered, the notes of the violins hesitated, but no one noticed. A second quiver of the ship, and the dancers paused to look at one another questioningly, then laughed and danced on.

Jasperson had been sitting beside the wall, vainly searching among the dancers for Tanya. He stood up, his forehead suddenly wet with sweat. Plowing through the dancers and out of the door, in the corridor he ran into Steward Davis, gliding along on silent, slippered feet.

"What was that, Davis?"

"Don't know, sir. Nothing serious, or the alarm lights would be on."

"Come with me."

He flung open the door of the Captain's cabin. It was empty. Stacey was not in the anteroom, and the inner cabin was silent.

The water carafe had been turned over on the desk, and a few papers lay scattered on the floor.

"They might be in Operations, sir."

"Show me the way!" They raced down the corridors, past the open door of the room where dancers still swayed and the orchestra still played. Through a hall, down an escalator, down, down, to the center of the ship.

Jasperson paused. "You needn't wait, Davis. But I may want you again. I'll let you know."

Pushing aside the crewmen who stood guard at the door, he rushed into the room.

"Josiah! What was that shock? I demand to know what's happened!"

Evans threw him a glance of pure, intense hatred, and then resumed his questioning of Chief Wyman.

"You say Number Ten just let go?"

"Not exactly, sir. For a couple of hours or so after we resumed speed, it stayed steady. All of a sudden, it started to climb. They called me, but by the time I got there it was already at critical level. We put in more dampers, but it kept going up and up, and I thought it might vaporize any minute. I hadn't any choice, sir. There wasn't time to call you and get orders. I had to drop it."

"Certainly. I'm not criticizing you. But there's one thing we hadn't counted on. Chief Thayer says Pile Ten took lifeboat C along with it."

"But how could that happen?"

"Boat C was just above, you remember. The heat triggered the release mechanism, and the boat launched itself into space."

Jasperson interrupted, trying to speak calmly. "What's happened? Tell me what's wrong?"

"We've hit the imaginary Thakura Ripples," Evans said savagely, "and they're tearing us apart!"

The plump soft body of Burl Jasperson seemed to deflate. The truculence drained from his face, leaving his skin a dirty white as he whispered, "Then the Thakura Ripples *are* real? And we're in danger?"

The Captain's laugh was bitter. "What do *you* think? Don't you want to give me the benefit of your advice now?"

Again the door burst open, and a crewman ran in.

"Captain Evans, sir. Piles Fourteen and Fifteen have started to heat. They're already at critical level."

"Dump them!"

The phone buzzed, and Evans listened with a face, which was turning a graveyard gray.

"If you can hold them down, keep them. If they pass the critical point, shoot them away." Turning, he looked straight into the dilated eyes of Jasperson; and spoke as if every word were a knife thrusting into the pudgy body.

"Everyone of the Piles is starting to heat. Every last one. One life boat is lost. That means fifteen hundred people to be crowded into five little boats!"

"What are you going to do?" croaked the little man.

"I've already reduced speed. I've sent out and am still sending out calls for help, over phase wave. We'll shift to normal space, and we'll launch the lifeboats as soon as they can be provisioned and loaded. And then we'll pray. And now, Burl Jasperson, how do you like the Thakura Ripples?"

Bracing himself against the desk, Burl tried to smile. "If there's any way I can help, of course, just let me know." With a feeble attempt at jauntiness, he staggered out of the cabin.

OPENING the long-closed shutter of the observation port, Captain Evans could see the suns of normal space glittering in the blackness about the ship, unfamiliar and alien. Before the shift to normal space he had sent out SOS calls throughout the galaxy, but he had not waited for any replies before shifting. He could not know whether the calls had been heard, or even whether there were any ships close enough to send help after hearing the calls. He hoped, with all his being, that they had come out in a region of inhabited planet systems, in a regular shipping lane, so that his passengers could be picked up and taken to port—any port.

He kept his line open to Operations, and every minute or so Wyman spoke to him, giving the data on the climbing piles. Ten had been jettisoned in hyperspace, and so had Fourteen and Fifteen. Since their shift to normal space, it had been necessary also to detach the entire bank of Nineteen, Twenty, and Twenty-one, whose index had risen at a terrifying rate.

Wyman's voice spoke in his ear. "One, Two, and Three are climbing fast, sir."

"Shoot them away!"

"No good, sir. I've tried. The release mechanism has fused, and those three Piles are welded to the ship!"

Evans closed his eyes. That meant that the life of the ship was doomed. There would be no way to save her. But the passengers could still be saved, if they got away soon enough, before the three Piles vaporized.

"Wyman!" he whispered despairingly, "is there any single Pile that isn't heating?"

"No, sir."

"Well is there any single Pile that's responding to your dampers?"

"No, sir, not one."

"Then, in your experience, they are all bound to go, sooner or later?"

"I've never seen anything like this in my experience, sir. It looks bad."

The door opened, and Jasperson slunk in. His skin had lost its cushioning, gray folds sagged under his cheekbones, and black hollows outlined his glittering blue eyes. The Captain ignored him, and spoke into the phone.

"Very well. In exactly fifteen minutes I shall sound the alarm and we'll abandon ship. I can't take a chance on waiting any longer. Keep a skeleton crew at work on those Piles to hold them down as much as possible, and have all other crewmen report to their lifeboat stations."

"Right, sir. But Boat C has gone, you remember. When we dumped Pile Ten."

"Yes. Distribute her passengers into the remaining boats."

He turned to look at Jasperson, who was shivering as though he were freezing.

"Is there no hope, Josiah? Is this the end?"

"The end of the *Star Lord*, yes. I hope to save the passengers. You heard me. In fifteen minutes all preparations should be finished, then I sound the alarm. Don't worry, Burl. There's room enough for everybody, your skin is safe."

"But won't the lifeboats be horribly crowded?"

"Crowded, yes, but not impossibly so. If they can carry two hundred and fifty people in fair comfort, they can jam in three hundred by squeezing a bit."

Jasperson shuddered. "So many people! And so close together! I can't bear crowds, Josiah, you know that. They make me feel sick and confused. It will be terrible!"

"Whether you like it or not, there's nothing else to do if we want to save lives. I'll sound the alarm in a quarter of an hour. Get yourself ready, but whatever you do, don't tell the others yet. I don't want a panic on my hands until I'm ready to deal with it."

Biting his lip, Jasperson turned, without a word, and shuffled out of the cabin.

ONCE in the corridor, he began to run, a shriveled old man waddling on wings of fear down the hall to the dining room where empty tables waited in the elegant silence of gleaming silver and crisp white linen for the breakfast hour.

Davis was standing at the sideboard, staring blankly at the flashing red light above the door.

Jasperson ran up to him and clutched his arm. Looking around cunningly to see that they were alone, he whispered.

"Davis, I want to talk to you."

"Later, sir. That red light means I'm wanted at the briefing room."

"Yes, but wait a minute!"

"I'm supposed to go at once, sir."

"A thousand credits if you'll listen to me a minute!"

As Davis hesitated, Burl went on. "Listen, Davis, the ship is in trouble. The Captain is going to launch the lifeboats. You're in charge of Boat F, aren't you? You know how to operate it?"

"Of course, Mr. Jasperson."

"Then come with me, and we'll take the boat now. I'll pay you well."

"But we can't do that!"

"Why not? *Star Lord* is doomed. In a few minutes this place will be a madhouse, and there may not be room for everybody. I want to get out of here before the mob. We'll take Boat F."

Steward Davis' eyes were thoughtful as he replied. "But sir, we can't just take a boat for ourselves, like that. There's two hundred and fifty people assigned to Boat F."

"Worse than that! Three hundred! One lifeboat has been lost already. It's dangerous to wait—there'll be a stampede and the lifeboats might even be wrecked. No, we must take her alone, Davis. I'll give you ten thousand credits if you'll do it, and as long as you live you'll have me as a friend."

The steward's little eyes looked sidewise at the pleading man. "But I'd be found out for sure, Mr. Jasperson. I'm sure I would, and then what would become of me? I'd never get another job for the rest of my life. I'd have to change my name, disguise myself, and maybe live on some other planet, and all that would take money. I'm a poor man, and I don't see how I could afford it."

"But if I have to squeeze into one of those boats with three hundred other people crowding against me, I'll go crazy! We'll go to some out-of-the-way planet, and you can change your identity and be perfectly safe. Can't you understand, man? My life is at stake, and my sanity. I'll give you fifteen thousand credits!"

"Well," said Davis. "Could you make it twenty-five?"

"Done! Meet me at Boat F in five minutes."

Jasperson rushed to his cabin. Yanking open the wall safe he dragged out his brief case and the locked memorandum book, thrust his pistol into his pocket, and ran to the door.

"Follow me!" he called to his startled secretary, and hurried from the room.

Running past the library door, he glimpsed Tanya at work, her auburn head bent over her sketching. On impulse, he stopped and ran back.

Panting from the physical punishment of running, nearly smothered by the pounding of his terrified heart, he gasped out his invitation.

"Tanya! The ship is going to blow up! Don't tell anyone. Come with me now, before the crowd, and I'll get you off safely in my lifeboat. I'll take care of you, Tanya."

She pulled away. "Have you lost your mind, Mr. Jasperson?"

"Don't argue. There's no time. Come, I'll protect you. We'll have plenty of room. If you wait, it may be too late."

"Go with you, and leave the others? You're mad!"

"But if you wait, you'll be trampled to death by the mob. I'm giving you a chance to save your life."

"But you can't take that boat for yourself. What would happen to the other people? That would be murder. Get away from me! I'm going to call Captain Evans."

As she ran to the phone and pressed the dial, he padded out of the door and resumed his flight to Boat F where Davis waited, peering nervously up and down the hall. Waving his secretary to follow, Jasperson rushed through the port.

"Everything ready, Davis? Provisions all in?"

"All set. I saw the tail end of the truck leaving just as I got here, but I'll just check—"

"Hurry, man! There's no time to waste." He cocked his head, listening to the low rumble of an approaching motor. Davis ran inside, and together they watched from the port.

Coming swiftly down the corridor was a small motor truck. It stopped, and the driver jumped out and shouted.

"Get out of that boat! She's not ready yet! What are you—"

With a steady hand Jasperson drew his pistol and pressed the trigger. The man fell without a sound.

"What are you waiting for, Davis? Shove off!"

The port door shut. A few seconds delay, and Lifeboat F, carrying three persons, shot away from the *Star Lord* into space.

ALARM bells rang, red lights flashed.

Sickening with the inexorable rise of her fevered power units, the *Star Lord* trembled with the clangor of bells ringing in library and nursery, in lounges and dance hall, in bar and cabins, in dining rooms and theaters. The orchestra crashed to a stop, the dancers halted, startled and vaguely frightened, half laughing at themselves as they listened to the bells.

Then silence, and the voice of Captain Evans.

"Ladies and gentlemen. Don't be alarmed. Because of certain mechanical difficulties the *Star Lord* has shifted to normal space. There's no immediate danger, but as a precautionary measure we shall launch the lifeboats. Remember, there is no danger, but I ask each of you to proceed at once, in calm orderly fashion, to the station to which you are assigned, and there obey the orders of the officer in charge. The passengers formerly assigned to Boat C will be placed in other boats. Do not wait to go to your cabins. Proceed immediately to your lifeboats."

The voice clicked off. A few seconds of silence, and then the quiet was broken by the patter of hurrying feet. In a moment, the public lounges were empty.

* * *

In the library, Tanya was still calling into the phone.

"Operator, operator!" she cried. "I must speak to the Captain. It's a matter of life and death!" But the phone was dead.

When the alarm bells rang, she listened to the announcement and then slowly put back the useless instrument. Back in her corner, she picked up her chalk, shuffled her drawings into an orderly heap, paused, and with a wry smile dropped them all to the floor and hurried away.

A sound of crying wailed from the open door of the playroom, and she looked in to see a group of children, none of them more than six, huddled together and sobbing. She walked up to them and smiled, hands on her hips.

"Well, small fry! What are you doing up so late? Why the big howls?"

Still they cried, ignoring their abandoned toys. Around the room hobby horses sat quietly, alphabet blocks lay scattered, and picture books and sprawling dolls littered the floor.

"So," she said. "Your nurses ran out on you, did they? Left you to shift for yourselves? Never mind, youngsters, Aunt Tanya will look after you. Take hands, now, and come with me."

CHAPTER EIGHT

WHEN the alarm rang in the Bar, a glass crashed to the floor as the only son of the deutonium millionaire jumped to his feet I and ran.

Professor Larrabee deliberately finished his drink, gently put down the glass, and stood up.

"Our final space-cap," he said. "Well, Alan, it's been a good trip, but I can't say I'm surprised at its ending. The ship had the wrong name, from the beginning."

"Let's hurry, Professor. We must find Tanya and the Halls."

"You're walking too fast for me, my boy. Don't worry. They're in Boat F, with us, and we're sure to find them there."

In the corridor leading to F station their way was blocked by the crowd, many of them still wearing the grotesque costumes of the masquerade dance, now pale and tawdry in the bright lights. Stunned with horror, they stared through the transparent wall at the gaping socket where the lifeboat had been. Crewmen formed a tight circle around the truck and the man who lay moaning on the floor. Pistols ready, they held back the crowd while Dr. Willoughby administered an intravenous shot of panedol, and Captain Evans, kneeling beside the dying man, tried to catch his whispers.

"It was Mr. Jasperson, sir. He got me before I could do a thing. I tried to stop him."

"You say you warned him?"

"I called to him, sir, and said, the boat wasn't ready. But he didn't give me a chance. He shot me."

The boy closed his eyes, and Evans stood up.

"Through an error, ladies and gentlemen, Boat F has already gone. You will please go to the other stations and wait for assignment to the other boats."

The crowd whispered, staring uncomprehendingly at the Captain's stony face.

"Did you ever teach mathematics, Professor?" Alan murmured.

"How do you divide fifteen hundred people among four boats?"

Larrabee only smiled, a faraway look in his eyes.

A frightened voice cried, high and loud, "But there won't be enough room!"

Someone screamed. Someone else started to run. In a few seconds a mob of running, panic-stricken people jammed the corridor, fighting their way out. Alan and the professor, an old man and an invalid, had no strength to resist and were helplessly carried along by the living wave.

"Stop those people!" shouted the Captain.

A gun fired into the air and the mob hesitated, then surged on, shouting, past the lounges, to join the throngs waiting at the other stations.

"It's no use," said Evans. "Chief Thayer. Send men to all the stations to guard the boats. You proceed to Boat E and load it first. If any person tries to force his way in, shoot to kill!"

IN their small cabin, Dorothy Hall raised herself on one elbow and looked down at her sleeping husband. His hair was rumpled, his face calm and placid.

"Tom," she whispered. "Wake up, Tom!" Mumbling sleepily, he opened his eyes, then smiled and tried to draw her down to him.

"Wait, Tom. Did you hear the Captain's message?"

"What message?"

"I was so sleepy I didn't understand it very well. Something about the ship, and we must all go to our lifeboats."

"You must have been dreaming. What time is it?"

"Not quite midnight. Do you think everything is all right?"

"Of course. You just had a bad dream. The *Star Lord* can't be in any trouble. You know that."

"Don't you think we ought to go see?"

Playfully he tousled her hair. "Trying to get away from your husband? Tired of me already?"

Relaxing, she snuggled down beside him with a happy sigh.

"I'd never be tired of you, Tom, in a million years. Wherever you are, that's where I want to be, always."

She closed her eyes.

*   *   *

The children were no longer afraid, and they had stopped crying. Leading them through the maze of corridors towards Boat station F, Tanya laughed and told them jokes until, reaching a corner, she suddenly found the passage blocked with a screaming mass of people, fighting, gouging, jamming the hall so that forward movement was almost impossible. She drew back, huddling the children behind her.

"No place for us here, youngsters," she said. "Let's go back, where it isn't so noisy."

Obediently they followed her back to the library, where she settled them in her favorite corner and picked up the abandoned chalk and paper.

"Now Aunt Tanya will tell you a story," she said. "And if you're very good and don't cry at all, I'll even draw you some pictures to go with the story. Once upon a time…"

*   *   *

There was not enough room. A lifeboat, which had been designed to carry two hundred and fifty persons, could not suddenly expand to take in three hundred and seventy-five, although Chief Thayer did his best. At Boat E he stood with drawn pistol, sorting the crowd, and ordering them one by one through the port according to custom as ancient as the race.

"Women and children first," he repeated, again and again. "*Women and children first!*"

They could hear from distant corridors an occasional shout and the clatter of running feet, but the first panic had subsided, and under the menace of the crew's guns the people had become subdued.

White-faced men stepped back and made themselves inconspicuous in the shadows, watching wives and children file through the port, and looking after them hungrily. One man screamed and tried to crash through the cordon. Thayer shot him, and he fell to the floor. Dr. Willoughby moved through the crowd, soothing the hysterical, jollying the frightened, until he spied Alan Chase standing at the edge of the group.

He pushed through to Alan and threw his arm around the bony shoulder, encouragingly.

"I'm assigned to this first boat, Chase, and they'll want you in one of the others. We want at least one medical man in each boat. But I must warn you—" he looked around cautiously, but they might have been alone in a desert for all chance there was of anyone's listening to them, "be sure to get off in Boats B or D. Don't wait for Boat A."

"What difference does it make?"

"Boat A lies above two of the Piles that had to be dumped, and the radioactivity index is sure to be high. Normal people won't be harmed in the brief time they'll be on board if they're rescued, and if they're not rescued, of course, it won't matter anyway. Even you might not be harmed, but with your condition you shouldn't take the risk."

"But does it really matter?"

"What do you mean?"

"I mean that we'd counted on my reaching Almazin III quickly and living in an inert atmosphere in order to cure the neosarcoma. Now that the *Star Lord* is wrecked, I may not be able to get there for months, and that will be too late. If I'm going to die, I'd rather stay with the ship and get it over with."

"Don't be an idiot, doctor! Don't you realize how much better you are? The mitosis was definitely decreasing the last time I checked you. This delay won't be fatal, I'm convinced."

Alan shook his head skeptically.

"Dr. Willoughby!" called Thayer. "Boat ready to launch!"

A grip of the hand, and he had gone. The port shut.

Boat E, jammed with three hundred and twenty-five persons, released itself and shot out into star-studded space.

BOAT B was the second to be launched, and soon Boat D followed.

Keeping to the back of the crowds, Alan watched, admiring the efficiency with which Chief Thayer worked, shouting, wheedling, cursing, until three hundred and thirty people were squeezed in, like frightened cattle in a pen.

There remained only Boat A, and from the shadows he watched nearly five hundred tense faces, drawn with the anxiety of wondering who was to go, and who remain.

Good thing the women and children had all been taken off in the earlier boats, Alan reflected thankfully. It would be heartbreaking enough for Thayer to have to choose among the men, and say to some, *Go*, and to some, *Stay*.

Captain Evans appeared, flanked by Thayer and Stacey, each with drawn pistol. He faced the silent crowd and spoke with terrifying calm.

"I will take charge here," he said. "I cannot ask Thayer to take on such a responsibility. I am sure it is not necessary to tell you that there is not room enough in this boat for all of you. If rescue ships arrive in time, those who must remain behind will be taken off. If not—I realize that no human being has the right arbitrarily to send some men to life and keep others for possible death. But since choice of some sort is necessary to avoid a panic, which might result in unnecessary deaths, I shall choose which ones are to enter this boat, as nearly as possible according to the random positions in which you are now standing. Anyone trying to change his place will be shot!"

No one moved. No one spoke.

"Thayer, you will send in two crewmen to help run the boat. You yourself will be the last man in, to take command. As for the rest —" He paused, wiped his hand over his reddened eyes, and staggered. In a few seconds he had regained control of himself, and with shoulders erect he pointed his arm and called out.

"You go, and you, and you, and you…"

Alan heard a low chuckle behind him, and turned to find

Professor Larrabee.

"What a climax, my boy! Do you believe in premonitions, now?"

"Why haven't you gone?"

"Too old, Alan. I don't want to go. My life is done. But I can't say I really mind. It's been a wonderful adventure, sharing the life and death of the *Star Lord*."

The boat was nearly half full when the tense quiet was broken by the treble voice of a child.

Captain Evans whirled to face the corridor, along which came Tanya, holding to the hands of the two smallest children, while the others clung tightly to the stiff folds of her taffeta gown.

His stare was ghastly. "Miss Taganova! I thought you'd gone! Where have you been? And why weren't these children sent off in the other boats? Didn't you hear the warnings?"

"Somebody's always scolding me for being late," said Tanya, lightly. "But I really couldn't help it. These children seem to have been abandoned by the nursemaids and lost or forgotten by their parents. I have been trying to amuse them until it seemed safe to bring them to you. If I'd come before they would have been trampled to death."

"Well, luckily it's not too late. In you go, the lot of you."

The six youngsters were scrambling through the port, and the Captain had resumed his "You, and you, and you..." when Alan darted forward and clasped Tanya's hand.

"I just want you to know," he whispered. "If the *Star Lord* had gone on to port I'd never have dared say it. But since it can't matter now, Tanya—I'd like you to know—"

She smiled. "I know, Alan. I've known it for many days. And I'd have made a good doctor's wife, I think!" Her lips were trembling as she turned away and entered the port.

"Dr. Chase!" roared the Captain. "What are you doing here? You were supposed to go on Boat D!"

"There isn't room for all of us, Captain. I thought the healthy men should have the preference. I prefer to stay here."

"Personal preferences mean nothing at all at this moment. Get into the boat."

"Let some one else have my place, sir. I haven't long to live anyway, you know. I don't mind staying behind."

THE Captain steadied his pistol.

"Get in. That's an order. This is no time for mock-heroics. You should have gone with Boat D to look after the women and children. Whether you live a month or a year doesn't matter to me, but it is important that you use your medical skill to take care of these people until they are rescued."

With a dazed look, Alan walked through the port.

"And you, and you, and you…"

Thayer called out at last. "That's all, sir. No more room."

"None at all? You're sure?"

"Certain, sir. The tally is three hundred and thirty…"

Nearly a hundred men remained in the corridor. Ashen-faced but calm, they stared at the rectangular doorway, which would have meant a chance to live.

"In you go, Thayer," said the Captain. "Prepare to release."

Into the tense silence broke the brittle clicking of high heels as Tom and Dorothy Hall sauntered up, arm in arm, a puzzled frown on their foreheads.

The Captain moaned. "Another woman! Wait, Thayer. We've one more woman here. Which one of you men in Boat A will volunteer to give up his place to young Mrs. Hall?"

An elderly man walked serenely back into the ship, and joined the others.

Dorothy looked bewildered. "But what's happened? We kept hearing so much noise we decided to get up. Is something wrong?"

"We're abandoning ship. This gentleman is giving up his place to you. Get in."

She clung to Tom's arm. "Not without my husband!"

"Mrs. Hall! We can't waste time on hysterics. This ship might be vaporized while we're talking. A man has given up his chance at life for you. Get in."

She held back. "And Tom?"

With a haggard smile, Tom patted her shoulder. "Never mind me, honey. You go jump in. I'll be all right."

"Mrs. Hall, I'm willing to deprive one man of his chance, because you are a woman. But I will not ask anyone else to give up his place to your husband. Every man in the lifeboat has as much right to his life as your husband, and so has every man who must be left behind. Go, now. It's your last chance!"

Her face had become calm and all hint of tears was gone. Without hesitating she looked up at her husband and spoke softly.

"Tell the man to go back. Whether we live or die, we'll do it together." Smiling at Tom, she took his hand to lead him away.

"Come, Tom. Let's go look at the sky. I believe these stars are real ones."

"Close the port!"

The door slid shut. A minute's long wait, then the boat released herself and shot out into the blackness. The last of the lifeboats was gone.

Professor Larrabee materialized from the shadows and approached Evans with outstretched hand.

"Well done, Captain!"

"You here? I'd hoped you'd gone with the others."

"What, for? My life is over. I've had my pleasures. And this way, I shall be seeing my wife all the sooner. She always loved adventure, and I shall tell her all about the Thakura Ripples. Will you join me in a drink, Captain Evans?"

"No, thank you." His voice broke. "No. I need to be alone." He turned and strode away.

In the privacy of his cabin he buzzed operations.

"What news, Wyman?"

"Slow, steady climb, sir. All piles have passed critical stage."

Slowly he replaced the phone, and covered his eyes.

HUDDLED against the wall of boat F, Burl Jasperson stared out of the observation port, his cold eyes intent on the distant, fast receding lights of the *Star Lord*. Now that he felt himself to be safe, he was weak and exhausted. Beside him sat his secretary, a wizened little man who stared numbly at his clasped hands.

Jasperson coughed.

"Yes, Mr. Jasperson?"

"Get me a panedol tablet and a glass of water. I don't suppose there's any ice, but if there is, put in some ice. I'm thirsty."

Meekly the secretary shuffled down the long length of the boat, solitary as a ghost, to the cubicle labeled Rations. He was gone a long time, thought Burl, and when at last he returned his feet were dragging more than ever.

"There isn't any water, Mr. Jasperson."

"You idiot! There's got to be water."

"I couldn't find any, Mr. Jasperson."

"Davis!" he roared. "Davis, get me a glass of water!"

Davis looked out from the control room. "Get it yourself. This isn't the ship's dining room any more, Jasperson. I've got other things to do now than taking orders from you."

"But I don't know where it is!"

"All right. I'll get it for you this time and show you where it's kept, but after this you wait on yourself."

Leading the way to Rations, he opened a steel cupboard and reached in. Suddenly anxious, he groped about frantically, then cried, "But there isn't any water!"

Jasperson swallowed, with dry throat.

"There isn't water?" he asked plaintively. "But I'm *thirsty!*"

As the hours crawled by, Jasperson sat in the vast emptiness of the boat and stared out at the alien stars. He could not bear to look at the long rows of empty seats, seats that might have been occupied by living men, two hundred and forty-seven silent, omni-present accusers. His eyes were glowing coals, his skin sagged in wrinkles over his haggard face, and his voice was a mere croak.

"Are you *sure* there's no water?" he asked again. "Are you certain?"

"Yes, I'm certain, as I've told you a thousand times," said Steward Davis. "Don't you suppose I'm thirsty too? If you hadn't been in such a hurry to sneak away we'd have been all right. That man you shot was probably getting ready to load the water tanks."

"But you told me the boat was all provisioned!"

"I thought it was, when I saw the tail-end of that truck! But you didn't give me time to check. Why did you have to be in such a hurry?"

Groaning, Jasperson turned again to peer at the unfamiliar suns.

"How long will it take us to reach an inhabited planet, do you think?"

"I don't know, because I don't know just where, we are. With luck, maybe a week, maybe two."

"How long can we live without water?"

"Longer than you'd think. Twelve to fifteen days if we don't move around. We may be able to land somewhere before then. If not—" His voice rose to a sudden shriek. *"What good are those twenty-five thousand credits going to do me now?"*

The secretary sat in numb collapse, but Jasperson prowled the room, up and down, up and down, past the rows of empty seats, while Davis sat and watched him with glittering eyes. Jasperson's head was aching, and he was aware, all at once, that he was out of breath, as though he had been climbing a steep hill under a broiling sun.

"Have to see to this," he muttered. "They can't treat me this way." Stumbling, he lurched down the aisle towards Davis, staggering like a drunken man.

"Got to have more air, Davis. This won't do."

Insolently, Davis got up and looked at the oxygen indicator set in the wall.

"Needle's falling a bit. I'll turn on another tank." He touched the switch, then sat down again.

Jasperson began to laugh.

"What's so funny?"

With shaking hand he pointed, laughing harder, his sagging cheeks quivering as he roared.

"It's those chairs! Ever see such silly chairs? The way they sit there, and look at you?"

"Hey, man, you're drunk! I wonder..."

He got up to look at the oxygen dial again. The needle had fallen still further.

"Where's that oxygen?" he shouted. He rushed into the inner compartment but soon returned, his eyes full of terror.

"No air reserve either! Only that one tank! You great, blundering, condemned fool! A man can live for fifteen days without water, but he can't live ten minutes without air. We're done for!"

Jasperson giggled.

Davis collapsed, and he, too, began to laugh, a helpless, gasping laugh. They had entirely forgotten the self-effacing secretary, but the noise of their dying laughter did not disturb him. He had already fallen sideways in his chair, and would never wake again.

ON the *Star Lord*, Tom and Dorothy sat in the empty lounge, looking through the observation port at the real stars that studded the void. They were holding hands. They were not afraid, and there was nothing they needed to say.

Some of the doomed passengers sat in the Bar, drinking steadily. Others sat and stared at nothingness. Professor Larrabee lay in his cabin, his face turned to the wall, his eyes closed. But he was not sleeping. He was thinking of his wife, and a smile clothed his face.

* * *

In his cabin Captain Josiah Evans waited alone. His hair was almost white, now, his cheeks were sunken, and all semblance of youth had left him. Knowing the futility of his action, nevertheless he completed the day's entry in the ship's log, and closed the volume.

As the hours crept by he noticed that the temperature in the room was rising. Once more, for the last time, he called Operations.

"It's no use, Wyman. Let the Piles alone. It's only a matter of hours now—or perhaps minutes."

"Shall I cast loose the other Piles, sir?"

"No, no use in that, since you can't jettison Piles One, Two and Three. When they go, we all go. It's impossible, now, that any rescue ship could get to us in time. You've done a good job, Wyman. You are now released from duty."

His hands were sweating, his whole body was wet from the high summer torridness of the room. Captain Evans wiped his sticky hands on his handkerchief and picked up the little red book, *Ley's Space Ships*. Opening the book, he read for the last time the well-loved page. Then he took up his pen and made a new notation in the margin.

"*Star Lord: Lost, May 26, 2421, on the Thakura Ripples.*"

He paused a moment, and then with firm, steady strokes he

wrote the final entry: *"Destroyed by the arrogance of her owners, and the criminal pride and weakness of her Captain."*

He put down the pen, and laid his head on his desk.

HOUR after hour Boat A circled the dying *Star Lord*, its weary passengers tense with hope for the all but impossible rescue. Alan sat next to Tanya, guarding the sleeping children.

Suddenly she sat up. "What's that? Out there?"

Over the loudspeaker came Thayer's voice. "We have successfully made contact with a rescue ship. A space cruiser will reach us in approximately eight hours."

Tanya scarcely heard him. She was still peering out, her eyes on the faint lights of the *Star Lord*.

"Look!" she cried.

"Shut your eyes!" shouted Thayer. "Everybody turn your head!"

Far out in space where the *Star Lord* had been was a brilliant red glow, like many suns. It changed, suddenly, to a blinding light, so bright that it was more blue than white, then vanished.

Man had not yet made himself Lord of the Stars.

THE END

If you've enjoyed this book, you will not want to miss these terrific titles…

ARMCHAIR SCI-FI & HORROR DOUBLE NOVELS, $12.95 each

D-1   **THE GALAXY RAIDERS** by William P. McGivern
        SPACE STATION #1 by Frank Belknap Long

D-2   **THE PROGRAMMED PEOPLE** by Jack Sharkey
        SLAVES OF THE CRYSTAL BRAIN by William Carter Sawtelle

D-3   **YOU'RE ALL ALONE** by Fritz Leiber
        THE LIQUID MAN by Bernard C. Gilford

D-4   **CITADEL OF THE STAR LORDS** by Edmund Hamilton
        VOYAGE TO ETERNITY by Milton Lesser

D-5   **IRON MEN OF VENUS** by Don Wilcox
        THE MAN WITH ABSOLUTE MOTION by Noel Loomis

D-6   **WHO SOWS THE WIND…** by Rog Phillips
        THE PUZZLE PLANET by Robert A. W. Lowndes

D-7   **PLANET OF DREAD** by Murray Leinster
        TWICE UPON A TIME by Charles L. Fontenay

D-8   **THE TERROR OUT OF SPACE** by Dwight V. Swain
        QUEST OF THE GOLDEN APE by Ivar Jorgensen and Adam Chase

D-9   **SECRET OF MARRACOTT DEEP** by Henry Slesar
        PAWN OF THE BLACK FLEET by Mark Clifton.

D-10   **BEYOND THE RINGS OF SATURN** by Robert Moore Williams
        A MAN OBSESSED by Alan E. Nourse

ARMCHAIR SCIENCE FICTION CLASSICS, $12.95 each

C-1   **THE GREEN MAN**
        by Harold M. Sherman

C-2   **A TRACE OF MEMORY**
        By Keith Laumer

C-3   **INTO PLUTONIAN DEPTHS**
        by Stanton A. Coblentz

ARMCHAIR MASTERS OF SCIENCE FICTION SERIES, $16.95 each

M-1   **MASTERS OF SCIENCE FICTION, Vol. One**
        Bryce Walton—"Dark of the Moon" and other tales

M-2   **MASTERS OF SCIENCE FICTION, Vol. Two**
        Jerome Bixby: "One Way Street" and other tales

If you've enjoyed this book, you will not want to miss these terrific titles…

ARMCHAIR SCI-FI & HORROR DOUBLE NOVELS, $12.95 each

D-11 **PERIL OF THE STARMEN** by Kris Neville
THE STRANGE INVASION by Murray Leinster

D-12 **THE STAR LORD** by Boyd Ellanby
CAPTIVES OF THE FLAME by Samuel R. Delany

D-13 **MEN OF THE MORNING STAR** by Edmund Hamilton
PLANET FOR PLUNDER by Hal Clement and Sam Merwin, Jr.

D-14 **ICE CITY OF THE GORGON** by Chester S. Geier and Richard Shaver
WHEN THE WORLD TOTTERED by Lester Del Rey

D-15 **WORLDS WITHOUT END** by Clifford D. Simak
THE LAVENDER VINE OF DEATH by Don Wilcox

D-16 **SHADOW ON THE MOON** by Joe Gibson
ARMAGEDDON EARTH by Geoff St. Reynard

D-17 **THE GIRL WHO LOVED DEATH** by Paul W. Fairman
SLAVE PLANET by Laurence M. Janifer

D-18 **SECOND CHANCE** by J. F. Bone
MISSION TO A DISTANT STAR by Frank Belknap Long

D-19 **THE SYNDIC** by C. M. Kornbluth
FLIGHT TO FOREVER by Poul Anderson

D-20 **SOMEWHERE I'LL FIND YOU** by Milton Lesser
THE TIME ARMADA by Fox B. Holden

ARMCHAIR SCIENCE FICTION CLASSICS, $12.95 each

C-4 **CORPUS EARTHLING**
by Louis Charbonneau

C-5 **THE TIME DISSOLVER**
by Jerry Sohl

C-6 **WEST OF THE SUN**
by Edgar Pangborn

ARMCHAIR SCI-FI & HORROR GEMS SERIES, $12.95 each

G-1 **SCIENCE FICTION GEMS, Vol. One**
Isaac Asimov and others

G-2 **HORROR GEMS, Vol. One**
Carl Jacobi and others

If you've enjoyed this book, you will not want to miss these terrific titles…

ARMCHAIR SCI-FI & HORROR DOUBLE NOVELS, $12.95 each

D-21 **EMPIRE OF EVIL** by Robert Arnette
THE SIGN OF THE TIGER by Alan E. Nourse & J. A. Meyer

D-22 **OPERATION SQUARE PEG** by Frank Belknap Long
ENCHANTRESS OF VENUS by Leigh Brackett

D-23 **THE LIFE WATCH** by Lester del Rey
CREATURES OF THE ABYSS by Murray Leinster

D-24 **LEGION OF LAZARUS** by Edmond Hamilton
STAR HUNTER by Andre Norton

D-25 **EMPIRE OF WOMEN** by John Fletcher
ONE OF OUR CITIES IS MISSING by Irving Cox

D-26 **THE WRONG SIDE OF PARADISE** by Raymond F. Jones
THE INVOLUNTARY IMMORTALS by Rog Phillips

D-27 **EARTH QUARTER** by Damon Knight
ENVOY TO NEW WORLDS by Keith Laumer

D-28 **SLAVES TO THE METAL HORDE** by Milton Lesser
HUNTERS OUT OF TIME by Joseph E. Kelleam

D-29 **RX JUPITER SAVE US** by Ward Moore
BEWARE THE USURPERS by Geoff St. Reynard

D-30 **SECRET OF THE SERPENT** by Don Wilcox
CRUSADE ACROSS THE VOID by Dwight V. Swain

ARMCHAIR SCIENCE FICTION CLASSICS, $12.95 each

C-7 **THE SHAVER MYSTERY, Book One**
by Richard S. Shaver

C-8 **THE SHAVER MYSTERY, Book Two**
by Richard S. Shaver

C-9 **MURDER IN SPACE** by David V. Reed
by David V. Reed

ARMCHAIR MASTERS OF SCIENCE FICTION SERIES, $16.95 each

M-3 **MASTERS OF SCIENCE FICTION, Vol. Three**
Robert Sheckley, "The Perfect Woman" and other tales

M-4 **MASTERS OF SCIENCE FICTION, Vol. Four**
Mack Reynolds, "Stowaway" and other tales

IT WAS THREE AGAINST INFINITY

It had finally happened, the Empire of Toromon had declared war. The attacks on its flying vessels had been nothing compared to the final insult—the kidnapping of the Crown Prince. It was felt that the enemy must be dealt with quickly and effectively; and when they were, Toromon would be able to get back on its economic feet.

But how would the members of this civilization—one of the few that survived the catastrophe of the Great Fire—get beyond that seemingly impenetrable wall in space, the deadly radiation barrier, behind which the enemy lay? And assuming the barrier could be breached, how would they deal with the enemy— The Lord of Flames—whose very presence was unknown to the people among whom he lived?

CAST OF CHARACTERS

JON KOSHAR
He was a prison escapee from the tetron mines. But glory awaited him on the far side of the Radiation Barrier.

PETRA
Was this Duchess just another pretty face in the Kingdom…or an active rebel leader?

TEL
This teenage runaway decided to take his chances in the city dregs known as the "Devil's Pot."

QUORL
It was the perfect job for a "gentle" giant—being guardian to a kidnapped princeling!

CLEA KOSHAR
Could this mathematical genius save her people from 60 years of scientific ignorance?

KING USKE
Useless, lazy and frivolous, he was king in name only.

PRINCE LET
Destined to lead. But first he had to experience life in the "real" world…

CAPTIVES OF
THE FLAME

By
SAMUEL R. DELANY

ARMCHAIR FICTION & MUSIC
PO Box 4369, Medford, Oregon 97504

*For more information about Armchair Books and products, visit our
website at…*

www.armchairfiction.com

Or email us at…

armchairfiction@yahoo.com

PROLOGUE

The green of beetles' wings...the red of polished carbuncle...a web of silver fire. Lightning tore his eyes apart, struck deep inside his body; and he felt his bones split. Before it became pain, it was gone. And he was falling through blue smoke. The smoke was inside him, cool as blown ice. It was getting darker.

He had heard something before, a...voice: the *Lord of the Flames...* Then:

Jon Koshar shook his head, staggered forward, and went down on his knees in white sand. He blinked. He looked up. There were two shadows in front of him.

To his left a tooth of rock jutted from the sand, also casting a double shadow. He felt unreal, light. But the backs of his hands had real dirt on them, his clothes were damp with real sweat, and they clung to his back and sides. He felt immense. But that was because the horizon was so close. Above it, the sky was turquoise—which was odd because the sand was too white for it to be evening. Then he saw the City.

It hit his eyes with a familiarity that made him start. The familiarity was a refuge, and violently his mind clawed at it, tried to find other familiar things. But the towers, the looped roadways, that was all there was—and one small line of metal ribbon that soared out across the desert, supported by strut-work pylons. The transit ribbon! He followed it with his eyes, praying it would lead to something more familiar. The thirteenth pylon—he had counted them as he ran his eyes along the silver length—was crumpled, as though a fist had smashed it. The transit ribbon snarled in mid-air and ceased. The abrupt end again sent his mind clawing back toward familiarity: *I am Jon Koshar* (followed by the meaningless number that had been part of his name for five years). *I want to be free* (and for a moment he saw again the dank, creosoted walls of the cabins of the penal camp, and heard the clinking chains of the cutter teeth as he had heard them for so many days walking to the mine entrance while the yard-high ferns brushed his thighs and forearms...but that was in his mind).

The only other things his scrambling brain could reach were facts of negation. He was some place he had *never* been before. He did *not* know how he had gotten there. He did *not* know how to get back. And the close horizon, the double shadows...now he realized that this was *not* Earth (Earth of the Thirty-fifth Century G. F.).

But the City... It was on earth, and he was on earth, and he was—had been—in it. Again the negations: the City was *not* a desert, nor could its dead, deserted towers cast double shadows, nor was the transit ribbon broken.

The transit ribbon!

No!

It couldn't be broken. He almost screamed. *Don't let it be broken, please...*

The entire scene was suddenly jerked from his head. There was nothing left but blue smoke, cool as blown ice, inside him, around him. He was spinning in blue smoke. Sudden lightning seared his eyeballs, and the shivering after-image faded, shifted, became...a web of silver fire, the red of polished carbuncle, the green of beetles' wings.

CHAPTER ONE

SILENT as a sleeping serpent for sixty years, it spanned from the heart of Telphar to the royal palace of Toromon. From the ashes of the dead city to the island capital, it connected what once had been the two major cities, the only cities of Toromon. Today there was only one.

In Telphar, it soared above ashes and fallen roadways into the night.

Miles on, the edge of darkness paled before the morning and in the faint shadow of the transit ribbon, at the edge of a field of lava, among the whispering, yard-high ferns, sat row on row of squat shacks, cheerless as roosting macaws. They stood near the entrance of the tetron mines.

A few moments before, the light rain had stopped. Water dribbled down the supporting columns of the transit ribbon, which made a black band on the fading night.

Now, six extraordinarily tall men left the edge of the jungle. They carried two corpses among them. Two of the tall men hung back to converse.

"The third one won't get very far."

"If he does," said the other, "he'll be the first one to get through the forest guards in twelve years."

"I'm not worried about his escaping," said the first. "But why has there been such an increase in attempts over the past year?"

The other one laughed. Even in the dull light, the three scars that ran down the side of his face and neck were visible. "The orders for tetron have nearly doubled."

"I wonder just what sort of leeches in Toran make their living off these miserable—" He didn't finish, but pointed ahead to the corpses.

"The hydroponic-growers, the aquarium manufacturers," answered the man with the scars. "They're the ones who use the ore. Then, of course, there's the preparation for the war."

"They say that since the artificial food growers have taken over, the farmers and fishermen near the coast are being starved out. And with the increased demand for tetron, the miners are dying off like flies here at the mine. Sometimes I wonder how they supply enough prisoners."

"They don't," said the other. Now he called out. "All right. Just drop them there, in front of the cabins."

The rain had made the ground mud. Two dull splashes came through the graying morning. "Maybe that'll teach them some sort of lesson," said the first.

"Maybe," shrugged the one with the scars.

Now they turned back toward the jungle.

Soon, streaks of light speared the yellow clouds and pried

apart the billowing rifts. Shafts of yellow sank into the lush jungles of Toromon, dropping from wet, green fronds, or catching on the moist cracks of boulders. Then the dawn snagged on the metal ribbon that arced over the trees, and webs of shadow from the immense supporting pylons fell across the few, gutted lava beds that dotted the forest.

A formation of airships flashed through a tear in the clouds like a handful of hurled, silver chips. As the buzz from their tetron motors descended through the trees, Quorl, the forest guard, stretched his seven-foot body and rolled over, crushing leaves beneath his shoulder. Instinctively his stomach tensed. But silence had returned. With large, yellow-brown eyes, he looked about the grove in which he had spent the night. His broad nostrils flared even wider. But the air was still, clean, safe. Above, the metal ribbon glinted. Quorl lay back on the dried leaves once more.

As dawn slipped across the jungle, more and more of the ribbon caught fire from beneath the receding shadows, till at last it soared above the yellow crescent of sand that marked the edge of the sea.

Fifty yards down the beach from the last supporting pylon whose base still sat on dry land, Cithon, the fisherman, emerged from his shack.

"Tel?" he called. He was a brown, wiry man whose leathery face was netted with lines from sand and wind. "Tel?" he called once more. Now he turned back into the cottage. "And where has the boy gotten off to now?"

Grella had already seated herself at the loom, and her strong hands now began to work the shuttle back and forth while her feet stamped the treadle.

"Where has he gone?" Cithon demanded.

"He went out early this morning," Grella said quietly. She did not look at her husband. She watched the shuttle moving back and forth, back and forth between the green and yellow threads.

"I can see he's gone out," Cithon snapped. "But where? The sun is up. He should be out with me on the boat. When will he be back?"

Grella didn't answer.

"When will he be back?" Cithon demanded.

"I don't know."

Outside there was a sound, and Cithon turned abruptly and went to the side of the shack.

The boy was leaning over the water trough, sloshing his face.

"Tel."

The boy looked up quickly at his father. He was perhaps fourteen, a thin child, with a shock of black hair, yet eyes as green as the sea. Fear had widened them now.

"Where were you?"

"No place," was the boy's quietly defensive answer. "I wasn't doing anything."

"Where were you?"

"No place," Tel mumbled again. "Just walking…"

Suddenly Cithon's hand, which had been at his waist jerked up and then down, and the leather strap that had been his belt slashed over the boy's wet shoulder.

The only sound was a sudden intake of breath.

"Now get down to the boat."

Inside the shack, the shuttle paused in Grella's fist the length of a drawn breath. Then it shot once more between the threads.

Down the beach, the transit ribbon leapt across the water. Light shook on the surface of the sea like flung diamonds, and the ribbon above was dull by comparison.

Dawn reached across the water till at last the early light fell on the shore of an island. High in the air, the ribbon gleamed above the busy piers and the early morning traffic of the wharf. Behind the piers, the towers of the City were lanced with gold, and as the sun rose, gold light dropped further down the building faces.

On the boardwalk, two merchants were talking above the

roar of tetron-powered winches and chuckling carts.

"It looks like your boat's bringing in a cargo of fish," said the stout one.

"It could be fish. It could be something else," answered the other.

"Tell me, friend," asked the portly one, whose coat was of cut and cloth expensive enough to suggest his guesses were usually right, "why do you trouble to send your boat all the way to the mainland to buy from the little fishermen there? My aquariums can supply the City with all the food it needs."

The other merchant looked down at the clipboard of inventory slips.

"Perhaps my clientele is somewhat different from yours."

The first merchant laughed. "You sell to the upper families of the City, who still insist on the doubtful superiority of your imported delicacies. Did you know, my friend, I am superior in every way to you? I feed more people, so what I produce is superior to what you produce. I charge them less money, and so I am financially more benevolent than you. I make more money than you do, so I am also financially superior. Also, later this morning my daughter is coming back from the university, and this evening I will give her a party so great and so lavish that she will love me more than any daughter has ever loved a father before."

Here the self-satisfied merchant laughed again, and turned down the wharf to inspect a cargo of tetron ore that was coming in from the mainland.

As the merchant of imported fish turned up another inventory slip, another man approached him. "What was old Koshar laughing about?" he asked.

"He was gloating over his good fortune in backing that harebrained aquarium idea. He was also trying to make me jealous of his daughter. He's giving her a party tonight to which I am no doubt invited; but the invitation will come late this afternoon with no time for me to reply properly.

The other man shook his head. "He's a proud man. But you

can bring him to his place. Next time he mentions his daughter, ask him about his son, and watch the shame storm into his face."

"He may be proud," said the other, "but I am not cruel. Why should I move to hurt him? Time takes care of her own. This coming war will see."

"Perhaps," said the other merchant. "Perhaps."

Once over the island city of Toron, capital of Toromon, the transit ribbon breaks from its even course and bends among the towers, weaves among the elevated highways, till finally it crosses near a wide splash of bare concrete, edged with block-long aircraft hangars. Several airships had just arrived, and at one of the passenger gates the people waiting for arrivals crowded closely to the metal fence.

Among them was one young man in military uniform. A brush of red hair, eyes that seemed doubly dark in his pale face, along with a squat, taurine power in his legs and shoulders; these were what struck you in the swift glance. A close look brought you the incongruity of the major's insignia and his obvious youth.

He watched the passengers coming through the gate with more than military interest.

Someone called, "Tomar!"

And he turned, a grin leaping to his face.

"Tomar," she called again. "I'm over here."

A little too bumptiously, he rammed through the crowd until at last he almost collided with her. Then he stopped, looking bewildered and happy.

"Gee, I'm glad you came," she said. "Come on. You can walk me back to father's." Her black hair fell close to broad, nearly oriental cheekbones. Then the smile on her first strangely, then attractively pale mouth fell.

Tomar shook his head, as they turned now, arm in arm, among the people wandering over the field.

"No?" she asked. "Why not?"

"I don't have time, Clea," he answered. "I had to sneak an hour off just to get here. I'm supposed to be back at the Military Ministry in forty minutes. Hey, do you have any bags I can carry?"

Clea held up a slide rule and a notebook. "I'm traveling light. In a week I'll be back at the university for summer courses, so I didn't bring any clothes. Wait a minute. You're not going to be too busy to get to the party Dad's giving me tonight, are you?"

Tomar shrugged.

Clea began a word, but pushed her tongue hard against the roof of her mouth. "Tomar?" she asked after a moment.

"Yes?" He had a rough voice, which, when he was sad, took on the undertones of a bear's growl.

"What's happening about the war? Will there really be one?"

Again he shrugged. "More soldiers, more planes, and at the Ministry there's more and more work to do. I was up before dawn this morning getting a fleet of survey planes off for a scouting trip to the mainland over the radiation barrier. If they come back this evening, I'll be busy all night with the reports and I won't be able to make the party."

"Oh," said Clea. "Tomar?"

"Yes, Clea Koshar?"

"Oh, don't be formal with me, please. You've been in the City long enough and known me long enough. Tomar, if the war comes, do you think they'll draft prisoners from the tetron mines into the army?"

"They talk about it."

"Because my brother…"

"I know," said Tomar.

"And if a prisoner from the mines distinguished himself as a soldier, would he be freed at the end of the war? They wouldn't send him back to the mines, would they?"

"The war hasn't even begun yet," said Tomar. "No one knows how it will end."

"You're right," she said, "as usual." They reached the gate. "Look, Tomar, I don't want to keep you if you're busy. But you've got to promise to come see me and spend at least an afternoon before I go back to school."

"If the war starts, you won't be going back to school."

"Why not?"

"You already have your degree in theoretical physics. Now you're only doing advanced work. Not only will they conscript prisoners from the mines, but all scientists, engineers, and mathematicians will have to lend their efforts to the cause as well."

"I was afraid of that," Clea said. "You believe the war will actually come, don't you, Tomar?"

"They get ready for it night and day," Tomar said. "What is there to stop it? When I was a boy on my father's farm on the mainland, there was too much work, and no food. I was a strong boy, with a strong boy's stomach. I came to the City and I took my strength to the army. Now I have work that I like. I'm not hungry. With the war, there will be work for a lot more people. Your father will be richer. Your brother may come back to you, and even the thieves and beggars in the Devil's Pot will have a chance to do some honest work."

"Perhaps," said Clea. "Look, like I said, I don't want to keep you—I mean I do, but—well, when will you have some time?"

"Probably tomorrow afternoon."

"Fine," said Clea. "We'll have a picnic then, all right?"

Tomar grinned. "Yes," he said. "Yes." He took both her hands, and she smiled back at him. Then he turned away, and was gone through the crowd.

Clea watched a moment, and then turned toward the taxi stand. The sun was beginning to warm the air as she pushed into the shadow of the great transit ribbon that soared above her between the towers.

Buildings dropped bands of shadow across the ribbon as it wound through the city, although occasional streaks of light from an eastward street still made silver half-rings around it. At the center of the city it raised a final two hundred feet and entered the window of the laboratory tower in the west wing of the royal palace of Toron.

The room in which the transit ribbon ended was deserted. At the end of the metal band was a transparent crystal sphere, fifteen feet in diameter, which hovered above the receiving platform. A dozen small tetron units of varying sizes sat around the room. The viewing screens were dead gray. On a control panel by one ornate window, a bank of forty-nine scarlet-knobbed switches pointed to off. The metal catwalks that ran over the receiving platform were empty.

In another room of the palace, however, someone was screaming.

"Tetron!"

"...if your Highness would only wait a moment to hear the report," began the aged minister, "I believe..."

"Tetron!"

"...you would understand the necessity," he continued in an amazingly calm voice, "of disturbing you at such an ungodly hour..."

"I never want to hear the word tetron again!"

"...of the morning."

"Go away, Chargill; I'm sleeping!" King Uske, who had just turned twenty-one though he had been the official ruler of Toromon since the age of seven, jammed his pale blond head beneath three over-stuffed pillows that lay about the purple silken sheets of his bed. With one too-slender hand he sought feebly around for the covers to hide himself completely.

The old minister quietly picked up the edge of the ermine-rimmed coverlet and held it out of reach. After several half-hearted swipes, the pale head emerged once more and asked in a coldly quiet voice, "Chargill, why is it that roads have been built, prisoners have been reprieved, and traitors have been disemboweled at every hour of the afternoon and evening without anyone expressing the least concern for what I thought? Now, suddenly, at—" Uske peered at the jewel-crusted chronometer by his bed in which a shimmering gold light fixed the hour. "—my God, ten o'clock in the morning! Why must I suddenly be consulted at every little twist and turn of empire?"

"First," explained Chargill, "you are now of age. Secondly, we are about to enter a war, and in times of stress, responsibility is passed to the top, and you, sir, are in that unfortunate position."

"Why can't we have a war and get it over with?" said Uske, rolling over to face Chargill and becoming a trifle more amenable. "I'm tired of all this idiocy. You don't think I'm a very good king, do you?" The young man sat up and planted his slender feet as firmly as possible on the three-inch thick fur rug. "Well, if we had a war," he continued, scratching his stomach through his pink sateen pajama top, "I'd ride in the first line of fire, in the most splendid uniform imaginable, and lead my soldiers to a *sweeping* victory." At the word sweeping, he threw himself under the covers.

"Commendable sentiment," stated Chargill dryly. "And seeing that there may just be a war before the afternoon arrives, why don't you listen to the report, which merely says that another scouting flight of planes has been crippled trying to observe the enemy just beyond the tetron mines over the radiation barrier."

"Let me continue it for you. No one knows how the planes have been crippled, but the efficacy of their methods has lead the council to suggest that we consider the possibility of open war even more strongly. Isn't this more or less what the reports have been for weeks?"

"It is," replied Chargill.

"Then why bother me. Incidentally, must we really go to that imbecilic party for that stupid fish-peddler's daughter this evening? And talk about tetron as little as possible, please."

"I need not remind you," went on the patient Chargill, "that this stupid fish-peddler has amassed a fortune nearly as large as that in the royal treasury—though I doubt if he is aware of the comparison—through the proper exploitation of the unmentionable metal. If there is a war, and we should need to 'borrow' funds, it should be done with as much good will as possible. Therefore, you will attend his party to which he has so kindly invited you."

"Listen a minute, Chargill," said Uske. "And I'm being serious now. This war business is completely ridiculous, and if you expect me to take it seriously, then the council is going to have to take it seriously. How can we have a war with whatever is behind the radiation barrier? We don't know anything about it. Is it a country? Is it a city? Is it an empire? We don't even know if it's got a name. We don't know how they've crippled our scouting planes. We can't monitor any radio communication. Of course we couldn't do that anyway with the radiation barrier. We don't even know if it's people. One of our silly planes gets its tetron (Pardon me. If you can't say it, I shouldn't say it either.) device knocked out and a missile hurled at it. Bango! The council says war. Well, I refuse to take it seriously. Why do we keep on wasting planes anyway? Why not send a few people through the transit ribbon to do some spying?"

Chargill looked amazed.

"Before we instituted the penal mines, and just after we annexed the forest people, the transit ribbon was built. Correct? Now, where does it go?"

"Into the dead city of Telphar," answered Chargill.

"Exactly. And Telphar was not at all dead when we built it, sixty years ago. The radiation hadn't progressed that far. Well, why not send spies into Telphar and from there, across the barrier and into enemy territory. Then they can come back and tell us everything." Uske smiled.

"Of course your Majesty is joking." Chargill smiled. "May I remind your Majesty that the radiation level in Telphar today is fatal to human beings. Completely fatal. The enemy seems to be well beyond the barrier. Only recently, with the great amount of tetron—eh, excuse me—coming from the mines have we been able to develop planes that can perhaps get over it. And that, when and if we can do it, is the only way."

Uske had started out smiling. It turned to a giggle. Then to a laugh. Suddenly he cried out and threw himself down on the bed. "Nobody listens to me! Nobody takes any of my suggestions!" He moaned and stuck his head under the pillows. "No one does anything but contradict me. Go away. Get out. Let me sleep."

Chargill sighed and withdrew from the royal bedchamber.

CHAPTER TWO

IT HAD BEEN silent for sixty years. Then, above the receiving stage in the laboratory tower of the royal palace of Toromon, the great transparent crystal sphere glowed.

On the stage a blue haze shimmered. Red flame shot through the mist, a net of scarlet, contracting, pulsing, outlining the recognizable patterning of veins and arteries. Among the running fires, the shadow of bones formed a human skeleton in the blue, till suddenly the shape was laced with sudden silver, the net of nerves that held the body imprisoned in sensation. The blue became opaque. Then the black-haired man, barefooted, in rags, staggered forward to the rail and held on for a moment. Above, the crystal faded.

He blinked his eyes hard before he looked up. He looked around. "All right," he said out loud. "Where the hell are you?" He paused. "Okay. Okay. I know. I'm not supposed to get dependent on you. I guess I'm all right now, aren't I?" Another pause. "Well, I feel fine." He let go of the rail and looked at his hands, backs and palms. "Dirty as hell," he mumbled. "Wonder where I can get washed up." He looked up. "Yeah, sure. Why not?" He ducked under the railing and vaulted to the floor. Once again he looked around. "So I'm really in the castle. After all these years. I never thought I'd see it. Yeah, I guess it really is."

He started forward, but as he passed under the shadow of the great ribbon's end, something happened.

He faded.

At least the exposed parts of his body—head, hands, and feet—faded. He stopped and looked down. Through his ghost-like feet, he could see the rivets that held down the metal floor. He made a disgusted face, and continued toward the door. Once in the sunlight, he solidified again.

There was no one in the hall. He walked along, ignoring the triptych of silver partitions that marked the consultant chamber. A stained glass window further on rotated by silent machinery flung colors over his face as he passed. A golden disk chronometer fixed in the ceiling behind a carved crystal face said ten-thirty.

Suddenly he stopped in front of a book cabinet and opened the glass door. "Here's the one," he said out loud again. "Yeah, I know we haven't got time, but it will explain it to you better than I can." He pulled a book from the row of books. "We used this in school," he said. "A long time ago."

The book was Catham's *Revised History of Toromon.* He opened the sharkskin cover and flipped a few pages into the text.

"...from a few libraries that survived the Great Fire (from which we will date all subsequent events). Civilization was reduced beyond barbarism. But eventually the few survivors on the Island of Toron established a settlement, a village, a city. Now they pushed to the mainland, and the shore became the central source of food for the island's population, which now devoted itself to manufacturing. On the coast, farms and fishing villages flourished. On the island, science and industry became sudden factors in the life of Toromon, now an empire.

"Beyond the plains at the coast, explorers discovered the forest people who lived in the strip of jungle that held in its crescent the stretch of mainland. They were a mutant breed, gigantic in physical stature, peaceful in nature. They quickly became part of Toromon's empire, with no resistance.

"Beyond the jungle were the gutted fields of lava and dead earth, and it was here that the strange metal tetron was discovered. A great empire has a great crime rate, and our penal system was used to supply miners for the tetron. Now technology leaped ahead, and we developed many uses for the power that could be released from the tetron.

"Then, beyond the lava fields, we discovered what it was that had enlarged the bodies of the forest people, what it was that had killed all green things beyond the jungle. Lingering from the days of the Great Fire, a wide strip of radioactive land still burned all around the lava fields, cutting us off from further expansion.

"Going toward that field of death, the plants became gnarled, distorted caricatures of themselves. Then only rock. Death was long if a man ventured in and came back. First immense thirst; then the skin dries out; blindness, fever, madness, at last death; this is what awaited the transgressor.

"It was at the brink of the radiation barrier, in defiance of death, that Telphar was established. It was far enough away to be safe, yet near enough to see the purple glow at the horizon over the broken hills. At the same time, experiments were being conducted with elementary matter transmission, and as a token to this new direction of science, the transit ribbon was commissioned to link the two cities. It was more a gesture of the solidarity of Toromon's empire than a practical appliance. Only three or four hundred pounds of matter could be sent at once, or two or three people. The transportation was instantaneous, and portended a future of great exploration to any part of the world, with theoretical travel to the stars.

"Then, at seven thirty-two on an autumn evening, sixty years ago, a sudden increase in the pale light was observed in the radiation-saturated west by the citizens of Telphar. Seven hours later the entire sky above Telphar was flickering with streaks of pale blue and yellow. Evacuation had begun already. But in three days, Telphar was dead. The sudden rise in radiation has been attributed to many things in theory, but as yet, an irrefutable explanation is still wanted.

"The advance of the radiation stopped well before the tetron mines; however, Telphar was not lost to Toron for good, and…"

Jon suddenly closed the book. "You see?" he said. "That's why I was afraid when I saw where I was. That's why…" He stopped, shrugged. "You're not listening," he said, and put the book back on the shelf.

Down the hallway fifty feet, two ornate stairways branched right and left. He waited with his hands shoved into his pockets, looking absently toward another window, like a person waiting for someone else to make up his mind. But the decision was not forthcoming. At last, belligerently he started up the stairway to the left. Halfway up he became a little more cautious, his bare feet padding softly, his broad hand preceding him wearily on the banister.

He turned down another hallway where carved busts and statues sat in niches in the walls, a light glowing blue behind those to the left, yellow behind those to the right. A sound from around a corner sent him behind a pink marble mermaid playing with a garland of seaweed.

The old man who walked by was carrying a folder and looked serenely and patiently preoccupied.

Jon waited without breathing the space of three ordinary breaths. Then he ducked out and sprinted down the hall. At last he stopped before a group of doors. "Which one?" he demanded.

This time he must have gotten an answer, because he went to one, opened it, and slipped in.

Uske had pulled the silken sheet over his head. He heard several small clicks and tiny brushing noises, but they came through the fog of sleep that had been washing back over him since Chargill's departure. The first sound definite enough to wake him was water against tile. He listened to it for nearly two minutes through the languid veil of fatigue. It was only when it stopped that he frowned, pushed back the sheet, and sat up. The door to his private bath was open. The light was off, but someone, or thing, was apparently finishing a shower. The windows of his room were covered with thick drapes; but he hesitated to push the button that would reel them back from the sun.

He heard the rings of the shower curtain sliding along the shower rod; the rattle of the towel rack; silence; a few whistled notes. Suddenly he saw that dark spots were forming on the great fur rug that sprawled across the black stone floor. One after another—footprints! Incorporeal footprints were coming toward him slowly.

When they were about four feet away from his bed, he slammed the flat of his palm on the button that drew back the curtains. Sunlight filled the room like bright water.

And standing in the last pair of footprints was the sudden, naked figure of a man. He leaped at Uske as the King threw himself face down into the mound of pillows and tried to scream at the same time. Immediately he was caught, pulled up, and the edge of a hand was thrust into his open mouth so that when he bit down, he chomped the inside of his cheeks.

"Will you keep still, stupid?" a voice whispered behind him. The King went limp.

"There, now just a second."

A hand reached past Uske's shoulder, pressed the button on the night table by the bed, and the curtains swept across the window. The hand went out as if it had been a flame.

"Now you keep still and be quiet."

The pressure released and the King felt the bed give as the weight lifted. He held still for a moment. Then he whirled around. There wasn't anyone there.

"Where do you keep your clothes, huh? You always were about my size."

"Over there…there in that closet."

The bodiless footprints padded over the fur rug, and the closet door opened. Hangers slid along the rack. The bureau at the back of the closet was opened. "This'll do fine. I didn't think I was ever going to get into decent clothes again. Just a second."

There was the sound of tearing thread.

"This jacket will fit me all right, once I get these shoulder pads out of it."

Something came out of the closet, dressed now: a human form, only with out head or hands.

"Now that I'm decent, open up those curtains and throw some light around the place." The standing suit of clothes waited. "Well, come on, open the curtains."

Slowly Uske reached for the button. A freshly shaven young man with black hair stood in the sunlight, examining his cuffs. An open brocade jacket with metalwork filigree covered a white silk shirt that laced over a wide V-neck. The tight gray trousers were belted with a broad strip of black leather and fastened with a gold disk. The black boots, opened at the toe and the heel, were topped with similar disks. Jon Koshar looked around. "It's good to be back."

"Who...what are you?" whispered Uske.

"Loyal subject of the crown," said Jon, "you squid-brained clam.

Uske sputtered.

"Think back about five years to when you and I were in school together."

A flicker of recognition showed in the blond face.

"You remember a kid who was a couple of years ahead of you, and got you out of a beating when the kids in the mechanics class were going to gang up on you because you'd smashed a high-frequency coil, on purpose. And remember you dared that same kid to break into the castle and steal the royal Herald from the throne room? In fact, you gave him the fire-blade to do it, too. Only that wasn't mentioned in the trial. Did you also alert the guards that I was coming? I was never quite sure of that part."

"Look..." began Uske. "You're crazy."

"I might have been a little crazy then. But five years out in the tetron mines has brought me pretty close to my senses."

"You're a murderer..."

"It was in self-defense, and you know it. Those guards that converged on me weren't kidding. I didn't kill him on purpose. I just didn't want to get my head seared off."

"So you seared one of their heads off first. Jon Koshar, I think you're crazy. What are you doing here anyway?"

"It would take too long to explain. But believe me, the last thing I came back for was to see you again."

"So you come in, steal my clothing..." Suddenly he laughed. "Oh, of course. I'm dreaming all this. How silly of me. I must be dreaming."

Jon frowned.

Uske went on. "I must be feeling guilty about that whole business when we were kids. You keep on disappearing and appearing. You can't possibly be more than a figment of my imagination. Koshar! The name! Of course. That's the name of the people who are giving the party that I'm going to once I wake up. That's the reason for the whole thing."

"What party?" Jon demanded.

"Your father is giving it for your sister. Yes, that's right. You had quite a pretty sister. I'm going back to sleep now. And when I wake up, you're to be gone, do you understand? What a silly dream."

"Just a moment. Why are you going?"

Uske snuggled his head into the pillow. "Apparently your father has managed to amass quite a fortune. Chargill says I have to treat him kindly so we can borrow money from him later on. Unless I'm dreaming that up too."

"You're not dreaming."

Uske opened one eye, closed it again. And rolled over onto the pillow. "Tell that to my cousin, the Duchess of Petra. She was dragged all the way from her island estate to come to this thing. The only people who are getting out of it are mother and my kid brother. Lucky starfish."

"Go back to sleep," said Jon.

"Go away," said Uske. He opened his eyes once more to see Jon push the button that pulled the curtains. And then the headless, handless figure went to the door and out. Uske shivered and pulled the covers up again.

Jon walked down the hall.

Behind the door to one room that he did not enter, the red-headed Duchess of Petra was standing by the window of her apartment, gazing over the roofs of the city, the great houses of the wealthy merchants and manufacturers, over the hive-like buildings, which housed the city's doctors, clerks, secretaries, and storekeepers, down to the reeking clapboard and stone alleys of the Devil's Pot.

The early sun lay flame in her hair and whitened her pale face. She pushed the window open a bit, and the breeze waved her blue robe as she absently fingered a smoky crystal set in a silver chain around her neck.

Jon continued down the hall.

Three doors away, the old queen lay on the heap of over-stuffed mattresses, nestled in the center of an immense fourposter bed. Her white hair was coiled in two buns on either side of her head, her mouth was slightly open and a faint breath hissed across the white lips. On the wall above the bed hung the portrait of the late King Alsen, sceptered, official, and benevolent.

In a set of rooms just beside the queen mother's chamber, Let, Prince of the Royal Blood, Heir Apparent to the Empire of Toromon, and half a dozen more, was sitting in just his pajama top on the edge of his bed, knuckling his eyes.

The thin limbs of the thirteen-year-old were still slightly akimbo with natural awkwardness and sleep. Like his brother, he was blond and slight.

Still blinking, he slipped into his underwear and trousers, pausing a moment to check his watch. He fastened the three snaps on his shirt, turned to the palace intercom, and pressed a button.

"I overslept, Petra," Let apologized. "Anyway, I'm up now."

"You must learn to be on time. Remember, you are heir to the throne of Toromon. You mustn't forget that."

"Sometimes I wish I could," replied Let. "Sometimes."

"Never say that again," came the sudden command through the tiny intercom. "Do you hear me? Never even let yourself think that for a moment."

"I'm sorry, Petra," Let said. His cousin, the Duchess, had been acting strangely since her arrival two days ago. Fifteen years his senior, she was still the member of the family to whom he felt closest. Usually, with her, he could forget the crown that was always being pointed to as it dangled above his head. His brother was not very healthy, nor even—as some rumored—all in his proper mind. Yet now it was Petra herself who was pointing out the gold circlet of Toroman's kingship. It seemed a betrayal. "Anyway," he went on. "Here I am. What did you want?"

"To say good morning." The smile in the voice brought a smile to Let's face too. "Do you remember that story I told you last night, about the prisoners in the tetron mines?"

"Sure," said Let, who had fallen asleep thinking about it. "The ones who were planning an escape." She had sat in the garden with him for an hour after dark, regaling him with the harrowing details of three prisoners' attempt to escape the penal mines. She had terminated it at the height of suspense with the three men crouching by the steps in the darkness and the drizzling rain, waiting to make their dash into the forest. "You said you were going to go on with it this morning."

"Do you really want to hear the end of the story?"

"Of course I do. I couldn't get to sleep for hours thinking about it."

"Well," said Petra, "when the guard changed, and the rope tripped him up when he was coming down the steps, the rear guard ran around to see what had happened, as planned, and they dashed through the searchlight beam, into the forest, and…" She paused. "Anyway, one of them made it. The other two were caught and killed."

"Huh?" said Let. "Is that all?"

"That's about it," said Petra.

"What do you mean?" Let demanded. Last night's version had contained detail upon detail of the prisoners' treatment, their efforts to dig a tunnel, the precautions they took, along with an uncannily vivid description of the scenery that had made him shiver as though he had been in the leaky, rotten-walled shacks. "You can't just finish it up like that," he exclaimed. "How did they get caught? Which one got away? Was it the chubby one with the freckles? How did they die?"

"Unpleasantly," Petra answered. "No, the chubby one with the freckles didn't make it. They brought him, and the one with the limp, back that morning in the rain and dropped them in the mud outside the barracks to discourage further escape attempts."

"Oh," said Let. "What about the one who did make it?" he asked after a moment.

Instead of answering, she said, "Let, I want to give you a warning." The prince stiffened a bit, but she began differently than he expected. "Let, in a little while, you may be going on quite an adventure, and you may want to forget some things, because it will be easier. Like being the prince of Toromon. But don't forget it, Let. Don't."

"What sort of adventure, Petra?"

Again she did not answer his question. "Let, do you remember how I described the prison to you? What would you do if you were king and those prisoners were under your rule, with their rotten food, the rats, their fourteen hours of labor a day in the mines…"

"Well, I don't know, Petra," he began, feeling as if something were being asked of him that he was reluctant to give. It was like when his history teacher expected him to know the answer on a question of government just because he had been born into it. "I suppose I'd have to consult the council, and see what Chargill said. It would depend on the individual prisoners, and what they'd done; and of course how the people felt about it. Chargill always says you shouldn't do things too quickly…"

"I know what Chargill says," said the Duchess quietly. "Just remember what I've said, will you?"

"What about the third man, the one who escaped?"

"He…came back to Toron."

"He must have had a lot more adventures. What happened to him, Petra? Come on, tell me."

"Actually," said Petra, "he managed to bypass most of the adventures. He came very quickly. Let me see. After they dashed across the search lit area, they ducked into the jungle. Almost immediately the three got separated. The black-haired one got completely turned around, and wandered in the wrong direction until he had gone past the mines, out of the forest, and across the rocky stretch of ground beyond a good five miles. By the time it was light enough to see, he suddenly realized he had been wandering toward the radiation barrier; because in the distance, like a black skeleton on the horizon, were the abandoned ruins of Telphar, the Dead City."

"Shouldn't he have been dead from the radiation?"

"That's exactly what he figured. In fact, he figured if he was close enough to see the place, he should have been dead a few miles back. He was tired. The food they'd taken kept him from being hungry. But he was definitely alive. Finally he decided that he might as well go toward the city. He took two steps more, when suddenly he heard something."

There was silence over the intercom.

After he had allowed sufficient time for a dramatic pause, Let asked, "What was it? What did he hear?"

"If you ever hear it," Petra said, "you'll know it."

"Come on, Petra, what was it?"

"I'm quite serious," Petra said. "That's all I know of the story. And that's all you need to know. Maybe I'll be able to finish it when I come back from the party tonight."

"Please, Petra…"

"That's it."

He paused for a minute. "Petra, is the adventure I'm supposed to have, the war? Is that why you're reminding me not to forget?"

"I wish it were that simple, Let. Let's say that's part of it."

"Oh," said Let.

"Just promise to remember the story, and what I've said."

"I will," said Let, wondering. "I will."

Jon walked down a long spiral staircase, nodded to the guard at the foot, passed into the castle garden, paused to squint at the sun, and went out the gate. Getting in was a lot more difficult.

CHAPTER THREE

THE DEVIL'S POT overturned its foul jelly at the city's edge. Thirteen alleys lined with old stone houses was its nucleus; many of them were ruined, built over, and ruined again. These were the oldest structures in Toran. Thick with humanity and garbage, it reached from the waterfront to the border of the hive houses in which lived the clerks and professionals of Toron. Clapboard alternated with hastily constructed sheet-metal buildings with no room between. The metal rusted; the clapboard sagged. The waterfront housed the temporary prison, the immigration offices, and the launch service that went out to the aquariums and hydroponics plants that floated on vast pontoons three miles away.

At the dock, a frog-like, sooty hulk had pulled in nearly an hour ago. But the passengers were only being allowed to come ashore now, and that after passing their papers through the inspection of a row of officials who sat behind a wooden table. A flimsy, waist-high structure of boards separated the passengers from the people on the wharf. The passengers milled.

A few had bundles. Many had nothing. They stood quietly, or ambled aimlessly. On the waterfront street, the noise was thunderous. Peddlers hawking, pushcarts trundling, the roar of arguing voices. Some passengers gazed across the fence at the sprawling slum. Most did not.

As they filed past the officers and onto the dock, a woman with a box of trinkets and a brown-red birthmark splashed over the left side of her face pushed among the new arrivals. Near fifty, she wore a dress and head rag, that were a well washed, featureless gray.

"And would you like to buy a pair of shoelaces, fine strong ones," she accosted a young man who returned a bewildered smile of embarrassment.

"I...I don't got any money," he stammered, though complimented by the attention.

Rara glanced down at his feet. "Apparently you have no shoes either. Well, good luck here in the New World, the Island of Opportunity." She brushed by him and aimed toward a man and woman who carried a bundle composed of a hoe, a rake, a shovel, and a baby. "A picture," she said, digging into her box, "of our illustrious majesty, King Uske, with a real metal frame, hand-painted in miniature in honor of his birthday. No true cosmopolitan patriot can be without one."

The woman with the baby leaned over to see the palm-sized portrait of a vague young man with blond hair and a crown. "Is that really the king?"

"Of course it is," declared the birthmarked vendress. "He sat for it in person. Look at that noble face. It would be a real inspiration to the little one there, when and if he grows up."

"How much is it?" the woman asked.

Her husband frowned.

"For a hand-painted picture," said Rara, "it's very cheap. Say, half a unit?"

"It's pretty," said the woman, then caught the frown on the man's face. She dropped her eyes and shook her head.

Suddenly the man, from somewhere, thrust a half-unit piece into Rara's hand. "Here." He took the picture and handed it to his wife. As she looked at it, he nodded his head. "It is pretty," he said. "Yes. It is."

"Good luck here in the New World," commented Rara. "Welcome to the Island of Opportunity." Turning, she drew out the next gee-gaw her hand touched, glanced at it long enough to see what it was, and said to the man she now faced. "I see you could certainly use a spool of fine thread to good purpose." She pointed to a hole in his sleeve. "There." A brown shoulder showed through his shirt, further up. "And there."

"I could use a needle too," he answered her. "And I could use a new shirt, and a bucket of gold." Suddenly he spat. "I've as much chance of getting one as the other with what I've got in my pocket."

"Oh, surely a spool of fine, strong thread…"

Suddenly someone pushed her from behind. "All right. Move on, lady. You can't peddle here."

"I certainly can," exclaimed Rara, whirling. "I've got my license right here. Just let me find it now…"

"Nobody has a license to peddle in front of the immigration building. Now move on."

"Good luck in the New Land," she called over her shoulder as the officer forced her away. "Welcome to the Island of Opportunity!"

Suddenly a commotion started behind the gate. Someone was having trouble with papers. Then a dark-haired, barefoot boy broke from his place in line, ran to the wooden gate, and vaulted over. The wooden structure was flimsy. As the boy landed, feet running, the fence collapsed.

Behind the fence they hesitated like an unbroken wave. Then they came. At the table the officials stood up, waved their hands, shouted, then stood on their benches and shouted some more. The officer who had shoved the vending woman disappeared in the wash of bodies.

Rara clutched her box of trinkets and scurried to the corner, then melded with the herding crowd for two blocks into the slums.

"Rara!"

She stopped and looked around. "Oh, there you are," she said, joining a young girl who stood back from the crowd, holding a box of trinkets like the other woman's.

"Rara, what happened?"

The birthmarked woman laughed. "You are watching the beginning of the transformation. Fear, hunger, a little more fear, no work, more fear, and every last one of these poor souls will be a first class, grade-A citizen of the Devil's Pot. How much did you sell?"

"Just a couple of units worth," the girl answered. She was perhaps sixteen, with a strange combination of white hair, blue eyes, and skin that had tanned richly and quickly, giving her the large-eyed look of an exotic snow-maned animal. "Why are they running?"

"Some boy started a panic. The fence gave way and the rest followed him." A second surge of people rounded the corner. "Welcome to the New Land, the Island of Opportunity," Rara called out. Then she laughed.

"Where are they all going to go?" Alter asked.

"Into the holes in the ground, into the cracks in the street. The lucky men will get into the army. But even that won't absorb them all. The women, the children...?" She shrugged.

Just then a boy's voice came from halfway down the block. "Hey!"

They turned.

"Why that's the boy that broke the fence down," exclaimed Rara.

"What does he want?"

"I don't know. Before this afternoon I'd never seen him in my life."

He was dark, with black hair; but as he approached, they saw that his eyes were water-green. "You're the woman who was selling things, huh?"

Rara nodded. "What do you want to buy?"

"I don't want to buy anything," he said. "I want to sell something to you." He was barefoot; his pants frayed into nothing at mid-calf, and his sleeveless shirt had no fastenings.

"What do you want to sell?" she asked, her voice deepening with skepticism.

He reached into his pocket, and brought out a rag of green flannel, which he unwrapped now in his hand.

They had been polished to a milky hue, some streaked with gold and red, others run through with warm browns and yellows. Two had been rubbed down to pure mother-of-pearl, rubbed until their muted silver surfaces were clouded with pastel lusters. There in the nest of green, they swirled around themselves, shimmering.

"They're nothing but sea shells," Rara said.

Alter reached her forefinger out and touched a white periwinkle. "They're lovely," she told him. "Where did you get them?" They ranged in size from the first joint of her thumb to the width of her pinky nail.

"By your departed mother, my own sister, we can't afford to give him a centiunit, Alter. I hardly sold a thing before that brute officer forced me away."

"I found them on the beach," the boy explained. "I was hiding on the boat and I didn't have nothing to do. So I polished them."

"What were you hiding for?" asked Rara, her voice suddenly sharp. "You don't mean you stowed away?"

"Uh-huh," the boy nodded.

"How much do you want for them?" Alter asked.

"How much? How much would it cost to get a meal and a place to stay?"

"Much more than we can afford to pay," interrupted Rara. "Alter, come with me. This boy is going to talk you out of a unit or two yet, if you keep on listening to him."

"See," said the boy, pointing to the shells, "I've put holes in them already. You can string them around your neck."

"If you want to get food and a place to sleep," said Alter, "you don't want money. You want friends. What's your name? And where are you from?"

The boy looked up from the handful of shells, surprised. "My name is Tel," he said after a moment. "I come from the mainland coast. And I'm a fisherman's son. I thought when I came here I could get a job in the aquariums. That's all you hear about on the coast."

Alter smiled. "First of all you're sort of young..."

"But I'm a good fisherman."

"...and also, it's very different from fishing on a boat. I guess you'd say that there were a lot of jobs in the aquariums and the hydroponics gardens. But with all the immigrants, there are three people for every job."

The boy shrugged. "Well, I can try."

"That's right," said Alter. "Come on. Walk with us."

Rara huffed.

"We'll take him back to Geryn's place and see if we can get him some food. He can probably stay there a little while if Geryn takes a liking to him."

"You can't just take every homeless barnacle you find back to Geryn's. You'll have it crawling with every shrimp in the Pot. And suppose he doesn't take a liking to him. Suppose he decides to kick us out in the street." The birthmark on her left cheek darkened.

"Aunt Rara, please," said Alter. "I'll handle Geryn."

Rara huffed once more. "How come when we're two weeks behind on the rent, you can't find a kind word in your mouth for the old man when he threatens to throw us onto the street? Yet for the sake of a handful of pretty shells..."

"*Please...*"

A breeze seeped through the narrow street, picked a shock of Alter's white hair and flung it back from her shoulder.

"Anyway, Geryn may be able to use him. If Tel stowed away, that means he doesn't have any papers."

Tel frowned with puzzlement.

Rara frowned with chastisement in her eyes. "You are not supposed to refer to that, ever."

"Don't be silly," said Alter. "It's just a fantasy of Geryn's anyway. It'll never happen. And without papers, Tel can't get a job at the aquariums, even if they wanted him. So if Geryn thinks he can fit him into his crazy plan, Tel will come out a lot better than if he had some old ten-unit-a-week factory job. Look, Rara, how can Geryn possibly kidnap..."

"Be quiet," snapped Rara.

"And even if he did, what good is it going to do? It's not as if it were the king himself."

"I don't understand," said Tel.

"That's good," said Rara. "And if you want to keep going with us, you won't try to find out."

"We can tell you this much," said Alter. "The man who owns the inn where we stay wants to do something. Now, he is a little crazy. He's always talking to himself, for example. But he needs someone who has no identification registered in the City. Now, if he thinks he can use you, you'll get free food and a place to sleep. He used to be the gardener on the island estate of the Duchess of Petra. But he drank a little too much and I guess at last he had to go. He still says she sends him messages though, about his plan. But..."

"You don't have to go any further," Rara said, curtly.

"You'll hear about it from him," said Alter. "Why did you stow away?"

"I just got fed up with life at home. We'd work all day to catch fish, and then have to leave them rotting on the beach because we could only sell a fifth of them, or sometimes none at all. Some people gave up; some only managed to get it in their heads that they had to work harder. I guess my father was like that. He figured if he worked enough, someone would just have to buy them. Only nobody did. My mother did some hand weaving and we were living mostly on that. Finally, I figured I was eating up more than I was worth. So I left."

"Just like that, and with no money?" asked Rara.

"Just like that," Tel said.

"You poor boy," said Rara, and in a sudden fit of maternal affection, she put her arm around his shoulder.

"Ow!" cried Tel, and winced.

Rara jerked her hand away. "What's the matter?"

"I...I got hurt there," the boy said, rubbing his shoulders gently.

"Hurt? How?"

"My father—he whipped me there."

"Ah," said Rara. "Now it comes out. Well, whatever the reasons you left, they're your own business. Anyway, I've never known anyone yet to do something for one reason alone. Don't lag behind, now. We'll be back at Geryn's in time for lunch."

"I thought if I could sneak aboard," went on Tel, "that they'd have to let me off in the City, even if I didn't have money. I didn't know about papers. And when I was in line, I figured I'd explain to the men at the desk. Or maybe I'd even give them my shells, and they would get the papers for me. But the guy ahead of me had a mistake in his. Some date was wrong, and they said they were going to send him back to the mainland and that he couldn't leave the ship. He said he'd give them real money, and even got it out of his pocket. But they started to take him away. That's when I ran out of line and jumped the fence. I didn't know everyone else would run too."

"Probably half their papers were out of order, too. Or forged. That's why they ran."

"You're a cynic, Aunt Rara."

"I'm a practical woman."

As they turned another corner, the boy's green eyes jumped at the blue-hazed towers of the palace, distant behind the wealthy roofs of merchants' mansions, themselves behind the hive houses and the spreading ruin of tenements. He tried to memorize the twisting street they followed. He couldn't.

There were two general, contradictory impressions in his mind: first, of being enclosed in these tiny alleys, some so small that two could not pass through them with arms held out; the second, of the spreading, immense endlessness of the city. He tried to tell Alter what he felt, but after a minute of broken sentences, she smiled at him and shook her head. "No, I don't understand. What do you mean?"

And a sudden picture of the seaside leapt into his head. The yellow length of the beach lashed across his mind so that it stung. He could see the salt-and-pepper rocks, shaling away and knobbed with periwinkle shells. He could see the brown and green fingers of seaweed clutching the sand when the waves went out. He blinked the gray city back into his eyes. Tears washed the broken curb, the cracked walls, washed the rusted metal window jamb sharp and clean again.

"He means he's homesick," Rara interpreted. "No, boy," she said. "It'll never go away. But it'll get less."

The street turned sharply twice, then widened.

"Well," said Alter. "Here we are."

A red, circular plaque hung over the door of the only stone building on the block. It was two stories, twice the height of the other structures. They entered.

Beams of real wood were set into the low ceiling. By one wall was a counter. There was a large table in the middle, and coming down into the room in a large V was a stairway.

Of the men and women sitting around the room, one caught Tel's eye immediately. He was perhaps seven feet and a handful of inches tall, and was sitting, spraddle-legged, at the table. He had a long, flat, equine face, and a triplex of scars started on his cheek, veered down to his neck, and disappeared under his collarless shirt. As Tel watched, he turned to a plate of food he was eating, so that his scars disappeared.

Suddenly, from the stair's top, a harpoon-straight old man appeared. He hurried down, his white hair spiking out in all directions. Reaching the bottom, he whirled around, darting black eyes to every person in the room. "All right," he said. "I've received the message. I've received the message. And it's time."

Alter whispered to Tel, "That's Geryn."

"Are we all here?" the old man demanded. "Are we all here now?"

A woman at the counter snickered. Suddenly Geryn turned

toward Tel, Alter, and Rara. "You!" he demanded. His pointing finger wavered so they could not tell which of the three he meant.

"You mean him?" asked Alter, pointing to Tel.

Geryn nodded vigorously. "What are you doing here? Are you a spy?"

"No, sir," said Tel.

Geryn stepped around the table and looked at him closely. The black eyes were two sharp spots of darkness in a face the color of shipboards gone two winters without paint.

"Geryn," Alter said. "Geryn, he isn't a spy. He's from the mainland. And Geryn, he doesn't have any papers, either. He stowed away."

"You're not a spy?" Geryn demanded again.

"No, sir," Tel repeated.

Geryn backed away. "I like you," he said. "I trust you." Slowly he turned away. Then he whirled back. "I have no choice, you see. It's too late. The message has come. So I need you." He laughed. Then the laugh stopped short as if sliced by a razor. He put his hands over his eyes, and then brought his finger down slowly. "I'm tired," he said. "Rara, you owe me rent. Pay up or I'll kick you all out. I'm tired." He walked heavily toward the bar. "Give me something to drink. In my own tavern you can give me something to drink."

Someone laughed again. Tel looked at Alter.

"Well," she said. "He likes you."

"He does?"

"Um-hm," she nodded.

"Oh," said Tel.

At the bar, Geryn drained a large glass of pale green liquid, slammed the empty glass on the board and cried out, "The war. Yes, the war!"

"Oh, here we go," Alter whispered.

Geryn ran his finger slowly along the rim of the glass. "The war," he said again. He turned suddenly. "It's coming!" he declaimed. "And do you know why it's coming? Do you know how it's coming? We can't stop it, not now, not any more. I've received the signal, so there's no hope left. We must just go ahead and try to save something, something to start and build from again." Geryn looked directly at Tel. "Boy, do you know what a war is?"

"No, sir," said Tel, which wasn't exactly true. He'd heard the word.

"Hey," someone cried from the bar. "Are we gonna get stories, great fires and destruction again?"

Geryn ignored the cry. "Do you know what the Great Fire was?"

Tel shook his head.

"The world was once much bigger than it is today," Geryn said. "Once man flew not just between island and mainland, island and island, but skirted the entire globe of the earth. Once man flew to the moon, even to the moving lights in the sky. There were empires, like Toromon, only bigger. And there were many of them. Often they fought with one another, and that was called a war. And the end of the final war was the Great Fire. That was over fifteen hundred years ago. Most of the world, from what little we know of it today, is scarred with strips of impassable land, the sea is run through with deadly currents. Only fragments of the earth, widely separated can hold life. Toromon may be the only one, for all we are sure of. And now we will have another war."

Someone from the bar yelled, "So what if it comes? It might bring some excitement."

Geryn whirled. "You don't understand!" He whipped one hand through his shocked white hair. "What are we fighting? We don't know. It's something mysterious and unnamable on the other side of the radiation barrier. Why are we fighting?"

"Because…" began a bored voice at the bar.

"Because," interrupted Geryn, suddenly pointing directly at Tel's face, "we have to fight. Toromon has gotten into a situation where its excesses must be channeled toward something external. Our science has outrun our economics. Our laws have become stricter, and we say it is to stop the rising lawlessness. But it is to supply workers for the mines that the laws tighten, workers who will dig more tetron, that more citizens shall be jobless, and must therefore become lawless to survive. Ten years ago, before the aquariums, fish was five times its present price. There was perhaps four percent unemployment in Toron. Today the prices of fish are a fifth of what they were, yet unemployment has reached twenty-five percent of the city's populace. A quarter of our people starve. More arrive every day. What will we do with them? We will use them to fight a war. Our university turns out scientists whose science we can not use lest it put more people out of work. What will we do with them? We will use them to fight a war. Eventually the mines will flood us with tetron, too much for even the aquariums and the hydroponic gardens. It will be used for the war."

"Then what?" asked Tel.

"We do not know who or what we are fighting," repeated Geryn. "We will be fighting ourselves, but we will not know it. According to the books, it is customary in a war to keep each side in complete ignorance of the other. Or give them lies like those we use to frighten children instead of truth. But here the truth may be…" His voice trailed off.

"What's your plan?" Tel asked.

There was another laugh at the bar.

"Somehow," and his voice was lower. "Somehow we must get ready to save something, salvage some fragment from the destruction that will come. There are only a few of us who know all this, who understand it, who know what…what has to be done."

"What is that?" Tel asked again.

Suddenly Geryn whirled. "Drinks!" he called. "Drinks all around!" The quiet amusement and general lethargy disappeared as the people moved to the bar. "Drink up, friends, my fellows!" cried Geryn.

"Your plan?" Tel asked again, puzzled.

"I'll tell you," answered the old man, almost in a whisper. "I'll tell you. But not just yet. Not just…" He turned back again. "Drink up!" Three men who already had their glasses gave a cheer.

"Are you with me, friends?" Geryn demanded.

"We're with you," six more cried, laughing, clinking their glasses hard on the table top as Tel looked from Alter to Rara and back.

"My plan…" began Geryn. "Have you all had a glass? All of you? Another round for everybody. Yes, a second round!"

There was a solid cheer, now. Glass bottoms turned toward the ceiling, then whammed on the counter top again.

"My plan is to—you understand it's not just my plan, but only a small part in a great plan, a plan to save us all—my plan is to kidnap Prince Let from the palace. That's the part that we must do. Are you with me, friends?" A yell rose, and somebody had started a friendly fight at the end of the bar. Then Geryn's voice suddenly broke through the sound, low, in a grating whisper that silenced them for seconds. "Because you must be with me! The time is tonight. I have… I have it planned." The voices halted, and then heaved to a roar. "Tonight," repeated Geryn, though hardly anyone could hear him. "I have it planned. Only you've got to be…be with me."

Tel frowned and Alter shook her head. The old man had closed his eyes for a moment. Rara was beside him, her hand on his shoulder. "You're going to get yourself sick with all this yelling. Let me get you up to your room."

As she turned him toward the stairs, the scarred giant who had been given a drink, now rose from the table, looked straight at Geryn, then drained his glass.

Geryn nodded, drew a breath through his teeth, and then allowed Rara to lead him up the stairs as Tel and Alter watched.

The noise among the drinking men and women at the bar increased.

CHAPTER FOUR

SHE MADE a note on her pad, put down her slide rule, and picked up a pearl snap with which she fastened together the shoulder panels of her white dress. The maid said, "Ma'am, shall I do your hair now?"

"One second," Clea said. She turned to page 328 of her integral tables, checked the increment of sub-cosine A plus B over the nth root of A to the nth plus B to the nth, and transferred it to her notebook.

"Ma'am?" asked the maid. She was a thin woman, about thirty. The little finger of her left hand was gone.

"You can start now." Clea leaned back in the beauty-hammock and lifted the dark mass of her hair from her neck. The maid caught the ebony wealth with one hand and reached for the end of the four yards of silver chain strung with alternate pearls and diamonds each inch and a half.

"Ma'am?" asked the maid again. "What are you figuring on?"

"I'm trying to determine the inverse sub-trigonometric functions. Dalen Golga, he was my mathematics professor at the university, discovered the regular ones, but nobody's come up with the inverses yet."

"Oh," said the maid. She ceased weaving the jeweled chain a moment, took a comb, and whipped it through a cascade of hair that fell back on Clea's shoulder. "Eh...what are you going to do with them, once you find them?"

"Actually," said Clea. "Ouch..."

"Oh, pardon me, I'm sorry, please..."

"Actually," went on Clea, "they'll be perfectly useless. At least as far as anyone knows now. They exist, so to speak, in a world that has little to do with ours. Like the world of imaginary numbers, the square root of minus one. Eventually we may find use for them, perhaps in the same way we use imaginary numbers to find the roots of equations of a higher order than two, because cosine theta plus I sine theta equals e to the I sine theta, which lets us..."

"Ma'am?"

"Well, that is to say they haven't been able to do anything like that with the sub-trigonometric functions yet. But they're fun."

"Bend your head a little to the left, ma'am," was the maid's comment.

Clea bent.

"You're going to look beautiful." Four and five fingers wove deftly in her hair. "Just beautiful."

"I hope that Tomar can get here. It's not going to be any fun without him."

"But isn't the King coming?" asked the maid. "I saw his acceptance note myself. You know it was on very simple paper. Very elegant."

"My father will enjoy that a good deal more than I will. My brother went to school with the King before...before his Majesty's coronation."

"That's amazing," said the maid. "Were they friends? Just think of it? Do you know whether they were friends or not?"

Clea shrugged.

"And, oh," said the maid, continuing, "have you seen the ballroom? All the hors d'oeuvres are real, imported fish. You can tell, because they're smaller than the ones your father grows."

"I know," smiled Clea. "I don't think I've ever eaten any of Dad's fish in my life, which is sort of terrible, actually. They're supposed to be, very good."

"Oh, they are, ma'am. They are. Your father is a fine man to grow such great, good fishes. But you must admit, there's something special about the ones that come from the coast. I tasted one on my way up through the pantry. So I know.

"What exactly is it?" Clea asked, turning around.

The maid frowned, and then smiled and nodded wisely. "Oh, I know. I know. You can tell the difference."

At that moment, Jon Koshar was saying, "Well, so far you've been right." He appeared to be more or less standing (the room was dim, so his head and hands were invisible), more or less alone ("Yeah, I trust you. I don't have much choice," he added.) in the pantry of his father's mansion.

Suddenly his voice took a different tone. "Look, I *will* trust you; with part of me, anyway. I've been caged up for nearly five years, for something stupid I did, and for something that no matter how hard I try, I can't convince myself was all my fault. I don't mean that Uske should be blamed. But chance, and all the rest...well, all I mean is it makes me want out that much more. I want to be *free*. I nearly got myself killed trying to escape from the mines. And a couple of people did get killed helping me. All right, you got me out of that stainless steel graveyard I wandered into back at the radiation barrier, and for that, thanks. I mean it. But I'm not free yet. And I still want out, more than anything in the world.

"Sure, I know that you want me to do something, but I don't understand it yet. You say you'll tell me soon. Okay. But you're riding around in my head like this, so I'm not free yet. If that's what I have to do to get free, than I'll do it. But I'm warning you. If I see another crack in the wall, another spot of light getting in, I'll claw my hands off trying to break through and to hell with what you want. Because while you're there, I can't be free."

Suddenly the light in the pantry flipped on. His sudden face went from the tautness of his last speech to fear. He had been standing by the side of a seven-foot porcelain storage cabinet. He jumped back to the wall. Whoever had come in, a butler or caterer, was out of sight on the other side. A hand came around the edge of the cabinet, reaching for the handle. The hand was broad, wiry with black hair, and sported a cheap, wide, brass ring set with an irregular shape of blue glass. As the door opened, the hand swung out of sight. There was a clatter of dishes on the shelves, the slide of crockery slipping over plastic racks, and a voice. "All right there. You carry this one." Then a grunt, and the *ker-flop* of the latch as the door slammed to.

A moment later, the light, and John Koshar's hands and head, went out. When Jon stepped forward again, he looked at the pantry, at the doors, the cabinets. The familiarity hurt. There was a door that opened into the main kitchen. (Once he had snagged a kharba fruit from the cook's table and ran, as behind him a wooden salad bowl crashed to the floor. The sound made him whirl, in time to catch the cook's howl and to see the pale shreds of lettuce strewn across the black tile floor. The bowl was still spinning. He had been nine.)

He started slowly for the door to the hallway that led to the dining room. In the hall was a red wood table on which sat a free form sculpture of aluminum rods and heavy glass spheres. That was unfamiliar. Not the table, the sculpture.

A slight highlight along the curve of crystal brought back to him for a moment the blue ceramic vase that had been there in his memory. It was coated with glaze that was shot through with myriad cracks. It was cylindrical, straight, then suddenly veering to a small mouth, slightly off center. The burnished red wood behind the vivid, turquoise blue was a combination that was almost too rich, too sensual. He had broken the vase. He had broken it in surprise when his sister had come in on him suddenly, the little girl with hair black as his own, only more of it, saying, "What are you doing, Jon?" and he had jumped, turned, and then the vase was lying in fragments on the floor, like a lot of bright, brittle leaves made out of stone. He remembered his first reaction had been, oddly, surprise at finding that the glaze covered the inside as well as the outside of the vase. He was fourteen.

He walked to the family dining room and stepped inside. With the ballroom in use, no one would come here. Stepping into the room was like stepping into a cricket's den, the subtle *tsk-tsk* of a thousand clocks repeated and repeated, overlapping and melting, with no clear, discernible rhythm. The wall by the door was lined with shelves and they were filled with his father's collection of chronometers. He looked at the clocks on the shelf level with his eye. The last time he had been in this room, it had been the shelf below. The light from the door made a row of crescents on the curved faces, some the size of his little finger nail, others the diameter of his head. Their hands were invisible, their settings were dim. (In his memory they went from simple gold to ornately carved silver, and one was set in an undersea bower with jeweled shells and coral branches.) There must be many new clocks after five years, he thought. If he turned on the light, how many would he recognize?

(When he was eighteen, he had stood in this room and examined the thin, double prong of a fire-blade. The light in the room was off, and as he flicked the button on the hilt, and the white sparks leaped out and up the length of the blade, the crescents flamed on the edges of the clock faces, all along the wall. Later, at the royal palace, with that same blade, there had been the same, sudden, clumsy fear at discovery, fear clotting into panic, the panic turning to confusion, and the confusion metastasizing into fear again, only fear all through him, dragging him down, so that when he tried to run down the vaulted hall, his feet were too heavy, so that when he tripped against the statue in the alcove, whirled upon the pursuing guard, and swung the white needle of energy down and the guard's flesh hissed and fell away—a moment of blood spurting under pale flame—almost immediately he was exhausted. They took him easily after that.)

Clumsy, he thought. Not with his fingers, (He had fixed many of these clocks when his father had acquired them in various states of disrepair.), but with his mind. His emotions were not fine and drawn, but rather great shafts of anger or fear fell about him without focus or apparent source. Disgust, or even love, when he had felt it was vague, liable to metamorphasize from one to the other. (School was great; his history teacher was very good…School was noisy; the kids were pushy and didn't care about anything. His blue parakeet was delicate and beautiful; he had taught it to whistle…there were always crumbs on the bottom of the cage; changing the paper was a nuisance.)

Then there had been five years of prison. And the first sharp feeling pierced his mind, as sharp as the uncoiled hairspring of a clock, as sharp as jewels in a poison ring. It was a wish, a pain, an agony for freedom. The plans for escape had been intricate, yet sharp as the cracks in blue ceramic glaze. The hunger for escape was a hand against his stomach, and as the three of them had, at last, waited in the rain by the steps, it had tightened unbearably. Then…

Then with all the sharpness, what had made him lose the others? Why had he wandered in the wrong direction? Clumsy! And he wanted to be free of that! And wonder if that was what he had wanted to be free of all along while he had sputtered at the prison guards, choked on the food, and could not communicate his outrage. Then, at the horizon, was the purple glow of something paler than sunrise, deadlier than the sea, a flickering, luminous purple gauze behind the hills. Near him were the skeletons of broken, century-ancient trees, leafless, nearly petrified. The crumbly dirt looked as if it had been scattered over the land in handfuls, loosely, bearing neither shrubs nor footprints. By one boulder a trickle of black water ran beneath a fallen log, catching dim light in the ripples on either side. He looked up.

On the horizon, against the lines of light, as though cut—no, torn—from carbon paper was the silhouette of a city. Tower behind tower rose against the pearly haze. A net of roadways wound among the spires.

Then he made out one minuscule thread of metal that ran from the city, in his general direction but veering to the right. It passed him half a mile away and at last disappeared into the edge of the jungle that he could see, now, behind him. *Telphar!* The word came to his mind as though on a sign attached with springs to his consciousness. The radiation! That was the second thing he thought of. Once more the name of the city shivered in his brain: *Telphar!* The certain, very certain death he had wandered into caught the center of his gut like a fist. It was almost as if the name were sounding out loud in his skull. Then he stopped. Because he realized he had heard something. A…a voice! Very definitely he heard it—

Music had started. He could hear it coming from the ball-room now. The party must be under way. He looked out into the hall. A fellow in a white apron, holding an empty tray on which were crumbs from small cakes, was coming toward him.

"Excuse me, sir," the man in the apron said. "Guests aren't supposed to be in this part of the house."

"I was trying to find the—eh—er…" Jon coughed.

The man in the apron smiled. "Oh. Of course. Go back into the ballroom and take the hall to your left down three doors."

"Thank you," Jon smiled back and hurried up the hallway. He entered the ballroom by way of a high, arched alcove in which were small white meat, red meat, dark meat of fish ground into patties, cut into stars, strips of fillet wound into imitation sea shells, tiny braised shrimp, and stuffed baby smelts.

A ten-piece orchestra—three bass radiolins, a theremin, and six blown shells of various sizes—was making a slow, windy music from the dais. The scattering of guests seemed lost in the great room. Jon wandered across the floor.

Here and there were stainless steel fountains in which blue or pink liquid fanned over mounds of crushed ice. Each fountain was rimmed with a little shelf on which was a ring of glasses. He picked a glass up, let a spout of pink fill it, and walked on, sipping slowly.

Suddenly, the loudspeaker announced the arrival of Mr. Quelor Da and party. Heads turned, and a moment later a complex of glitter, green silk, blue net, and diamonds at the top of the six wide marble steps across the room resolved into four ladies and their escorts.

Jon glanced up at the balcony that ran around the second story of the room. A short gentleman in a severe, unornamented blue suit was coming toward the head of the steps, which expanded down toward the ballroom floor with the grace, and approximate shape of a swan's wing. The gentleman hurried down the pale cascade.

Jon sipped his drink. It was sweet with the combined flavors of a dozen fruits, with the whisper of alcohol bitter at the back of his tongue. The gentleman hurried across the floor, passing within yards of him.

Father! The impact was the same as the recognition of Telphar. The hair was thinner than it had been five years ago. He was much heavier. His—father—was at the other side of the room already, checking with the waiters. Jon pulled his shoulders in, and let his breath out. It was the familiarity, not the change that hurt.

It took some time before the room filled. There was a lot of space. One guest Jon noted was a young man in military uniform. He was powerful, squat in a taurine way usually associated with older men. There was a major's insignia on his shoulder. Jon watched him a while, empathizing with his occasional looks that told how out of place he felt. He took neither food nor drink, but prowled a ten-foot area by the side of the balcony steps. Waiting, Jon thought.

A half an hour later, the floor was respectably populated. Jon had exchanged a few words at last with the soldier. (Jon: "A beautiful party, don't you think?" Soldier, with embarrassment: "Yes, sir." Jon: "I guess the war is worrying all of us." Soldier: "The war? Yes." Then he looked away, not inclined to talk more.) Jon was now near the door. Suddenly the loudspeaker announced: "The Party of His Royal Majesty, the King."

Gowns rustled, the talk rose, people turned, and fell back from the entrance. The King's party, headed by himself and a tall, electric-looking redheaded woman, his senior by a handful of years, appeared at the top of the six marble steps. As they came down, right and left, people bowed. Jon dropped his head, but not before he realized that the King's escort had given him a very direct look. He glanced up again, but now her emerald train was sweeping down the aisle the people had left open. Her insignia, he remembered, told him she was a duchess.

Coming up the aisle in the other direction now between the bowing crowds was old Koshar. He bowed very low, and the pale blond young man raised him and they shook hands, and Koshar spoke. "Your Majesty," he began warmly.

"Sir," answered the King, smiling.

"I haven't seen you since you were a boy at school."

The King smiled again, this time rather wanly. Koshar hurried on.

"But I would like to introduce my daughter to you, for it's her party. Clea—." The old man turned to the balcony stairs, and the crowd's eyes turned with him.

She was standing on the top step, in a white dress made of panel over silken panel, held with pearl clasps. Her black hair cascaded across one shoulder, webbed and re-webbed with a chain of silver strung with pearls. Her hands at her sides, she came down the stairs. People stepped back; she smiled, and walked forward. Jon watched while at last his sister reached his father's side.

"My daughter Clea," said old Koshar to the King.

"Charmed."

Koshar raised his left hand, and the musicians began the introduction to the changing partners dance. Jon watched the King take Clea in his arms, and also saw the soldier move toward them, and then stop. A woman in a smoky gray dress suddenly blocked his view, smiled at him, and said, "Will you dance?" He smiled back, to avoid another expression, and she was in his arms. Apparently the soldier had had a similar experience, for at the first turn of the music, Jon saw the soldier was dancing too. A few couples away, Clea and the King turned round and round, white and white, brunette and blond. The steps came back to Jon like a poem remembered, the turn, the dip, separate, and join again. When a girl does the strange little outward step, and the boy bows, so that for a moment she is out of sight, her gown always swishes just so. Yes, like that! This whole day had been filled with the sudden remembrances of tiny facts like that, forgotten for five years, at once relearned with startling vividness that shocked him. The music signaled for partners to change. Gowns whirled into momentary flowers, and he was dancing with the brown-haired woman the soldier had been dancing with a moment before. Looking to his left, he saw that the soldier had somehow contrived to get Clea for a partner. Moving closer, he overheard.

"I didn't think you were going to get here at all. I'm so glad," from Clea.

"I could have even come earlier," Tomar said. "But you'd have been busy."

"You could have come up."

"And once I got here, I didn't think we'd get a chance to talk, either."

"Well, you've got one now. Better make it quick. We change partners in a moment. What happened to the scouting planes?"

"All crippled. Didn't sight a thing. They got back to base almost before I did this morning. The report was nothing. What about the picnic, Clea?"

"We can have it on…"

A burst of music signaled the change. Jon did not hear the day, but expected his sister to whirl into his arms. But instead (he saw her white dress flare and turn by him) an emerald iridescence caught in his eye, then rich mahogany flame. He was dancing with the Duchess. She was nearly his height, and watched him with a smile hung in the subtle area between friendship and knowing cynicism. She moved easily, and he had just remembered that he ought to smile back to be polite when the music sounded the change. The instant before she whirled away, he heard her say, very distinctly, "Good luck, Jon Koshar."

His name brought him to a halt, and he stared after her. When he did turn back to his new partner, surprise still on his face, his eyes were filled with sudden whiteness. It was Clea.

He should have been dancing, but he was standing still. When she looked at his face to discover why, she suddenly drew a breath. At first he thought his head had disappeared again. Then, as shock and surprise became suddenly as real as her wide eyes, her open mouth, he whispered, "Clea!" And her hand went to her mouth.

Clumsy! he thought, and the word was a sudden ache in his hands and chest. Reach for her. Dance. As his hands went out, the music stopped, and the languid voice of the King came over the loudspeaker.

"Ladies and gentlemen, citizens of Toromon, I have just received a message from the council that necessitates an announcement to you as my friends and loyal subjects. I have been requested by the council to make their declaration of war official by my consent. An emergency meeting over sudden developments has made it imperative that we begin immediate action against our most hostile enemies on the mainland. Therefore, before you all, I declare the Empire of Toromon to be at war."

In the silence, Jon looked for his sister, but she was gone. Someone near the microphone cried out, "Long live the King." Then the cry echoed again. The musicians started the music once more, partners found one another, and the talking and laughing grew in his ears like waves, like crumbling rock, like the cutter teeth clawing into the rock face of the ore deposits...

Jon shook his head. But he was in his own house, yes. His room was on the second floor and he could go up and lie down. And by his bed would be the copper night table, and the copy of *Delcord the Whaler* which he had been reading the night before.

He'd left the ballroom and gotten halfway down the hall before he remembered that his room was probably not his room any longer. And that he certainly couldn't go up to it and lie down. He was standing in front of the door of one of the sitting rooms that opened off the hall. The door was ajar, and from it he heard a woman's voice.

"Well, can't you do something about his index of refraction?

If he's going to be doing any work at night, you can't have him popping on and off like a cigarette lighter." There was silence. Then: "Well, at least don't you think he should be told more than he knows now? Fine. So do I, especially since the war has been officially declared."

Jon took a breath and stepped in.

Her emerald train whirled across the duller green of the carpet as she turned. The bright hair, untonsured save by two coral combs, fell behind her shoulders. Her smile showed faint surprise. Very faint. "Who were you talking to?" Jon Koshar asked.

"Mutual friends," the Duchess said. They were alone in the room.

After a moment, Jon said, "What do they want us to do? It's treason, isn't it?"

The Duchess' eyes went thin, "Are you serious?" she asked. "You call that treason, keeping these idiots from destroying themselves, eating themselves up in a war with a nameless enemy, something so powerful that if there were any consideration of real fighting, we could be destroyed with a thought. Do you remember who the enemy is? You've heard his name. There are only three people in Toromon who have, Jon Koshar. Everyone else is ignorant. So we're the only ones who can say we're fully responsible. That responsibility is to Toromon. Have you any idea what state the economy is in? Your own father is responsible for a good bit of it; but if he closed down his aquariums now, the panic he would cause would equal the destruction their being open already causes. The empire is snowballing toward its own destruction, and it's going to take it out in the war. You call trying to prevent it treason?"

"Whatever we call it, we don't have much choice, do we?"

"With people like you around, I'm not sure it isn't a bad idea."

"Look," said Jon. "I was cooped up in a prison mine way out beyond nowhere for five years. All I wanted was out, see.

All I wanted was to get free. Well, I'm back in Toron and I'm still not free."

"First of all," said the Duchess, "if it wasn't for them, you wouldn't be as free as you are now. After a day of clean clothes and walking in fresh air, if you're not well on the road to what you want, then I'd better change some ideas of my own. I want something too, Jon Koshar. When I was seventeen, I worked for a summer in your father's aquarium. My nine hours a day were spent with a metal spoon about the size of your head scraping the bottoms of the used tank tube of the stuff that even the glass filters were too touchy to take out. Afterwards I was too tired to do much more than read. So I read. Most of it was about Toromon's history. I read a lot about the mainland expeditions. Then, in my first winter out of school, I lived in a fishing village at the edge of the forest, studying what I could of the customs of the forest people. I made sketches of their temples, tried to map their nomadic movements. I even wrote an article on the architecture of their temporary shelters that was published in the university journal.

"Well, what I want is for Toromon to be free, free of its own ridiculous self-entanglements. Perhaps coming from the royal family, I had a easier path toward a sense of Toromon's history. At its best, that's all an aristocracy is good for anyway. But I wanted more than a sense, I wanted to know what it was worth. So I went out and looked, and I found, found out it was worth a whole lot. Somehow Toromon is going to have to pick itself up by the back of the neck and give itself a shaking. If I have to be the part that does the shaking, then I will. That's what I want, Jon Koshar, and I want it as badly as you want to be free."

Jon was quiet a moment. Then he said, "Anyway, to get what we want, I guess we more or less have to do the same thing. All right, I'll go along. But you're going to have to explain some things to me. There's a lot I still don't understand."

"A lot we both don't," the Duchess said. "But we know this: they're not from Earth, they're not human, and they come from very far away. Inconceivably far."

"What about the rest?"

"They'll help us help Toromon if we help them. How, I still don't understand for sure. Already I've arranged to have Price Let kidnapped."

"Kidnapped? But why?"

"Because if we get through this, Toromon is going to need a strong king. And I think you'll agree that Uske will never quite make that. Also, he's ill, and under any great strain, might die in a moment, not to mention the underground groups that are bound to spring up to undermine whatever the government decides to do, once the war gets going. Let is going where he can become a strong man, with the proper training, so that if anything happens to Uske, he can return and there'll be someone to guide the government through its crises. After that, how we're to help them, I'm not sure."

"I see," said Jon. "How did they get hold of you, anyway? For that matter, how did they get me?"

"You? They contacted you just outside of Telphar, didn't they? They had to rearrange the molecular structure of some of your more delicate proteins and do a general overhaul on your sub-crystalline structure so the radiation wouldn't kill you. That, unfortunately had the unpleasant side effect of booting down your index of refraction a couple of points, which is why you keep fading in dim light. In fact, I got a blow-by-blow description of your entire escape from them. It kept me on the edge of my seat all night. How was I contacted? The same way you were, suddenly, and with those words: *Lord of the Flames.* Now, your first direct assignment will be…"

In another room, Clea was sitting on a blue velvet hassock with her hands tight in her lap. Then suddenly they flew apart like springs, shook beside her head, and then clasped again. "Tomar," she said. "Please, excuse me, but I'm upset. It was so strange. When I was dancing with the King, he told me how he had dreamed of my brother this morning. I didn't think anything of it. I thought it was just small talk. Then, just after I changed partners for the third time, there I was, staring into a face that I could have sworn was Jon's. And the man wasn't dancing, either. He was just looking at me, very funny, and then he said my name. Tomar, it was the same voice Jon used to use when I'd hurt myself and he wanted to help. Oh, it couldn't have been him, because he was too tall, and too gaunt, and the voice was just a little too deep. But it was so much like what he might have been. That was when the King made his announcement. I just turned and ran. The whole thing seemed supernatural. Oh, don't worry, I'm not superstitious, but it unnerved me. And that plus what you said this morning."

"What I said?" asked Tomar. He stood beside the hassock in the blue-draped sitting room, his hands in his pockets, listening with animal patience.

"About their drafting all the degree students into the war effort. Maybe the war is good, but Tomar, I'm working on another project, and all at once, the thing I want most in the world is to be left alone to work on it. And I want you, and I want to have a picnic. I'm nearly at the solution now, and to have to stop and work on bomb sightings and missile trajectories... Tomar, there's a beauty in abstract mathematics that shouldn't have to be dulled with that sort of thing. Also, maybe you'll go away, or I'll go away. That doesn't seem fair either. Tomar, have you ever had things you wanted, had them in your hands, and suddenly have a situation come up that made it look like they might fly out of your grip forever?

Tomar rubbed his hand across his brush-cut red hair and shook his head. "There was a time once, when I wanted things. Like food, work, and a bed where all four legs touched the ground. So I came to Toron. And I got them. And I got you, and so I guess there isn't anything else to want, or want that bad." He grinned, and the grin made her smile.

"I guess," she started. "...I guess it was just that he looked so much like my brother."

"Clea," Tomar said. "About your brother. I wasn't going to

tell you this until later. Maybe I shouldn't say it now. But you were asking whether or not they were going to draft prisoners into the army; and whether at the end of their service, they'd be freed. Well, I did some checking. They are going to, and I sent through a recommendation that they take your brother among the first bunch. In three hours I got a memorandum from the penal commissioner. Your brother's dead."

She looked at him hard, trying to hold her eyes open and to prevent the little snarl of sound that was a sob from loosening in the back of her throat.

"In fact it happened last night," Tomar went on. "He and two others attempted an escape. Two of their bodies were found. And there's no chance that the third one could have escaped alive."

The snarl collapsed into a sound she would not make. She sat for a moment. Then she said, "Let's go back to the party." She stood up, and they walked across the white rug to the door. Once she shook her head and opened her mouth. Then she closed it again and went on. "Yes. I'm glad you said it. I don't know. Maybe it was a sign...a sign that he was dead. Maybe it was a sign..." She stopped. "No. It wasn't. It wasn't anything, was it? No." They went down the steps to the ballroom once more. The music was very, very happy.

CHAPTER FIVE

A FEW hours earlier, Geryn gave Tel a kharba fruit. The boy took the bright-speckled melon around the inn, looking for Alter. Unable to find her, he wandered onto the street and up the block. Once a cat with a struggling gray shape in its teeth hurtled across his path. Later he saw an overturned garbage can with a filigree of fish bones ornamenting the parti-colored heap. Over the house roofs across the street, the taller buildings and towers of Toron paled to blue, with sudden yellow rectangles of window light scattered unevenly over their faces.

Turning down another block, he saw Rara standing on the

corner, stopping the occasional passers-by. Tel started up to her, but she saw him and motioned him away. Puzzled, he went to a stoop and sat down to watch. As he ran his thumbnail along the orange rind, and juice oozed from the slit, he heard Rara talking to a stranger.

"Your fortune, sir. I'll spread your future before you like a silver mirror…" The stranger passed. Rara turned to a woman now coming toward her. "Ma'am, a fragment of a unit will spread your life out like a patterned carpet where you may trace the designs of your fate. Just a quarter of a unit…" The woman smiled, but shook her head. "You look like you come from the mainland," Rara called after her. Well, good luck here in the New World, sister, the Island of Opportunity." Immediately she turned to another man, this one in a deep green uniform. "Sir," Tel heard her begin. Then she paused as she surveyed his costume. "Sir," she continued, "for a single unit I will unweave the threads of your destiny from eternity's loom. Would you like to know the promotion about to come your way? How many children you'll…"

"Come on, lady," said the man in uniform. "It's illegal to tell fortunes here."

"But I've got my license," declared Rara. "I'm a genuine clairvoyant. Just a second…" And her hands began to plunge into the seams and pockets of her gray rags.

"Never mind, lady. Just get moving," and he gave her a push. Rara moved.

Tel peeled back the strip of rind he'd loosened from the kharba fruit, licked the juice from the yellow wound, and followed Rara.

"Son of an electric eel," she said when Tel reached her, her birthmark scarlet. "Just trying to make a living, that's all."

"Want a bite?"

Rara shook her head. "I'm too angry," she said. They walked back to the inn.

"Do you know where Alter is?" Tel asked. "I was looking for her."

"She's not in the inn?"

"I couldn't find her there."

"Did you look on the roof?" Rara asked.

"Oh," said Tel. "No." They turned into the tavern and Tel went upstairs. It was not until he was halfway up the ladder on the second floor that went to the trap door in the ceiling that he wondered why she was on the roof. He pushed the trap door back and hoisted himself to the dusty, weathered rim.

Alter was hanging head and white hair down from a pipe that went from the stone chimney to a supporting pipe that was fastened by a firm collar to the roof.

"What are you doing?" Tel asked.

"Hi," she smiled down at him. "I'm practicing."

"Practicing what?"

She was hanging double from her waist over the pipe. Now she grabbed the bar close to her waist and somersaulted forward, letting her feet slowly and evenly to the ground, her legs perfectly straight. "My stunts," she said. "I'm an acrobat." She did not let go of the bar, but suddenly swung her legs up so that her ankles nearly touched her hands, and then whipped them down again, ending the kip by supporting herself upright on the metal perch. Then she flung her legs back (Tel jumped because she looked like she was going to fall) and went out and down, then under, swung up, arced over, and went down again in a giant circle. She circled once more, then doubled up, caught one knee over the bar, reversed direction, and suddenly was sitting on top of the rod with one leg over.

"Gee," Tel said. "How did you do that?"

"It's all timing," Alter said. Suddenly she threw her head back, and circled the bar once more, hanging from her hands and one knee. Then the knee came loose, and her feet came slowly to the ground. "You've just got to be strong enough to hold up your own weight. Maybe a little stronger. But the rest is all timing."

"You mean I could do that?"

"You want to try something?"

"Like what?"

"Come here and grab hold of the bar."

Tel came over and grabbed. He could just keep his feet flat on the tar-papered roof and still hold on. "All right," he said.

"Now pull yourself up and hook your left knee around the bar."

"Like this?" He kicked up once, missed, and tried again.

"When you kick, throw your head back," she instructed. "You'll balance better."

He did, pulled up, and got his foot through his arms, and suddenly felt the bar slide into the crook of his knee. He was hanging by his left knee and hands. "Now what do I do?" he asked, swaying back and forth.

Alter put her hand on his back to steady him. "Now straighten your right leg, and keep your arms fairly straight." He obeyed. "Now swing your right leg up and down, three times, and then swing it down real hard." Tel lifted his leg, dropped it, and at once began swinging back and forth beneath the pole. "Keep the leg straight," Alter said. "Don't bend it, or you'll loose momentum."

He got to the third kick, and then let go (with his thigh muscles, not his hands) and at once the sky slipped back behind him and his body swung upward away from the direction of the kick. "Whoooo," he said, and then felt an arm steadying his wrist. He was sitting on top of the bar with one leg over it. He looked down at Alter. "Is that what was supposed to happen?"

"Sure," she said. "That's how you mount the bar. It's called a knee mount."

"I guess it's easier than climbing. Now what do I do?"

"Try this. Straighten out your arms. And make sure they stay straight. Now straighten your back leg behind you." As he tried, he felt her hand on his knee, helping. "Hey…" he said. "I'm not balanced."

"Don't worry," she said. "I'm holding you. Keep those arms straight. If you don't obey instructions you'll have a head full of tarpaper. Seven feet isn't very high, but head first it's sort of uncomfortable."

Tel's elbows locked.

"Now when I count three, kick the leg I'm holding under you and throw your head back as hard as you can. One…"

"What's supposed to happen?" Tel demanded.

"Follow instructions," replied Alter. "Two…three!"

Tel threw and kicked, and felt Alter give his leg an extra push. He had planned to close his eyes, but what he saw kept them open. Sky and then roof were coming at him, fast. Then they veered away, along with Alter's face (which was upside down), till an instant later the pale blue towers of Toron, all pointing in the wrong direction, pierced his sight. Righting themselves, they jerked out of his line of vision and he was looking straight up at the sky (there was a star out, he noted before it became a meteor and flashed away) until it was replaced by the roof and Alter's face (laughing now) and then once more everything swept into its proper position for a moment.

He clamped his stinging hands tightly on the bar, and when he felt himself stop, he hunched forward and closed his eyes. "Mmmmmmmmmmmm," he said. Alter's hand was on his wrist, very firm, and he was sitting on top of the bar again.

"You just did a double back knee circle," she said. "You did it very well too." Then she laughed. "Only it wasn't supposed to be double. You just kept going."

"How do I get down?" Tel asked.

"Arms straight," said Alter.

Tel straightened his arms.

"Put this hand over here." She patted the bar on the other side of his leg. Tel transferred his grip. "Now bring your leg off the bar." Tel hoisted his leg back so that he was supported by just his hands. "Now bend forward and roll over, slowly if you can." Tel rolled, felt the bar slip from where it was pressed against his waist, and a moment later his feet were brushing back and forth over the tarpaper. He let go and rubbed his hands together. "Why didn't you tell me what I was gonna do?"

"Because then you wouldn't have done it. Now that you know you can, the rest will be easier. You've got three stunts now in less than five minutes. The knee mount, back knee circle, and the forward dismount. And that was the best I've ever seen anybody do for a first try."

"Thanks," said Tel. He looked back up at the horizontal bar. "You know, it feels real funny, doing that stuff. I mean you don't really do it. You do things and then it happens to you."

"That's right," Alter said. "I hadn't thought of it like that. Maybe that's why a good acrobat has to be a person who can sort of relax and just let things happen. You have to trust both your mind and your body."

"Oh," said Tel. "I was looking for you when I came up here. I wanted to give you something."

"Thank you," she smiled, brushing a shock of white hair from her forehead.

"I hope it didn't get broken." He reached into his pocket and pulled out a handful of something sinewy; he had strung the shells on lengths of leather thong. There were three loops of leather, each longer than the one before, and the shells were spread apart and held in place by tiny knots. "Geryn gave me the thong, and I put it together this afternoon. It's a necklace, see?"

She turned while he tied the ends behind her neck. Then she turned back to him, touching the green brilliance of one frail cornucopia, passing to the muted orange of another along the brown leather band. "Thank you," she said. "Thank you very much, Tel."

"You want some fruit?" he said, picking up the globe and beginning to peel the rest of it.

"All right," she said. He broke it open, gave her half, and they went to the edge of the roof and leaned on the balustrade, looking to the street below, then over the roofs of the other houses of the Devil's Pot and up to the darkening towers.

"You know," Tel said. "I've got a problem."

"No identification papers, no place to go. I should say you

do."

"Not like that," he said. "But that's part of it, I guess. I guess it's a large part of it. But not all."

"Then what is it?"

"I've got to figure out what I want. Here I am, in a new place, with no way to get anything for myself; I've got to figure a goal."

"Look," said Alter, assuming the superiority of age and urban training, "I'm a year older than you, and I don't know where I'm going yet. But when I was your age, it occurred to me it would probably all take care of itself. All I had to do was ride it out. So that's what I've been doing, and I haven't been too unhappy. Maybe it's the difference between living here or on the seashore. But here you've got to spend a lot of time looking for the next meal. At least people like you and me have to. If you pay attention to that, you'll find yourself heading in the right direction soon enough. Whatever you're going to be, you're going to be, if you just give yourself half a chance."

"Like a big acrobatic stunt, huh?" asked Tel. "You just do the right things and then it happens to you."

"Like that," said Alter. "I guess so."

"Maybe," said Tel. The kharba fruit was cool, sweet like honey, orange, and pineapple.

A minute later someone was calling them. They turned from the balustrade and saw Geryn's white head poking from the trap door. "Come down," he demanded. "I've been looking all over for you. It's time."

They followed him back to the first floor. Tel saw that the scarred giant was still sitting at the table, his hands folded into quiet hammers before him.

"Now, everyone," Geryn called as he sat down at the table. Somewhat reluctantly people left the bar. Geryn dropped a sheaf of papers on the table. "Come, around, everyone." The top sheet was covered with fine writing and careful architectural drawing; so were the other sheets, when Geryn turned them over. "Now this is the plan. First, I'll divide you into groups."

He looked at the giant across the table. "Arkor, you take the first group." He picked out six more men and three women. He turned to the white-haired girl now. "Alter, you'll be with the special group." He named six more people. Tel was among them. A third group was formed which Geryn himself was to lead. Arkor's group was for strong-arm work. Geryn's was for guard duty and to keep the way clear while the prince was being conveyed back to the inn. "The people in the special group already know what to do."

"Sir," said Tel, "you haven't told me, yet."

Geryn looked at him. "You have to get caught."

"Sir?"

"You go past the guards, and make enough noise so that they catch you. Then, when they're occupied with you, we'll break in. Because you have no papers, they won't be able to trace you."

"Am I supposed to stay caught?"

"Of course not. You'll get away when we distract them."

"Oh," said Tel. Geryn went back to the papers.

As the plan was reviewed, Tel saw two things. First the completeness of the research, information, and attention to detail—habits of individual guards: one who left at the first sound of the change signal; another who waited a moment to exchange greetings with his replacement, a friend from his military academy days. Second, he saw its complexity. There were so many ins and outs, gears that had to mesh, movements to be timed within seconds, that Tel wondered if everything could possibly go right.

While he was wondering, they were suddenly already on their way, each one with a bit of the plan fixed firmly in his mind, no one with too clear a picture of the entire device. The groups were to split into subgroups of two or three, then reconvene at appointed spots around the castle. Tel and Alter found themselves walking through the city with the giant. Occasional streetlights wheeled their shadows over the cracked pavement.

"You're from the forest, aren't you?" Tel finally asked the

giant.

He nodded.

"Why did you come here?" Tel asked, trying to make conversation as they walked.

"I wanted to see the city," he said, raising his hand to his scars with a small chuckle. After that, he said nothing.

Prime Minister Chargill took his evening constitutional along the usually deserted Avenue of the Oyster at about this time every night. Prime Minister Chargill always carried on him a complete set of keys to the private suites of the royal family. This evening, however, a drunk in rags reeled out of a side street and collided with the old man. A moment later, making profuse apologies, he backed away, ducking his head, his hands behind his back. When the drunk returned to the side street, his weaving gait ceased, his hand came from behind his back, and in it was a complete set of keys to the private suites of the royal family.

The guard who was in charge of checking the alarm system loved flowers. He could be—(and had been)—observed going to the florist's at least once a week on his time off. So when the old woman with a tray of scarlet anemones came by and offered them for his perusal, it is not surprising that he lowered his head over the tray and filled his lungs with that strange, pungent smell somewhere between orange rind and the sea wind. Forty-seven seconds later, he yawned. Fourteen seconds after that, he was sitting on the ground, his head hung forward, snoring. Through the gate two figures could be seen at the alarm box...had anyone been there to look.

At another entrance to the castle, two guards converged on a fourteen-year-old boy with black hair and green eyes who was trying to climb the fence.

"Hey, get down from there! All right, come on. Where're your papers? What do you mean you don't have any? Come on with us. Get the camera out, Jo. We'll have to photograph him and send the picture to Chief Records Headquarters. They'll tell us who you are, kid. Now hold still."

Behind them, a sudden white-haired figure was out of the shadows and over the gate in a moment. The guards did not see her.

"Hold still now, kid, while I get your retina pattern."

Later on a bunch of rowdies, led by a giant, started to raise hell around the palace. They hadn't even gotten the kid to the guardhouse yet, but somehow in the confusion the boy got away. One guard, who wore a size seventeen uniform was knocked unconscious, but no one else was hurt. They dispersed the rowdies, carried the guard to the infirmary, and left. The doctor saw him in the waiting room, then left him there momentarily to look for an accident report slip in the supply room at the other side of the building. He could have sworn that a whole pad of them had been lying on the desk when he'd stepped out for a bit ten minutes ago. When the doctor returned with the slip the soldier was still there—only he was stark naked.

A minute later, an unfamiliar guard, wearing a size seventeen uniform, saluted the guard at the gate, and marched in.

Two strange men behind the gate flung a cord with a weight on one end over a third story cornice. They missed once, then secured it the second time and left it hanging there.

A guard wearing a size seventeen uniform came down the hall of the west wing of the castle, stopped before a large double door on which was a silver crown, indicating the room of the Queen Mother; he took a complete set of keys to the private suites of the royal family from his cloak, and locked her Majesty firmly in her room. At the next door, he locked Prince Let securely in his. Then he went rapidly on.

Tel ran till he got to the corner, rounded it, and checked the street sign. It was correct. So he went to a doorway and sat down to wait.

At the same time, Prince Let, getting ready for bed and wearing nothing but his undershirt, looked out the window and saw a girl with white hair hanging head down outside, the shutter. He stood very still. The upside down face smiled at him. Then the hands converged at the window lock, did something, and the two glass panels came open. The girl rolled over once, turned quickly, and suddenly she was crouching on the window ledge.

Let snatched up his pajama bottoms first, and ran to the door second. When he couldn't open it, he whirled around and pulled on his pajama pants.

Alter put her finger to her lips as she stepped down into his room. "Keep quiet," she whispered. "And relax," she added. "The Duchess of Petra sent me. More or less." She had been instructed to use that name to calm the prince. It seemed to work a trifle.

"Look," explained Alter, "you're being kidnapped. It's for your own good, believe me." She watched the blond boy come away from the door.

"Who are you?" he asked.

"I'm a friend of yours if you'll let me be."

"Where are you going to take me?"

"You're going to go on a trip. But you'll come back, eventually."

"What has my mother said?"

"Your mother doesn't know. Nobody knows except you and the Duchess, and the few people who're helping her."

Let appeared to be thinking. He walked over to his bed, sat down, and pressed his heel against the sideboard. There was a tiny click. Nothing else happened. "Why won't they open the door?" he asked.

"It's been locked," Alter said. Suddenly she looked at the clock beside the Prince's bed, and turned to the window. Light from the crystal chandelier caught on the shells that were strung on leather thongs around her neck as she turned.

Let put his hand quietly on the newel post of his bed and pressed his thumb hard on the purple garnet that encrusted the crowning ornamental dolphin. Nothing happened except a tiny click.

At the window, Alter reached out her hand, just as a bundle appeared outside on a lowered rope. She pulled them in, untied them, and shook them out as the rope suddenly flew out the window again. "Here," she said. "Get into these." It was a suit of rags. She tossed them to him.

Finally Let slipped out of his pajama pants and into the suit.

"Now look in your pocket," Alter said.

The boy did and took out a bunch of keys.

"You can open the door with those," Alter said. "Go on."

Let paused, then went to the door. Before he put the key in the lock though, he bent down and looked through the keyhole. "Hey," he said, looking back at the girl. "Come here. Do you see anything?"

Alter crossed the room, bent down, and looked. The only motion Let made was to lean against one of the panels on the wall, which gave a slight click. Nothing happened.

"I don't see anything," Alter said. "Open the door."

Let found the proper key, put it in the lock, and the door swung back.

"All right, you kids," said the guard who was standing on the other side of the door (who incidentally wore a size seventeen uniform), "you come along with me." He took Let firmly by one arm and Alter by the other and marched them down the hall. "I'm warning you to keep quiet," the guard said to Let as they turned the last corner.

Three minutes later they were outside the castle. As the guard passed another uniformed man at the Sentry's post, he said, "More stupid kids trying to break into the palace."

"What a night," said the guard and scratched his head. "A girl too?"

"Looks like it," said the guard who was escorting Alter and the Prince. "I'm taking them to be photographed."

"Sure," answered the guard, and saluted.

The two children were marched down the street toward the guardhouse. Before they got there, they were turned off into a side street. Then suddenly the guard was gone. A black-haired boy with green eyes was coming toward them.

"Is this the Prince?" Tel asked.

"Uh-huh," said Alter.

"Who are you?" Let asked. "Where are you taking me?"

"My name is Tel. I'm a fisherman's son."

"My name is Alter," Alter introduced herself.

"She's an acrobat," Tel added.

"I'm the Prince," Let said. "Really. I'm Prince Let."

The two others looked at the blond boy who stood in front of them in rags like their own. Suddenly they laughed. The Prince frowned. "Where are you taking me?" he asked again.

"We're taking you to get something to eat and where you can get a good night's sleep," Alter answered. "Come on."

"If you hurt me, my mother will put you in jail."

"Nobody's going to hurt you, silly," Tel said. "Come on."

CHAPTER SIX

THE DUCHESS OF PETRA said; "Now, your first direct assignment will be…"

Then, the sudden green of beetles' wings; the red of polished carbuncle; a web of silver fire; lightning and blue smoke. Columns of jade caught red light through the great crack in the roof. The light across the floor was red. Jon felt that there were others with him, but he could not be sure. Before him, on a stone platform, three marble crescents were filled with pulsating shadows. Jon Koshar looked at them, and then away. There were many more columns, most broken.

He saw a huge break in the sanctuary wall. Outside he could

look down on an immense red plain. At a scribed line, the plain changed color to an even more luminous red. Near the temple a few geometrical buildings cast maroon pinions of shadow over the russet expanse. Suddenly he realized that the further half of the plain was an immense red sea, yet with a perfectly straight shoreline. Calmly it rippled toward the bright horizon.

At the horizon, filling up nearly a quarter of the sky, was what seemed to be a completely rounded mountain of dull red. No, it was a segment of a huge red disk, a great dull sun lipping the horizon of the planet. Yet it was dim enough so that he could stare directly at it without blinking. Above it, the atmosphere was a rich purple.

Then there was a voice from behind him, and he turned to the triple throne once more.

"Hail, hosts of Earth," the voice began. The very shadows of the room were like red bruises on the stone. "You are in the halls of an extinct city on Creton III. Twelve million years ago this planet housed a civilization higher than yours today. Now it is dead, and only we are left, sitting on their thrones in the twilight of their dying, ruddy sun."

"Who are you?" demanded Jon, but his voice sounded strange, distorted. As he bit the last word off, another voice broke in.

"What do you really want from us?"

Then a third voice.

"What are you going to do with us?"

Jon looked around but saw no one else. Suddenly another picture, the picture of a world of white desert where the sky was deep blue and each object cast double shadows, filled his mind. "This isn't the world you took me to before..." he exclaimed.

"No," came the quiet voice, "this is not the world we took you to before. Listen. We are homeless wanderers of space. Our origin was not only in another galaxy, but in another universe, eternities ago. By way of this universe we can move from star to star without transversing any segment of time, unless we desire. Thus we have dwelt quietly in the dead cities of myriad suns till now. We have never tampered with any living species, though there is something in us that yearns for the extinct cultures.

"Recently according to our standards, though still much older than your solar system, a dark force has come into the universe. It has evolved similarly to us, and also leaps among galaxies in moments. Yet it holds no culture sacred that it finds, and has already tampered with a score of civilizations. It is younger than we are, and can only exist in one individual at a time, while our entity has three lobes, so to speak. This rival thinks nothing of completely changing the mind of its host, giving deadly information, even new powers. We are bound only to ride with your minds, warn you, guide you, but changing your body before your minds, and that only to keep you from death. So it will be your own greed, your own selflessness that will eventually win or loose this battle. Therefore it will be won or lost within the framework of your own civilization."

"Then tell us this," came a voice that was not Jon's. "What is on the other side of the radiation barrier?"

"But we have told you already. And you have guessed. Toromon is at war with an economic condition. Beyond the barrier is a civilization, which is controlled by the Lord of the Flames. He is only in one member of their number, and any time he may move to another, although it is not likely."

"Are they our enemies?"

"Your only enemies are yourselves. But he must be evicted none the less. To do that, all you must do is confront the individual who is bearing him, the three of you together. But you must all be within seeing distance of him at once. For we work through your minds. What you cannot perceive, we cannot affect."

"How will we do this?"

"One of you has already been made immune to the radiation barrier. So will the rest of you when it becomes necessary. This is what you will do for us, and it will also remove the threatening element of the unknown that distracts Toromon from her own problems."

"But why our planet?" a voice asked.

"Yours is an ideal experimenting ground. Because of the Great Fire, your planet has many civilizations that are now completely isolated from one another; many, however, are on a fairly high level. The radiation barriers that lace your planet will keep you isolated from them for some time. When the Lord of the Flames is finished with one empire, he may wish to try a different method on a basically similar civilization. For all your isolated empires had the same base. Marinor, Letpar, Calcivon, Aptor—these are all empires on your planet of which you have never heard. But your first concern is Toromon."

"Will we remember all this?" Jon asked.

"You will remember enough. Good-bye; you know your task." The red haze in the deserted temple pulsed and the jade columns flickered. Hands of blue smoke caught him and flung him through a lightning flash. Whirled through a net of silver, he dropped through red into the vivid green of beetles' wings.

Jon blinked. The Duchess took a step backwards. The green carpet, the rich wood-paneled walls, the glass-covered desk: they were in a sitting room of his father's house, again.

Finally Jon asked, "Now just what am I supposed to do, again? And explain it very carefully."

"I was going to say," said the Duchess, "that you were to get to the Prince, who is being kept at an inn in the Devil's Pot, and accompany him to the forest people. I want him to stay there until this war is over. They live a different life from any of the other people of this empire. They will give him something he'll be able to use. I told you I spent some time there when I was younger. I can't explain exactly what it is, but it's certain ruggedness, a certain strength. Maybe they won't give it to him, but if he's got it in him, they'll bring it out."

"What about…the Lord of the Flames?"

"I don't—do you have any idea, Jon?"

"Well, assuming we get beyond the radiation barrier, assuming we find what people we're fighting, assuming we find which one of them is carrying around the Lord of the Flames, and assuming we can all three of us get to him at once—assuming all that, there's no problem. But we can't, can we? Look, I'll be going to the forest, so I'll be closest to the radiation barrier. I'll try to get through, see what the situation is, and then the two of you can come on. All right?"

"Fine."

"If nothing else, it'll put me closer to the Lord of the Flames...and my freedom."

"How are you not free now, Jon Koshar?" the Duchess asked.

Instead of answering, he said, "Give me the address of the inn at the Devil's Pot."

Going down the hall, with the address, Jon increased his pace. His mind carried an alien mind that had saved him from death once already. How could he be free? The...obligation? That couldn't be the word.

Around the corner he heard a voice. "And now would you please explain it to me? It's not every day that I'm called on to declare war. I think I did it rather eloquently. Now tell my why."

(Jon remembered the trick of acoustics, which as a child enabled him to stand in this spot and overhear his sister and her girlfriends' conversation just as they came into the house.)

"It's your brother," came the other voice. "He's been kidnapped."

"He's been what?" asked the King. "And why? And by whom?"

"We don't know," answered the official. "But the council thought it was best to get you to declare war."

"Oh," said the King. "So that's why I made that little speech in there. What does mother say?"

"It wouldn't be polite to repeat, sir. She was locked in her room, and very insulted."

142

"She would be," said Uske. "So, the enemy has infiltrated and gotten my silly brother."

"Well," said the voice, "they can't be sure. But what with the planes this morning, they thought it was best."

"Oh, well," said the King. There were footsteps. Then silence.

Coming round the corner, Jon saw the coat closet was ajar. He opened the door, took out a great cape and hood, and wrapped it around him, pulling the hood close over his head. He stepped into the foyer and went out past the doorman.

At the edge of the Devil's Pot, the woman with the birthmark on the left side of her face was tapping a cane and holding out a tin cup. She had put on a pair of dark glasses and wandered up one street and down another. "Money for a poor blind woman," she said in a whiny voice. "Money for the blind." As a coin clinked into her cup, she nodded, smiled, and said, "Welcome to the New World. Good luck in the Island of Opportunity."

The man who had given her the coin walked a step, and then turned back. "Hey," he said to Rara. "If you're blind, how do you know I'm new here?"

"Strangers are generous," Rara explained, "while those who live here are too frozen to give."

"Look," said the man, "I was told to watch out for blind beggars who weren't blind. My cousin, he warned me..."

"Not blind!" cried Rara. "Not blind? Why my license is right here. It permits me to beg in specified areas because of loss of sight. If you keep this up, I'll be obliged to show it to you." She turned away with a huff and began in another direction. The man scratched his head, then hurried off.

A few moments later, a man completely swathed in a gray cloak and hood came around the corner and stopped in front of the woman.

"Money for the blind?"

"Can you use this?" the man said. From his cloak he held

out a brocade jacket, covered with final metal work.

"Of course," said Rara softly.   Then she coughed. "Er…what is it?"

"It's a jacket," Jon said. "It's made pretty well. Maybe you can sell it?"

"Oh, thank you. Thank you, sir."

A few blocks later, a ragged boy, who looked completely amazed, was handed a white silk shirt by the man in the gray cloak. In front of a doorway two blocks on, a pair of open-toed black boots with gold disks were left—and stolen from that doorway exactly forty seconds later by a hairdresser who was returning to her home in Devil's Pot. She was missing the little finger of her left hand. Once the gray cloaked figure paused in an alley beneath a clothesline. Suddenly he flung up a ball of gray cloth, which caught on the line, unrolled, and became identifiable as a pair of dark gray trousers. A block later the last minor articles of clothing were hurled unceremoniously through an open window. As Jon turned another corner, he glimpsed a figure ducking into a doorway down the dim street. The man was apparently following him.

Jon walked very slowly down the next block, ambling along in the shadow. The hoodlum crept up behind him, then grabbed his cloak, ripped it away, and leaped forward.

Only there wasn't anything there. The mugger stood for a moment, the cape dangling from his hand, blinking at the place a man should have been. Then something hit him in the jaw. He staggered back. Something else hit him in the stomach. As he stumbled forward now, beneath the street lamp, a transparent human figure suddenly formed in front of him. Then it planted its quite substantial fist into his jaw again, and he went back, down, and out.

Jon dragged the man back to the side of the alley, fading out completely as he did so. Then he took the hoodlum's clothes, which were ragged, smelly, and painfully nondescript. The shoes, which were too small for him, he had to leave off. Then he flung the cape back around his shoulders and pulled the hood over his head.

For the next six blocks he was lost because there were no street signs. When he did find the next one, he realized he was only a block away from the inn.

As he reached the stone building, he heard a thud in the tiny alleyway beside it. A moment later a girl's voice called softly, "There. Just like that. Only you better do exactly as I say or you'll break your arms or legs, or back."

He walked to the edge of the building and peered into the alley.

Her white hair loose, Alter stood looking up at the roof. "All right, Tel," she called. "You next."

Something came down from the roof, flipped over on the ground at her feet, rolled away, and then suddenly unwound to standing position. The black-haired boy ran his fingers through his hair. "Wow," he said. Then he shook his head. "Wow."

"Are you all right?" Alter asked. "You didn't pull anything, did you?"

"No," he said. "I'm all right. I think. Yeah, everything's in place." He looked up at the roof again, two stories above.

"Your turn, Let," Alter called up.

"It's high," came a childish voice from the roof.

"Hurry up," said Alter, her voice becoming authoritative. "When I count three. And remember, knees up, chin down, and roll quick. One, two, three!" There was the space of a breath, and then it fell, rolled, bounced unsteadily to its feet, and resolved into another boy, this one blond, and slighter than the first.

"Hey, you kids," Jon said.

They turned.

Jon looked at the smaller boy. His slight blond frame, less substantial then even Alter's white-haired loveliness was definitely of the royal family. "What are you doing out here, anyway?" Jon asked. "Especially you, your Highness."

All three children jumped.

It looked like they might balk, and after that descent from the roof, he wasn't sure where they might balk to. So he said, "Incidentally, the Duchess of Petra sent me. How did you do that fall?"

His Highness was the only one to relax appreciably.

"And are you sure you're supposed to be outside?"

"We were supposed to stay on the top floor," Tel said. "But him," he pointed to his ragged Highness, "he got restless, and we started telling him about the tricks, and so we went up to the roof, and Alter said she could get us down."

"Can you get them back up?" Jon asked.

"Sure," said Alter, "all we do is climb…"

Jon held up his hand. "Wait a minute," he said. "We'll go inside and talk to the man in charge. Don't worry. No one'll be mad."

"You mean talk to Geryn?" said Alter said.

"I guess that's what his name is."

They started back out of the alley. "Tell me," Jon said, "just what sort of person is Geryn?"

"He's a strange old man. He talks to himself all the time," said Alter. "But he's smart."

Talks to himself, Jon reflected, and nodded. When they reached the door of the inn, Jon pulled his cape off and stepped into the light. A few people at the bar turned around, and when they saw the children, they looked askance at one another.

"Geryn's probably upstairs," Alter said. They went to the second floor. Jon let the children go ahead of him as they passed into the shadow of the hall. He only stepped up to them when Alter pushed open the door at the end of the hall and bright light from Geryn's room fell full across them.

"What is it?" Geryn snapped. And then, "What is it, quick?" He whirled around in the chair at the rough wooden desk when they entered. The giant was standing by the window. Geryn's gray eyes fidgeted back and forth. Finally he said, "Why are you out here? And who is he? What do you want?"

"I'm from the Duchess of Petra," Jon said. "I've come to

take Let to the forest people."

"Yes," said the old man. "Yes." Then suddenly his face twisted as if he were trying to remember something. Then shook his head. "Yes." Suddenly he stood up. "Well, go on. I've done my part, I tell you. I've done. Every minute he's in my house he endangers my boarders, my friends. Take him. Go on."

The giant turned from the window. "I am to go with you. My name is Arkor."

Jon frowned. For the first time the scarred giant's height struck him. "Why...?" he started.

"It is my country that we go to," said Arkor. "I know how to get there. I can take you through it. Geryn says it is part of the plan."

Jon felt a sudden knot of resentment tighten inside him. These plans—the Duchess', Geryn's, even the plans of the triple beings who inhabited them—they trapped him. Freedom. The word went in and out of his mind like a shadow. He said, "When do we go then, if you know how to get there?"

"In the morning," said Arkor.

"Alter, take him to a room. Get him out of here. Quick. Go on." They backed from the room and Alter hurried them up the hall.

Jon was thinking. After delivering Let to the forest people, he was going further. Yes. He would go on, try to get through the radiation barrier. But all three of them had to get through if they were to do any good. So why wasn't Geryn coming instead of sending the giant? If Geryn came, then there'd be two people near the Lord of the Flames. But Geryn was old. Maybe the Duchess could bring him with her when she came. Mentally he smashed a fist into his thoughts and scattered them. Don't think. Don't think. Thinking binds up your mind, and, you can never be— He stopped. Then another thought wormed into his skull, the thought of five years of glittering hunger.

That night he slept well. Morning pried his eyes open with blades of light that fell through the window. It was very early.

He had been up only a minute when there was a knock on his door. Then it opened, and Arkor directed the dwarfed form of the Prince into Jon's room, then turned and left.

"He says to meet him downstairs in five minutes," Let said.

"Sure," said Jon. He finished buttoning up the ragged shirt stolen from the mugger the night before, and looked at the boy by the door. "I guess you're not used to these sort of clothes," he said. "Once I wasn't either. Pretty soon they begin to take."

"Huh?" said Let. Then, "Oh."

"Is something wrong?"

"Who are you?"

Jon thought for a moment. "Well," he said. "I'm sort of a friend of your brother. An acquaintance, anyway. I'm supposed to take you to the forest."

"Why?"

"You'll be safe there."

"Could we go to the sea instead?"

"My turn for a 'why'?" Jon asked.

"Because Tel told me all about it last night. He said it was fun. He said there were rocks all different colors. And in the morning, he said, you can see the sun come up like a burning blister behind the water. He told me about the boats, too. I'd like to work on a boat. I really would. They don't allow me to do anything at home. Mother says I might get hurt. Will I get a chance to work someplace?"

"Maybe," Jon said.

"Tel had some good stories about fishing. Do you know any stories?"

"I don't know," Jon said. "I never tried telling any. Hey, come on. We better get started."

"I like stories," Let said. "Come on. I'm just trying to be friendly."

Jon laughed, then thought a minute. "I can tell you a story, about a prison mine. Do you know anything about the prison mines beyond the forest?"

"Some," said Let.

"Well, once upon a time, there were three prisoners in that prison camp." They started out in the hall. "They'd been there a long time, and they wanted to get out. One was…well, he looked like me, let's pretend. Another had a limp…"

"And the third one was chubby, sort of," interrupted Let. "I know that story."

"You do?" asked Jon.

"Sure," Let said.

"Then you go on and tell it." Jon was a little annoyed.

Let told it to him.

They were outside waiting for Arkor when the boy finished. "See," Let said. "I told you I knew it."

"Yeah," said Jon quietly. He stood very still. "You say the other two…didn't make it?"

"That's right," Let said. "The guards brought them back and dumped their bodies in the mud so that…"

"Shut up," Jon said.

"Huh?" asked Let.

He was quiet for a few breaths. "Who told you that…story?"

"Petra," Let answered. "She told it to me. It's a good story, huh?"

"Incidentally," Jon said. "I'm the one that got away."

"You mean?" The boy stopped. "You mean it really happened?"

The early light warmed the deserted street now as Arkor came to the door of the inn and stepped into the street.

"All right," he said. "Come on."

CHAPTER SEVEN

THE NEWS service of Toromon in the city of Toron was a public address system that flooded the downtown area, and a special printed sheet that was circulated among the upper families of the city. On the mainland it was a fairly accurate brigade of men and women who transported news orally from settlement to settlement. All announced simultaneously that morning:

CROWN PRINCE KIDNAPPED KING DECLARES WAR!

In the military ministry, directives were issued in duplicate and redelivered in triplicate. At eight-forty, the 27B Communications Sector became hopelessly snarled. This resulted in the shipment of a boatload of prefabricated barracks foundations to a port on the mainland sixty-two miles from the intended destination.

Let, Jon, and Arkor were just mounting the private yacht of the Duchess of Petra, which was waiting for them at the end of the harbor. Later, as the island of Toron slipped across the water, Let mentioned to Jon, leaning against the railing, that there was an awful lot of commotion on the docks.

"It's always like that," Jon told him, remembering the time he'd gone with his father in the morning to the pier. "They're inspecting cargoes. But it does look awfully busy."

Which was a euphemism. One group of military directives, which had been quite speedily and accurately delivered, were the offers of contracts, primarily for food, and secondarily for equipment. Two of the distributors of imported fish who had absolutely no chance of receiving the contracts sent in a bid accompanied by a letter which explained (with completely fraudulent statistics) how much cheaper it would be to use imported fish rather than those from the aquariums. Then they commandeered a group of ruffians who broke into the house of old Koshar's personal secretary, who was still sleeping after the previous night's party, which he had helped out with. (So far he has appeared in this story only as a hand seen around the edge of a storage cabinet door, a broad hand, with wiry black hair, on which there was a cheap, wide, brass ring in which was set an irregular shape of blue glass.)

They tied him to a chair, punched him in the stomach, and in the head, and in the mouth until there was blood running down his trimmed, black beard; and he had given the information they wanted—information that enabled them to sink three of the Koshar cargo fleet that was just coming into dock.

The Duchess' private yacht made contact with a tetron--tramp returning to the mainland and Let, Jon, and Arkor changed ships. Coming from the yacht in bare feet and rags gave them an incongruous appearance. But on the tramp, among those passengers who were returning for their families, they quickly became lost.

On Toron, the pilot of the shuttle boat that took workers from the city to the aquariums found a clumsily put-together, but nevertheless unmistakable, bomb hidden in the lavatory. It was dismantled. There was no accident. But an authority, Vice-Supervisor Nitum of Koshar Synthetic Food Concerns (whose name you do not need to remember, as he was killed three days later in a street brawl) clenched his jaw (unshaven; he had been called to the office a half an hour early over the sunken cargo boats), nodded his head, and issued a few non-official directives himself. Twenty minutes later, Koshar Synthetic Food Concerns was officially given the government contract to supply the armies of Toromon with food. Because the two rival bidders, the import merchants, had ceased to exist about twelve minutes previously, having suddenly been denied warehouse space, and their complete storage dumped into the streets to rot (nearly seven tons of frozen fish) because the refrigeration lockers, and the refrigeration buildings, and the refrigeration trucks had all been rented from Rahsok Refrigeration, and nobody had ever thought of spelling Rahsok backwards.

In the military ministry, Captain Clemen, along with Major Tomar, was called away from his present job of completing the evacuation of the top four floors of an adjacent office building to accommodate the new corps of engineers, mathematicians, and physicists that the army had just enlisted. Apparently riots had started in the streets around the old Rahsok Refrigeration Houses. The warehouses were just a few blocks away from the official boundary of the Devil's Pot.

They got there ten minutes after the report came in. "What the hell is going on?" Clemen demanded, from the head of the City Dispersal Squad. Behind the line of uniformed men, masses of people were pushing and calling out. "And what's that stench?" added Clemen. He was a tiny man, exactly a quarter of an inch over the minimum for military acceptance— 4' 10".

"Fish, sir," the Dispersal Chief told him. "There's tons of it all over the street. The people are trying to take it away."

"Well, let them have it," Clemen said. "It'll clear the streets of the mess and maybe do some good."

"You don't understand, sir," the head of Dispersal explained. "It's been poisoned. Just before it was dumped, it was soaked with buckets of barbitide. Half a ton of the stuff's already been carried away."

Clemen turned. "Tomar," he said. "You get back to headquarters and see personally that a city-wide announcement goes out telling about the poisoned fish. Call General Medical, find out the antidote, and get the information all over the city. See to it personally, too."

Tomar got back to headquarters, got General Medical, got the antidote, which was expensive, complicated, and long, and drafted his announcement.

WARNING! Any citizen who has taken fish from the street in the area of Rahsok Refrigeration is in immediate danger of death. The fish has been treated with the fatal poison barbitide. No fish other than that directly traceable to the Synthetic Markets should be eaten. WARN YOUR NEIGHBORS! If fish has been eaten, go directly to the General Medical building (address followed). Symptoms of barbitide poisoning: intense cramps about two hours after ingestion, followed by nausea, fever, and swollen lymph nodes. Death results in twenty minutes after onset of cramps under normal conditions. Foods with high calcium contents prolong spasms to a maximum hour and a half (foods such as milk, ground egg shell). General

Medical has been alerted. There you will receive injections of
Calcium Silicate and Atropayic Acid which can counteract the
effects of the poison up until the last five or ten minutes.

Tomar personally sent the directive through Communications Center 27B, marked urgent and emergency. Ten minutes
later he received a visiphone call from the Communications
Engineer saying that 27B had been hopelessly snarled all
morning. In fact so had 26B, 25B. In further fact, said the
engineer, the only available sectors open were 34A and 42A,
none of which, incidentally, had access to complete city lines.

Tomar made a triplicate copy of the warning and sent it out,
nonetheless, through Sectors 40A, 41A, and 42A. A half an
hour later the secretary to the Communications Engineer called
and said, "Major Tomar, I'm sorry, I just got back from my
break and I didn't see your message until just now. Because of
the tie-ups, we've received instructions only to let authorized
persons have access to the available sectors."

"Well, who the hell is authorized," Tomar bellowed. "If you
don't put that through and quick, half the city may be dead by
this evening."

The secretary paused a minute. Then he said, "I'm sorry, sir,
but…well, look. I'll give it directly to the Communications
Engineer when he gets back."

"When is he getting back?" Tomar demanded.

"I…I don't know."

"Who is authorized?"

"Only generals, sir, and only those directly concerned with
the war effort."

"I see," Tomar said, and hung up.

He had just dispatched seven copies of the announcement
with an explanatory note to seven of the fourteen generals in the
ministry when the Communications Engineer called again.
"Major, what's all this about a bushel of fish?"

"Look, there are seven tons of the stuff all over the streets."

"And poisoned?"

"Exactly. Will you please see that this message gets out over every available piece of city-wide communication as fast as possible? This is really life and death."

"We're just allowed to work on getting war messages through. But I guess this takes priority. Oh, that explains some of the messages we've been getting. I believe there's even one for you."

"Well?" asked Tomar after a pause.

"I'm not allowed to deliver it, sir."

"Why not?"

"You're not authorized, sir."

"Look, damn it, get it right now and read it to me."

"Well…er…it's right here sir. It's from the chief of the City Dispersal Squad."

The message was, in brief, that twenty-three men, among them Captain Clemen, had been trampled to death by an estimated two and a half thousand hungry residents of the Devil's Pot, most of them immigrants from the mainland.

A ton and a half of fish was finally removed from the streets and disposed of. But five and a half tons had made its way through the city. The Communications Engineer also added that while they'd been talking, a memorandum had come through that Sectors 34A to 42A were now out of commission, but that the major should try 27B again, because it might have cleared up.

The second shift of workers that day was arriving at the aquariums. In the great pontooned building, vast rows of transparent plastic tubes, three feet in diameter, webbed back and forth among the tetron pumps. Vibrator nets cut the tubes into twenty-foot compartments. Catwalks strung the six-story structure, all flooded with deep red light that came from the phosphor-rods that stuck up from the pumps. Light toward the blue end of the spectrum disturbed the fish, who had to be visible at all times, to be moved, or to be checked for any sickness or deformity. In their transparent tubes, the fish floated in a state near suspended animation, vibrated gently, were kept at a constant 82^0, were fed, were fattened, were sorted according to age, size, and species; then slaughtered. The second shift of workers moved into the aquarium, relieving the first shift.

They had been on about two hours when a sweating hulk of a man who was an assistant feeder reported to the infirmary, complaining of general grogginess. Heat prostration was an occasional complaint in the aquarium.

The doctor told him to lie down for a little while. Five minutes later he went into violent cramps. Perhaps the proper attention would have been paid to him had not a few minutes later a woman fallen from a catwalk at the top of the aquarium and broken one of the plastic arteries and her skull, six stories below.

In the red light the workers gathered around her broken body that lay at the end of a jagged plastic tube. In the spreading water, dozens of fish, fat and ruddy-skinned, flapped their gills weakly.

The woman's co-workers said she had complained of not feeling well, when suddenly she went into convulsions while crossing one of the catwalks. By the time the doctor got back to the infirmary, the assistant feeder had developed a raging fever, and the nurse reported him violently nauseated. Then he died.

In the next two hours, out of the five thousand two hundred and eighty people who worked at the aquariums, three hundred and eighty-seven were taken with cramps and died in the next two hours, the only exception being an oddball physical culture enthusiast who always drank two quarts of milk for lunch; he lasted long enough to be gotten onto the shuttle and back to General Medical on Toron, where he died six minutes after admittance, one hour and seventeen minutes after the onset of the cramps. That was the first case that General Medical actually received. It was not until the sixteenth case that the final diagnosis of barbitide poisoning was arrived at. Then someone remembered the query that had come in by phone from the military ministry that morning about the antidote.

"Somehow," said Chief Toxicologist Oona, "the stuff has gotten into some food or other. It may be all over the city." Then he sat down at his desk and drafted a warning to the citizens of Toron containing a description of the effects of barbitide poisoning, antidote, and instructions to come to the General Medical building, along with a comment on high calcium foods. "Send this to the Military Ministry and get it out over every available source of public communications, and quick," he told his secretary.

When the Assistant Communications Engineer (the first having gone off duty at three o'clock) received the message, he didn't even bother to see who it was from, but balled it up in disgust and flung it into a wastepaper basket and mumbled something about unauthorized messages. Had the janitor bothered to count that evening, he would have discovered that there were now thirty-six copies of Major Tomar's directive in various wastebaskets around the ministry.

Only a fraction of the barbitide victims made it to General Medical, but the doctors were busy. There was just one extraordinary incident, and among the screams of cramped patients, it was not given much thought. Two men near the beginning of the rush of patients, gained access to the special receiving room. They managed to get a look at all the women who arrived. One of the patients who was wheeled by them was a particularly striking girl of about fifteen with snow white hair and a strong, lithe body, now knotted with cramps. Sweat beaded her forehead, her eyelids, and through her open collar you could see she wore a leather necklace of shells.

"That's her," one of the men said. The other nodded, then went to the doctor who was administering the injections, and whispered to him.

"Of course not," the doctor said indignantly in a clear voice. "Patients need at least forty-eight hours rest and careful observation after injection of the antidotes. Their resistance is extremely low and complications…"

The man said something else to the doctor and showed him a set of credentials. The doctor stopped, looked scared, then left the patient he was examining and went to the bed of the new girl. Quickly he gave her two injections. Then he said to the men, "I want you to know that I object to this completely and I will—"

"All right, Doctor," the first man said. Then the second hoisted Alter from the cot and they carried her out of the hospital.

The Queen Mother had her separate throne room. She sat in it now, looking at photographs. In bright colors, two showed the chamber of the Crown Prince. In one picture the Prince was seated on his bed in his pajama pants with his heel against the sideboard; standing by the window was a white-haired girl with a leather necklace strung with tiny, bright shells. The next showed the Prince still sitting on the bed, this time with his hand on the newel dolphin. The girl was just turning toward the open window.

The third picture, which from the masking, seemed to have been taken through a keyhole, showed what seemed to be an immense enlargement of a human pupil; mistily discernible through the iris were the dottings and tiny pathways of a retina pattern. On the broad arm of the Queen Mother's throne was a folder marked: ALTER RONID.

In the folder were a birth certificate, a clear photograph of the same retina pattern, a contract in which a traveling circus availed itself of the service of a group of child acrobats for the season, a school diploma, copies of receipts covering a three-year period of gymnastic instruction, a copy of a medical bill for the correction of a sprained hip, and two change of address slips. Also there were several cross reference slips to the files of Alla Ronid (mother, deceased) and Rara Ronid (maternal aunt, legal guardian).

The Queen put the photographs on top of the folder and turned to the guards. There were thirty of them lined against the walls of the room. She lifted up the heavy, jeweled scepter and said, "Bring her in." She touched the two buns of white hair on the sides of her head, breathed deeply, and straightened in the chair, as two doors opened at the other end of the room.

Two blocks had been set up in the middle of the room, about four feet high and a foot apart.

Alter stumbled once, but the guard caught her. They walked her between the blocks, which came to just below her shoulders, spread her arms over the surface and strapped them straight across the tops at the biceps and wrist.

The Queen smiled. "That's only a precaution. We want to help you." She came down the steps of the throne, the heavy jeweled rod cradled in her arm. "Only we know something about you. We know that you know something, which if you tell me, will make me feel a great deal better. I've been very upset, recently. Did you know that?"

Alter blinked and tried to get her balance. The blocks were just under the proper height by half an inch so that she could neither stand completely nor could she sag.

"We know you're tired, and after your ordeal with the barbitide—you don't feel well, do you?" asked the Queen, coming closer.

Alter shook her head.

"Where did you take my son?" the Queen asked.

Alter closed her eyes, then opened them wide and shook her head.

"Believe me," said the Queen, "we have ample proof. Look." She held up the photographs for Alter to see. "My son took these pictures of the two of you together. They're very clear, don't you think?" She put the pictures back in the quilted pocket of her robe.

"Aren't you going to tell me, now?"

"I don't know anything," Alter said.

"Come now. That room had as many cameras as a sturgeon has eggs. There are dozens of hidden switches. Somehow the alarms connected with them didn't go off, but the cameras still worked."

Alter shook her head again.

"You don't have to be afraid," said the Queen. "We know you're tired and we want to get you back to the hospital as soon as possible. Now. What happened to my son, the Prince?"

Silence.

"You're a very sweet girl. You're an acrobat too?"

Alter swallowed, and then coughed.

The Queen gave a puzzled smile this time. "Really, you don't have to be afraid to answer me. You are an acrobat, isn't that right?"

Alter nodded.

The Queen reached out and slowly lifted the triplet leather necklace with its scattering of shells in her fingers. "This is a beautiful piece of jewelry." She lifted it from Alter's neck. "An acrobat's body must be like a fine jewel, fine and strong. You must be very proud of it." Again she paused and tilted her head. "I'm only trying to put you at ease, dear, make conversation." Smiling, she lifted the necklace completely from around Alter's neck. "Oh, this is exquisite…"

Suddenly the necklace clattered to the ground, the shells making an almost miniature sound against the tiles.

Alter's eyes followed the necklace to the floor.

"Oh," the Queen said. "I'm terribly sorry. It would be a shame to break something like this." With one hand the Queen drew back her robes until her shoe was revealed. Then she moved her foot forward until her raised toe was over the necklace. "Will you tell me where my son is?"

There was seven, eight, ten seconds of silence. "Very well," the Queen said, and brought her foot down. The sound of crushed shells was covered by Alter's scream. Because the Queen had brought down the scepter, too, the full arc of its swing, onto Alter's strapped forearm. Then she brought it down again. The room was filled with the scream and the crack of the jeweled scepter against the surface of the block. Then the Queen smashed Alter's upturned elbow joint.

When there was something like silence, the Queen said, "Now, where is my son?"

Alter didn't say for a long while; when she did, they were ready to believe anything. So what she told them didn't do much good when they had time to check it. Later, unconscious, she was carried into the General Medical building wrapped in a gray blanket.

"Another fish poison case?" asked the clerk.

The man nodded. The doctor, who had been there when Alter was removed from the hospital, had been working steadily for six hours. When he unwrapped the blanket, he recognized the girl. When he unwrapped it further, the breath hissed between his lips, and then hissed out again, slowly. "Get this girl to emergency surgery," he said to the nurse. "Quickly!"

In the Devil's Pot, Tel had just gotten over a case of the runs, which had kept him away from food all day. Feeling hungry, now, he was foraging in the cold storage cabinet of the inn's kitchen. In the freezing chest he found the remains of a baked fish, so he got a sharp knife from over the sink, and cut a piece. Then the door opened and the barmaid came in. She was nearly seventy years old and wore a red scarf around her stringy neck. Tel had cut a slice of onion and was putting it on top of the fish when the barmaid ran forward and knocked the dish from his hand.

"Ouch," Tel said, and jumped, though nothing had hurt him.

"Are you completely crazy?" the woman asked. "You want to be carried out of here like the rest of them?"

Tel looked puzzled as Rara entered the kitchen. "Good grief," she declared. "Where is everybody? I'm starved. I started selling that homebrew tonic of mine that I made up yesterday, and around noon, suddenly everybody was buying the stuff. They wanted something for cramps, and I guess my Super Aqueous Tonic is as good as anything else. I couldn't even get back to eat. Is there some sort of epidemic? Say, that looks good," and she went for the fish.

The old barmaid snatched up the dish and carried it to the disposal can. "It's poisoned, don't you understand?" She dumped it into the chute. "It's got to be the fish that's causing it. Everybody who ate it has been carried off to General Medical with cramps. Lots of them died, too. The woman who lives across the street and me, we figured it out. We both bought it from the same woman this morning, and that's all it could be."

"Well, I'm still hungry," Tel said.

"Can we have some cheese and fruit?" asked Rara.

"I guess that's safe," the woman said.

"Who was carried out?" Tel wanted to know, looking back in the cabinet.

"Oh, that's right," the barmaid said, "you've been upstairs sick all day." And then she told him.

At about the same time, an observer in a scouting plane noticed a boat bearing prefabricated barracks foundations some sixty miles away from any spot that could possibly be receiving such a shipment. In fact, he had sent a corrective order on a typographical error concerning...yes, it must be, that same boat. He'd sent it that morning through Communication Sector 27B. They were near the shore, one of the few spots away from the fishing villages and the farm communes where the great forest had crept down to the edge of the water itself. A tiny port, occasionally used as an embarkation for the families of emigrants going to join people in the city, was the only point of civilization between the rippling smoke-green sea on one side and the crinkling deep green of the forest tree tops on the other. The observer also noted that a small tetron tramp was about to dock also. But that transport ship... He called the pilot and requested contact be made.

The pilot was shaking his head, groggily.

The co-pilot was leaning back in his seat, his mouth opened, his eyes closed. "I don't feel too..." The pilot started, and then reached forward absently to crumple a sheet of tin foil he had left on the instrument panel, in which, a few hours ago, had been a filet sandwich that he and the co-pilot had shared between them.

Suddenly the pilot fell forward out of his chair, knocking the control stick way to the left. He clutched his stomach as the plane banked suddenly to the right. In the observation blister, the observer was thrown from his chair and the microphone fell from his hand.

The co-pilot woke up, belched, grabbed for the stick, which was not in its usual place, and so missed. Forty-one seconds later, the plane had crashed into a dock some thirty feet from the mooring tetron tramp.

CHAPTER EIGHT

THERE WAS a roaring in the air. Let cried out and ran forward. Then shadow. Then water. His feet were slipping on the deck as the rail swung by. Then thunder. Then screaming. Something was breaking in half.

Jon and Arkor got him out. They had to jump overboard with the unconscious Prince, swim, climb, and carry. There were sirens at the dock when they laid him on the dried leaves of the forest clearing.

"We'll leave him here," Arkor said.

"Here? Are you sure?" Jon asked.

"They will come for him. You must go on," he said softly. "We'll leave the Prince now, and you can tell me of your plan.

"My plan..." Jon said. They walked off through the trees.

Dried leaves tickled one cheek, a breeze cooled the other. Something touched him on the side, and he stretched his arms, scrunched his eyelids, then curled himself into the comfortable dark. He was napping in the little park behind the palace. He would go in for supper soon. The leaf smell was fresher than it had ever... Something touched him on the side again.

He opened his eyes, and bit off a scream. Because he wasn't

in the park, he wasn't going in to supper, and there was a giant standing over him.

The giant touched the boy with his foot once more.

Suddenly the boy scrambled away, then stopped, crouching, across the clearing. A breeze shook the leaves like admonishing fingers before he heard the giant speak. The giant was silent. Then the giant spoke again.

The word the boy recognized in both sentences was, "...Quorl..."

The third time he spoke, he merely pointed to himself and repeated, "Quorl."

Then he pointed to the boy and smiled questioningly.

The boy was silent.

Again the giant slapped his hand against his naked chest and said, "Quorl." Again he extended his hand toward the boy, waiting for sound. It did not come. Finally the giant shrugged, and motioned for the boy to come with him.

The boy rose slowly, and then followed. Soon they were walking briskly through the woods.

As they walked, the boy remembered: the shadow of the plane out of control above them, the plane striking the water, water becoming a mountain of water, like shattered glass rushing at them across the sea. And he remembered the fire. Hadn't it really started in his room at the palace, when he pressed the first of the concealed micro-switches with his heel? The cameras were probably working, but there had been no bells, no sirens, no rush of guards. It had tautened when he pushed the second switch in the jeweled dolphin on his bedpost. It nearly snapped with metallic panic when he had to maneuver the girl into position for the retina photograph. Nothing had happened. He was taken away, and his mother stayed quietly in her room. What was supposed to happen was pulling further and further away from the reality. How could anybody kidnap the Prince?

His treatment by the boy who told him about the sea and the girl who taught him to fall pulled it even tighter. *If* the Prince *were* kidnapped, certainly his jailers should not tell him stories of beautiful mornings and sunsets, or teach him to do impossible things with his body.

He was sure that the girl had meant him to die when she had told him to leap from the roof. But he had to do what he was told. He always had. (He was following the giant through the dull leaves because the giant had told him to.) When he had leapt from the roof, then rolled over and sprung to his feet alive, the shock had turned the rack another notch and he could feel the threads parting.

Perhaps if he had stayed there, talked more to the boy and girl, he could have loosened the traction, pulled the fabric of reality back into the shape of expectation. But then the man with the black hair and the scarred giant had come to take him away. He'd made one last volitional effort to bring "is" and "suppose" together. He'd told the man the story of the mine prisoners, the one cogent, connected thing he remembered from his immediate past, a real good "suppose" story. But the man turned on him and said that "suppose" wasn't "suppose" at all, but "is." A thread snapped here, another there.

(Over the deck of the boat there was roaring in the air. He had cried out. Then shadow. Then water. His feet were slipping and the rail swung by. Then thunder. Then screaming, his screaming: *I can't die! I'm not supposed to die!* Something tore in half.)

The leaves were shaking, the whole earth trembled with his tired, unsteady legs. As they walked through the forest, the last filament went, like a thread of glass under a blowtorch flame. The last thing to flicker out, like the fading end of the white hot strand, was the memory of someone, somewhere, entreating him not to forget something, not to forget it no matter what...but what it was, he wasn't sure.

Quorl, with the boy beside him, kept a straight path through the forest. The ground sloped up now. Boulders lipped with moss pushed out here and there. Once Quorl stopped short; his arm shot in front of the boy to keep him from going further.

Yards before them the leaves parted, and two great women

walked forward. Everything about them was identical, their blue-black eyes, flatnoses, broad cheek ridges. Twin sisters, the boy thought. Both women also bore a triplex of scars down the left sides of their faces. They paid no attention to either Quorl or the boy, but walked across into the trees again. The moment they were gone, Quorl started again.

Much later they turned onto a small cliff that looked across a great drop to another mountain. Near a thick tree trunk was a pile of brush and twigs. The boy watched Quorl drop to his knees and begin to move the brush away. The boy crouched to see better.

The great brown fingers tipped with bronze-colored nails gently revealed a cage made of sticks tied together with dried vines. Something squeaked in the cage, and the boy jumped.

Quorl in a single motion got the trap door opened and his hand inside. The next protracted squeak suddenly turned into a scream. Then there was silence. Quorl removed a furry weasel and handed it to the boy.

The pelt was feather soft and still warm. The head hung crazily to the side where the neck had been broken. The boy looked at the giant's hands again.

Veins roped across the ligaments' taut ridges. The hair on the joints of the fingers grew up to edge of the broad, furrowed knuckles. Now the fingers were pulling the brush back over the trap. They crossed the clearing and Quorl uncovered a second trap. When the hand went into the trap and the knot of muscle jumped on the brown forearm (Squeeeeeeeraaaaa!), the boy looked away, out across the great drop.

The sky was smoke gray to the horizon where a sudden streak of orange marked the sunset. The burning copper disk hung low in the purple gap of the mountains. A fan of lavender drifted above the orange, and then white, faint green… The gray wasn't really gray, it was blue-gray. He began to count colors, and there were twelve distinct ones (not a thousand). The last one was a pale gold that tipped the edges of the few low clouds that clustered near the burning circle.

A touch on the shoulder made the boy turn back. Quorl handed him the second animal, and they went back into the woods. Later, they had built a small fire and had skinned and quartered the animals on the scimitar-like blade that the giant wore. They sat in the diminishing shell of light with the meat on forked sticks, turning it over the flame. The boy watched the gray-maroon fibers go first shiny with juice, and then darken, turn crisp and brown. When the meat was done, Quorl took a piece of folded skin from his pouch and shook some white powder onto it. Then he passed the leather envelope to the boy.

The boy poured a scattering of white powder into his palm, then carefully put his tongue to it. It was salt.

When they had nearly finished eating the forest had grown cooler and still. Fire made the leaves around them into flickering shingles on the darkness. Quorl was cleaning the last, tiny bone with big, yellow teeth when there was a sound. They both turned.

Another branch broke to their left. "Tloto," Quorl called harshly, followed by some sort of invective.

It moved closer, the boy could hear it moving, closer until the boy saw the tall shadow at the edge of the ring of light.

With disgust—but without fear, the boy could see—Quorl picked up a stick and flung it. The shadow dodged and made a small mewing sound.

"Di ta klee, Tloto," Quorl said. "Di ta klee."

Only Tloto didn't *di ta klee*, but came forward instead, into the light.

Perhaps it had been born of human parents, but to call it human now... It was bone naked, hairless, shell white. It had no eyes, no ears, only a lipless mouth and slitted nostril flaps. It sniffed toward the fire.

Now the boy saw that both the feet were clubbed and gnarled. Only two fingers on each hand were neither misshapen nor stiffly paralyzed. It reached for Quorl's pile of bones, making the mewing sound with its mouth.

With a sudden sweep of his hand, Quorl knocked the

paraplegic claw away and shouted another scattering of indifferent curses. Tloto backed away, turned to the boy, and came forward, its nostril slits widening and contracting.

The boy had eaten all he could and had a quarter of his meat still left. It's only a head or two taller than I am, he thought. If it's from this race of giants, perhaps it's still a child. Maybe it's my age. He stared at the blank face. It doesn't know what's going on, the boy thought. It doesn't know what's supposed to be happening.

Perhaps it was just the sound of the word in his head that triggered off the sudden panic. (Or was it something else that caught in his chest?) Anyway, he took the unfinished meat and extended it toward Tloto.

The claw jumped forward, grabbed, and snatched back. The boy tried to make his mouth go into a smile. But Tloto couldn't see, so it didn't matter. He turned back to the fire, and when he looked up again, Tloto was gone.

As Quorl began to kick dirt onto the coals, he lectured the boy, apparently on Tloto and perhaps a few other philosophical concepts. The boy listened carefully, and understood at least that Tloto was not worth his concern. Then they lay down beside the little cyst of embers, the glowing scab of light on the darkness, and slept.

When the giant's hand came down and shook his shoulder, it was still dark. He didn't jump this time but blinked against the night and pulled his feet under him. It had grown colder, and dark wind brushed his neck and fingered his hair. Then a high sound cut above the trees and fell away. Quorl took the boy's arm and they started through the dark trees quickly.

Gray light filtered from the left. Was it morning? No. The boy saw it was the rising moon. The light became white, then silver white. They reached a cliff at last, beyond that was the dark sea. Broken rock spilled to ledges below. Fifty feet down, but still a hundred feet above the water, was the largest table of rock. The moon was high enough to light the entire lithic arena as well as the small temple at its edge.

In front of the temple stood a man in black robes who blew on a huge curved shell. The piercing wail sliced high over the sea and the forest. People were gathering around the edge of the arena. Some came in couples, some with children, but most were single men and women.

The boy started to go down, but Quorl held him back. They waited. From sounds about them, the boy realized there were others observing from the height also. On the water, waves began to glitter with broken images of the moon. The sky was speckled with stars.

Suddenly a group of people were led from the temple onto the platform. Most of them were children. One was an old man whose beard twitched in the light breeze. Another was a tall stately woman. All of them were bound, all of them were near naked, and all except the woman shifted their feet and looked nervously about.

The priest in the black robe disappeared into the temple, and emerged again with something that looked to the boy from this distance for all the world like a back-scratcher. The priest raised it in the moonlight, and a murmur rose and quieted about the ring of people. The boy saw that there were three close prongs on the handle, each snagging on the luminous beams of the moon, betraying their metallic keenness.

The priest walked to the first child and caught the side of her head in his hand. Then he quickly drew the triple blade down the left side of her face. She made an indefinite noise, but it was drowned in the rising whisper of the crowd. He did the same to the next child who began to cry, and to the next. The woman stood completely still and did not flinch when the blades opened her cheek. The old man was afraid. The boy could tell because he whimpered and backed away.

A man and a woman stepped from the ring of people and held him for the priest. As the blade raked the side of his face, his high senile whine turned into a scream. The boy thought for a moment of the trapped animals. The old man staggered away from his captors and no one paid him any more attention. The priest raised the shell to his mouth once more, and the high, brilliant sound flooded the arena.

Then, as they had come, silently the people disappeared into the woods. Quorl touched the boy's shoulder and they too went into the woods. They boy looked at the giant with a puzzled expression, but there was no explanation. Once the boy caught sight of a white figure darting at their left as a shaft of moonlight slipped across a naked shoulder. Tloto was following them.

The boy spent his days learning. Quorl taught him to pull the gut of animals to make string. It had to be stretched a long time and then greased with hunks of fat. Once learned it became his job; as did changing the bait in the traps; as did cutting willow boughs to make sleeping pallets; as did sorting the firewood into piles of variously sized wood; as did holding together the sticks while Quorl tied them together and made a canopy for them, the night it rained.

He learned words, too. At least he learned to understand them. *Tike*—trap. *Di'tika*—a sprung trap, *Tikan*—two traps. One afternoon Quorl spent a whole six hours teaching words to the boy. There were lots of them. Even Quorl, who did not speak much, was surprised how many had to be learned. The boy did not speak at all. But soon he understood.

"There is a porcupine," Quorl would say, pointing.

The boy would turn his eyes quickly, following the finger, and then look back, blinking quietly in comprehension.

They were walking through the forest that evening, and Quorl said, "You walk as loud as a tapir." The boy had been moving over dry leaves. Obediently he moved his bare feet to where the leaves were damp and did not crackle.

Sometimes the boy went alone by the edge of the stream. Once a wild pig chased him and he had to climb a tree. The pig tried to climb after him and he sat in the crotch of the branch looking quietly down into the squealing mouth, the warty gray face; he could see each separate bristle stand up and lie down as the narrow jaw opened and closed beneath the skin. One yellow tusk was broken.

Then he heard a mewing sound away to his left. Looking off he saw slug-like Tloto coming towards his tree. A sudden urge to sound pushed him closer to speech (*Stay away! Stay Back!*) than he had been since his arrival in the woods. But Tloto could not see. Tloto could not hear. His hands tightened until the bark burned his palm.

Suddenly the animal turned from the tree and, took off after Tloto. Instantly the slug-man turned and was gone.

The boy dropped from the tree and ran after the sound of the pig's crashing in the underbrush. Twenty feet later after tearing through a net of thick foliage, he burst onto a clearing and stopped.

In the middle of the clearing, the pig was struggling half above ground and half under. Only it wasn't ground. It was some sort of muckpool covered by a floating layer of leaves and twigs. The pig was going under fast.

Then the boy saw Tloto on the other side of the clearing, his nostrils quivering, his blind head turning back and forth. Somehow the slug-man must have maneuvered the animal into the trap. He wasn't sure how, but that must have been what had happened.

The urge that welled in him now came too fast to be stopped. It had too much to do with the recognition of luck, and the general impossibility of the whole situation. The boy laughed.

He startled himself with the sound, and after a few seconds stopped. Then he turned. Quorl stood behind him. (Squeeeee…Squeeee…*raaaaaaa!* Then a gurgle, then nothing.)

Quorl was smiling too, a puzzled smile.

"Why did you—?" (The last word was new. He thought it meant laugh, but he said nothing.)

The boy turned back now. Tloto and the pig were gone.

Quorl walked the boy back to their camp. As they were

nearing the stream Quorl saw the boy's footprints in the soft earth and frowned. "To leave your footprints in wet earth is dangerous. The vicious animals come to drink and they will smell you, and they will follow you, to eat. Suppose that pig had smelled them and been chasing you, instead of running into the pool? What then? If you must leave your footprints, leave them in dry dust. Better not to leave them at all."

The boy listened, and remembered. But that night, he saved a large piece of meat from his food. When Tloto came into the circle of firelight, he gave it to him.

Quorl gave a shrug of disgust and flung a pebble at the retreating shadow. "He is useless," Quorl said. "Why do you waste good food on him? To throw away good food is a—." (Unintelligible word) "You do not understand—." (Another unintelligible word.)

The boy felt something start up inside him again. But he would not let it move his tongue; so he laughed. Quorl looked puzzled. The boy laughed again. Then Quorl laughed too. "You will learn. You will learn at last." Then the giant became serious. "You know, that is the first—sound I have heard you make since coming here."

The boy frowned, and the giant repeated the sentence. The boy's face showed which word baffled him.

The giant thought a minute, and then said, "You, me, even Tloto, are *malika*." That was the word. Now Quorl looked around him. "The trees, the rocks, the animals, they are not *malika*. But the laughing sound, that was a *malika* sound."

The boy thought about it until perhaps he understood. Then he slept.

He laughed a lot during the days now. Survival had come as close to routine as it could here in the jungle, and he could turn his attention to more *malika* concerns. He watched Quorl when they came on other forest people. With single men and women there was usually only an exchange of ten or twelve friendly words. If it were a couple, especially with children, he would give them food. But if they passed anyone with scars, Quorl would freeze until the person was by.

Once the boy wandered to the temple on the arena of rock. There were carvings on much of the stone. The sun was high. The carvings represented creatures somewhere between fish and human. When he looked up from the rock, he saw that the priest had come from the temple and was staring at him. The priest stared until he went away.

Now the boy tried to climb the mountain. That was hard because the footing was slippery and the rocks kept giving. At last he stopped on a jutting rock that looked down the side of the mountain. He was far from any place he knew. He was very high. He stood with hand against the leaning trunk of a near rotten tree, breathing deep and squinting at the sky. (Three or four times Quorl and he had taken long hunting trips: one had taken them to the edge of a deserted meadow across which was a crazily sagging farmhouse. There were no people there. Another had taken them to the edge of the jungle, beyond which the ground was gray and broken, and row after row of unsteady shacks sat among clumps of slithering ferns. Many of the forest people living there had scars and spent more time in larger groups.) The boy wondered if he could see to the deserted meadow from here, or to the deadly rows of prison shacks. A river, a snake of light, coiled through the valley toward the sea. The sky was very blue.

He heard it first, and then he felt it start. He scrambled back toward firmer ground but didn't scramble fast enough. The rock tilted, tore loose, and he was falling. (It pierced through his memory like a white fire-blade hidden under canvas: "...knees up, chin down, and roll quick," the girl had said a long time ago.) It was perhaps twenty feet to the next level. Tree branches broke his fall and he hit the ground spinning, and rolled away. Something else, the rock or a rotten log, hit the ground a moment later where he had been. He uncurled too soon, reaching out to catch hold of the mountain as it tore by him. Then he hit something hard; then something hit him back, and he sailed off into darkness in a web of pain.

Much later he shook his head, opened his eyes, then chomped his jaws on the pain. But the pain was in his leg, so chomping didn't help. He moved his face across crumbling dirt. The whole left side of his body ached, the type of ache that comes when the muscles are tensed to exhaustion but will not relax.

He tried to crawl forward, and went flat down onto the earth, biting up a mouthful of dirt. He nearly tore his leg off.

He had to be still, calm, find out exactly what was wrong. He couldn't tear himself to pieces like the wildcat who had gotten caught in the sprung trap and who had bled to death after gnawing off both hind legs. He was too *malika*.

But each movement he made, each thought he had, happened in the blurring green haze of pain. He raised himself up and looked back. Then he lay down again and closed his eyes. A log the thickness of his body lay across his left leg. Once he tried to push it away but only bruised his palm against the bark, and at last went unconscious with the effort.

When he woke up, the pain was very far away. The air was darkening. No, he wasn't quite awake. He was dreaming about something, something soft, a little garden, with shadows blowing in at the edge of his vision swift and cool, a little garden behind the—

Suddenly, very suddenly, it struck him what was happening, the slowing down of thoughts, his breathing, maybe even his heart. Then he was struggling again, struggling hard enough that had he still the strength, he would have torn himself in half, knowing while he struggled that perhaps the wildcat had been *malika* after all, or not caring if he were less, only fighting to pull himself away from the pain, realizing that blood had begun to seep from beneath the log again, just a tiny trickle.

Then the shadows overtook him, the dreams, the wisps of forgetfulness gauzing his eyes.

Tloto nearly had to drag Quorl halfway up the mountain before the giant got the idea. When he did, he began to run.

Quorl found the boy; just before sunset. He was breathing in short gasps, his fists clenched, his eyes closed. The blood on the dirt had dried black.

The great brown hands went around the log, locked, and started to shift it; the boy let out a high sound from between his teeth.

The hands, roped with vein and ridged with ligament, strained the log upward; the sound became a howl.

The giant's feet braced against the dirt, slid into the dirt, and the hands that had snapped tiny necks and bound sticks together with gut string, pulled; the howl turned into a scream. He screamed again. Then again.

The log coming loose tore away nearly a square foot of flesh from the boy's leg. Then, Quorl went over and picked him up.

This is the best dream, the boy thought, from that dark place he had retreated to behind the pain, because Quorl is here. The hands were lifting him now, he was held close, warm, somehow safe. His cheek was against the hard shoulder muscle, and he could smell Quorl too. So he stopped screaming and turned his head a little to make the pain go away. But it wouldn't go. It wouldn't. Then the boy cried.

The first tears through all that pain came salty in his eyes, and he cried until he went to sleep.

Quorl had medicine for him the next day ("From the priest," he said.) which helped the pain and made the healing start. Quorl also had made the boy a pair of wooden crutches that morning. Although muscle and ligament had been bruised and crushed and the skin torn away, no bone had broken.

That evening there was a drizzle and they ate under the canopy. Tloto did not come, and this time it was Quorl who saved the extra meat and kept looking off into the wet gray trees. Quorl had told the boy how Tloto had led him to him; when they finished eating, Quorl took the meat and ducked into the drizzle.

The boy lay down to sleep. He thought the meat was a

reward for Tloto. Only Quorl had seemed that night full of more than usual gravity. The last thing he wondered before sleep flooded his eyes and ears was how blind, deaf Tloto had known where he was anyway.

When he woke it had stopped raining. The air was damp and chill. Quorl had not come back.

The sound of the blown shell came again. The boy sat up and flinched at the twinge in his leg. To his left the moon was flickering through the trees. The sound came a third time, distant, sharp, yet clear and marine. The boy reached for his crutches and hoisted himself to his feet. He waited till the count of ten, hoping that Quorl might suddenly return to go with him.

A last he took a deep breath and started haltingly forward. The faint moonlight made the last hundred yards easy going. Finally he reached a vantage where he could look down through the wet leaves onto the arena of stone.

The sky was sheeted with mist and the moon was an indistinct pearl in the haze. The sea was misty. People were already gathered at the edge. The boy looked at the priest and then ran his eye around the circle of people. One of them was Quorl!

He leaned forward as far as he could. The priest sounded the shell again and the prisoners came out of the temple: first three boys, then an older girl, then a man. The next one...Tloto! It was marble-white under the blurred moon. Its clubbed feet shuffled on the rock. Its blind head ducked right and left with bewilderment.

As the priest raised the long three-pronged knife, the boy's hands went tight around the crutches. He passed from one prisoner to the next. Tloto cringed, and the boy sucked in a breath as the knife went down, feeling his own flesh part under the blades. Then the murmur died, the prisoners were unbound, and the people filed from the rock back into the forest.

The boy waited to see which way Quorl headed before he

started through moon-dusted bushes as fast as his crutches would let him. There were many people on the webbing of paths that came from the temple rock. There was Quorl!

When he caught up, Quorl saw him and slowed down. Quorl didn't look at him, though. Finally the giant said, "You don't understand. I had to catch him. I had to give him to the old one to be marked. But you don't understand." The boy hardly looked at all where they were going, but stared up at the giant.

"You don't understand," Quorl said again. Then he looked at the boy and was quiet for a minute. "No, you don't," he repeated. "Come." They turned off the main path now, going slower. "It's a...custom. An important custom. Yes, I know it hurt him. I know he was afraid. But it had to be. Tloto is one of those who—." (The word was some inflection of the verb to know.) Quorl was silent for a moment. "Let me try to tell you why I had to hurt your friend. Yes, I know he is your friend, now. But once I said that Tloto was *malika*. I was wrong. Tloto is more than *malika*—he and the others that were marked. Somehow these people know things. That was how Tloto survived. That's how he knew where you were, when you were hurt. He knew inside your head, he heard inside your head. Many are born like that, more of them each year. As soon as we find out, we mark them. Many try to hide it, and some succeed for a long time. Can you understand? Do you? When Tloto showed me where you were, he knew that I would know, that he would be caught and marked. Do you understand?"

Again he paused and looked at the boy. The eyes still showed puzzled hurt. "You want to know why. I...we... Long ago we killed them when we found out. We don't any more. The mark reminds them that they are different, and yet the same as we. Perhaps it is wrong. It doesn't hurt that much, and it heals. Anyway, we don't kill them any more. We know they're important..." Suddenly, having gone all through it with this strange boy, it seemed twisted to the giant, incorrect. Then he gave the boy what the boy had been sent to the forest to get, what the Duchess had found and knew was necessary. "I was wrong," Quorl said. "I'm sorry. I will speak to the priest tomorrow."

They walked until the dawn lightened the sky behind the trees. Once Quorl looked around and said, "I want to show you something. We are very near, and the weather is right."

They walked a few minutes more till Quorl pointed to a wall of leaves, and said, "Go through there."

As they pressed through the dripping foliage, bright light burnished their faces. They were standing on a small cliff that looked down the mountain. Fog the color of pale gold, the same gold the boy had seen so rarely in the sunset, rolled across the entire sky. The center flamed with the misty sun, and way below them through the fog was the shattered traces of water, the color of magnesium flame on copper foil, without edge or definition.

"That's a lake that lies between this mountain and the next," Quorl said, pointing to the water.

"I thought..." the boy started softly, his tongue rough against the new language. "I thought it was the sea."

Beside them appeared the crouching figure of Tloto. Drops from the wet leaves burned on his neck and back, over the drying blood. He turned his blank face left and right in the golden light, and with all his knowing could communicate no awe.

CHAPTER NINE

CLEA KOSHAR had been installed in her government office for three days. The notebook in which she had been doing her own work in inverse sub-trigonometric functions had been put away in her desk for exactly fifty-four seconds when she made the first discovery that gave her a permanent place in the history of Toromon's wars as its first military hero. Suddenly she pounded her fist on the computer keys, flung her pencil across the room, muttered, "What the hell is this!" and dialed the military ministry.

It took ten minutes to get Tomar. His red-haired face came in on the visiphone, recognized her, and smiled. "Hi," he said.

"Hi, yourself," she said. "I just got out those figures you people sent us about the data from the radiation barrier, and those old readings from the time Telphar was destroyed. Tomar, I didn't even have to feed them to the computer. I just looked at them. That radiation was artificially created. Its increment is completely steady. At least on the second derivative. Its build-up pattern is such that there couldn't be more than two simple generators, or one complexed on..."

"Slow down," Tomar said. "What do you mean, generators?"

"The radiation barrier, or at least most of it, is artificially maintained. And there are not more than two generators, and possibly one, maintaining it."

"How do you generate radiation?" Tomar asked.

"I don't know," Clea said. "But somebody has been doing it."

"I don't want to knock your genius, but how come nobody else figured it out?"

"I just guess nobody thought it was a possibility, or thought of gratuitously taking the second derivative, or bothered to look at them before they fed them into the computers. In twenty minutes I can figure out the location for you."

"You do that," he said, "and I'll get the information to whomever it's supposed to get to. You know, this is the first piece of information of import that we've gotten from this whole battery of slide-rule slippers up there. I should have figured it would have probably come from you. Thanks, if we can use it."

She blew him a kiss as his face winked out. Then she got out her notebook again. Then minutes later the visiphone crackled at her. She turned to it and tried to get the operator. The operator was not to be gotten. She reached into her desk and got out a small pocket tool kit and was about to attack the housing of the frequency-filterer when the crackling increased and she heard a voice. She put the screw driver down and put the instrument back on the desk. A face flickered onto the screen and then flickered off. The face had dark hair, seemed perhaps familiar. But it was gone before she was sure she had made it out.

Crossed signals from another line, she figured. Maybe a short in the dialing mechanism. She glanced down at her notebook and took up her pencil when the picture flashed onto the screen again. This time it was clear and there was no static. The familiarity, she did not realize, was the familiarity of her own face on a man.

"Hello," he said. "Hello. Hello, Clea?"

"Who is this?" she asked.

"Clea, this is Jon."

She sat very still, trying to pull two halves of something back together (as in a forest, a prince had felt the same things disengage). Clea succeeded. "You're supposed to be...dead. I mean I thought you were. Where are you, Jon?"

"Clea," he said. "Clea—I have to talk to you."

There was a five-second silence.

"Jon, Jon, how are you?"

"Fine," he said. "I really am. I'm not in prison any more. I've been out a long time, and I've done a lot of things. But Clea, I need your help."

"Of course," she said. "Tell me how? What do you want me to do?"

"Do you want to know where I am?" he said. "What I've been doing? I'm in Telphar, and I'm trying to stop the war."

"In Telphar?"

"There's something behind that famed radiation barrier, and it's a more or less civilized race. I'm about to break through the rest of the barrier and see what can be done. But I need some help at home. I've been monitoring phone calls in Toron. There's an awful lot of equipment here that's more or less mine if I can figure out how to use it. And I've got a friend here who knows more in that line than I gave him credit for. I've overheard some closed circuit conference calls, and I'm talking to you by the same method. I know you've got the ear of Major Tomar and I know he's one of the few trustworthy people in that whole military hodgepodge. Clea, there is something hostile to Toromon behind that radiation barrier, but a war is not the answer. The thing that's making the war is the unrest in Toromon. And the war isn't going to remedy that. The emigration situation, the food situation, the excess manpower, the deflation: that's what's causing your war. If that can be stopped, then the thing behind the barrier can be dealt with quickly and peacefully. There in Toron you don't even know what the enemy is. They wouldn't let you know even if they knew themselves."

"Do you know?" Clea asked.

Jon paused. Then he said, "No, but whatever it is, it's people with something wrong among them. And warring on them won't exorcise it."

"Can you exorcise it?" Clea asked.

Jon paused again. "Yes. I can't tell you how; but let's say what's troubling them is a lot simpler than what's troubling us in Toromon."

"Jon," Clea asked suddenly, "what's it like in Telphar? You know I'll help you if I can, but tell me."

The face on the visiphone was still. Then it drew a deep breath. "Clea, it's like an open air tomb. The city is very unlike Toron. It was planned, all the streets are regular, there's no Devil's Pot, nor could there ever be one. Roadways wind above ground among the taller buildings. I'm in the Palace of the Stars right now. It was a magnificent building." The face looked right and left. "It still is. They had amazing laboratories, lots of equipment, great silvered meeting halls under an immense ceiling that reproduced the stars on the ceiling. The electric plants still work. Most houses you can walk right in and turn on a light switch. Half the plumbing in the city is out, though. But everything in the palace still works. It must have been a beautiful place to live in. When they were evacuating during the radiation rise, very little marauding took place…"

"The radiation…" began Clea.

Jon laughed. "Oh, that doesn't bother us. It's too complicated to explain now, but it doesn't."

"That's not what I meant," Clea said. "I figured if you were alive, then it obviously wasn't bothering you. But Jon, and this isn't government propaganda, because I made the discovery myself: whatever is behind the barrier caused the radiation rise that destroyed Telphar. Some place near Telphar is a projector that caused the rise, and it's still functioning. This hasn't been released to the public yet, but if you want to stop your war, you'll never do it if the government can correctly blame the destruction of Telphar on the enemy. That's all they need."

"Clea, I haven't finished telling you about Telphar. I told you that the electricity still worked. Well, most houses you go into, you turn on the light and find a couple of sixty-year-old corpses on the floor. On the roads you can find a wreck every hundred feet or so. There're almost ten thousand corpses in the Stadium of the Stars. It isn't very pretty. Arkor and I are the only two humans who have any idea of what the destruction of Telphar really amounted to. And we still believe we're in the right."

"Jon, I can't hold back information…"

"No, no," Jon said. "I wouldn't ask you to. Besides, I heard your last phone call. So it's already out. I want you to do two things for me. One has to do with Dad. The other is to deliver a message. I overheard a conference call between Prime Minister Chargill and some of the members of the council. They're about to ask Dad for a huge sum of money to finance the first aggressive drive in this war effort. Try and convince him that it'll do more harm than good. Look, Clea, you've got a mathematical mind. Show him how this whole thing works. He doesn't mean to be, but he's almost as much responsible for this thing as anyone individual could be. See if he can keep production from flooding the city. And for Toromon's sake, keep an eye, a close eye on his supervisors. They're going to tilt the island into the sea with all their cross-purposes intrigues. All I can do is start you on the right track, Sis, and you'll have to take it from there.

"Now for the message. The one circuit I can't break in on is the Royal Palace system. I can just overhear. Somehow I've got to get a message to the Duchess of Petra. Tell her to get to Telphar in the next forty-eight hours by way of the transit ribbon. Tell her there are two kids she owes a favor to. And tell her the girl she owes four or five favors. She'll be able to find out who they are."

Clea was scribbling. "Does the transit ribbon still work?" she asked.

"It was working when I escaped from prison," Jon said. "I don't see why it should have stopped now."

"You used it?" Clea said. "That means you *were* in Toron!"

"That's right. And I was at your party too."

"Then it was…" She stopped. Then laughed, "I'm so glad, Jon. I'm so glad it was you after all."

"Come on, Sis, tell me about yourself," Jon said. "What's been happening in the real world. I've been away from it a long time. Here in Telphar I don't feel much closer. Right now I'm walking around in my birthday suit. On our way here we got into a shadowy situation and I had to abandon my clothes for fear of getting caught. I'll explain that later, too. But what about you?"

"Oh, there's nothing to tell. But to you I guess there is. I graduated, with honors. I've grown up. I'm engaged to Tomar. Did you know that? Dad approves, and we're to be married as soon as the war's over. I'm working on a great project, to find the inverse sub-trigonometric functions. Those are about the most important things in my life right now. I'm suppose to be working on the war effort, but except for this afternoon, I haven't done much."

"Fine," Jon said. "That's about the right proportions."

"Now what about you? And the clothes?" She grinned into

the visaphone, and he grinned back.

"Well—no, you wouldn't believe it. At least not if I told it that way. Arkor, the friend who's with me, is one of the forest people. He left the forest to spend some time in Toron, which is where I met him. Apparently he managed to accumulate an amazing store of information, about all sorts of things— electronics, languages, even music. You'd think he could read minds. Anyway, here we are, through the forest, across the prison mines, and in Telphar."

"Jon, what were the mines like? It always made me wonder how Dad could use tetron when he knew that you were being whipped to get it."

"You and I'll get drunk some evening and I'll tell you what it was like," Jon said. "But not until. When you're trying to convince Dad, bring that up about me and the mines."

"Don't worry," she said. "I will."

"Anyway," Jon went on, "we had to get through the forest without being seen and with all those leaves it was pretty dark. Arkor could get through because he was a forest man and nobody would stop him. But because they'd have seen me, I had to go most of the way naked as a jaybird."

Clea frowned. "I don't understand. You sure you're all right?"

Jon laughed. "Of course I'm all right. I can't really explain to you just yet. I'm just so happy to see you again, to be able to talk to you. Sis, I've wanted to be free for so long, to see you and Dad again, and—there's nothing wrong with me—except the sniffles."

It welled up in her like a wave and the tears flooded her lower lids, and then one overflowed and ran down the left side of her nose. "You see what you're doing," she said. And they laughed once more. "To see you again, Jon is so...*fine*."

"I love you, Sis," Jon said. "Thanks, and so long for a little while."

"I'll get your message out. So long." The phone blinked dark and she sat there wondering if perhaps the tension wasn't too much. But it wasn't, and she had messages to deliver.

CHAPTER TEN

DURING THE next couple of hours, two people died, miles apart.

"Don't be silly," Rara was saying in the inn at the Devil's Pot. "I'm a perfectly good nurse. Do you want to see my license?"

The white-haired old man sat very straight in his chair by the window. Blue seeped like liquid across the glass. "Why did I do it?" he said. "It was wrong. I—I love my country."

Rara pulled the blanket from the back of the chair and tucked it around the stiff, trembling shoulders. "What are you talking about?" she said, but the birthmark over her face showed deep purple with worry.

He shook the blanket off and flung his hand across the table where the news directive lay.

CROWN PRINCE KIDNAPPED! KING DECLARES WAR!

The trembling in Geryn's shoulders became violent shaking.

"Sit back," said Rara.

Geryn stood up.

"Sit down," Rara repeated. "Sit down. You're not well. Now sit down!"

Geryn lowered himself stiffly to the chair. He turned to Rara. "Did I start a war? I tried to stop it. That was all I wanted. Would it have happened if..."

"Sit back," Rara said. "If you're going to talk to somebody, talk to me. I can answer you. Geryn, you didn't start the war."

Geryn suddenly rose once more, staggered forward, slammed his hands on the table and began to cough.

"For pity's sake," Rara cried, trying to move the old man back into his chair, "will you sit down and relax! You're not well! You're not well at all!" From above the house came the faint beat of helicopter blades.

Geryn went back to his chair. Suddenly he leaned his head back, his sharp Adam's apple shooting high in his neck and quivering. Rara jumped forward and tried to bring his head up. "Dear heavens," she breathed. "Stop that. Now stop it, or you'll hurt yourself."

Geryn's head came up straight again. "A war," he said. "They made me start the—"

"No one made you do anything," Rara said. "And you didn't start the war."

"Are you sure?" he asked. "No. You can't be sure. No one can. Nobody…"

"Will you please try to relax," Rara repeated, tucking at the blanket.

Geryn relaxed. It went all through his body, starting at his hands. The stiff shoulders dropped a little, his head fell forward, the wall of muscle quivering across his stomach loosened, the back bent; and that frail fist of strength that had jarred life through his tautened body for seventy years, shaking inside his chest, it too relaxed. Then it stopped. Geryn crumpled onto the floor.

The shifting body pulled Rara down with him. Unaware that he was dead, she was trying to get him back into the chair, when the helicopter blades got very loud.

She looked up to see the window darken with a metal shadow. "Good lord," she breathed. Then the glass shattered.

She screamed, careened around the table, and fled through the door, slamming it behind her.

Over the flexible metal ramp that hooked onto the windowsill two men entered the room. Fire-blades poised, they walked to the crumpled body, lifted it between them, and carried it back to the window. Their arm bands showed the royal insignia of the palace guards.

Tel was running down the street because someone was following him. He ducked into a side alley and skittered down a flight of stone steps. Somewhere overhead he heard a helicopter.

His heart was pounding like explosions in his chest, like the sea, like his ocean. Once he had looked through a six-inch crevice between glassy water and the top of a normally submerged cave and seen wet, orange starfish dripping from the ceiling and their reflections quivering with his own breath. Now he was trapped in the cave of the city, the tide of fear rising to lock him in. Footsteps passed above him.

Nearby was a ladder that led to a trap door which would put him in the hall of a tenement. He climbed it, emerged, and then turned up the regular steps to the roof. He walked across the tar-paper surface to the edge, leaned over, and peered into the alley. Two men, who may have been the people following him, approached from opposite ends of the alley. The sky was deepening toward evening and it was cool. The two men met, and then one pointed to the roof.

"Damn," Tel muttered, ducked backward, and bit his tongue with surprise. He opened his mouth and breathed hard, holding the side of his jaw. The helicopter was coming closer.

Then something very light fell over him. He forgot his bitten tongue and struck out with his hands. It was strong, too. It jerked at his feet and he fell forward. It was not until it lifted him from the roof that he realized he was caught in a net. He was being drawn up toward the sound of the whirling helicopter blades.

Just about that time the order came through. He didn't even have time to say good-bye to Clea. Two other mathematicians in the corps had shown appropriate awe at Clea's discovery and proceeded to locate the generator. The next-in-charge general, working on a strategy Tomar did not quite understand, decided that now was the time for an active strike. "Besides," he added, "if we don't give them some combat soon, we'll lose—and I mean lose as in 'misplace'—the war."

The shadow of the control tower fell through the windshield

and slipped across Tomar's face. He pulled up his goggles and sighed. Active combat. What the hell would they be combating? The disorder, the disorganization was beginning to strike him as farcical. Though after the poisoned fish, the farcical was no longer funny.

The buildings on the airfield sunk back and down. The transit ribbon fell below him and the six other planes in the formation pulled up behind him. A moment later the island was a comb of darkness on the glittering foil of the evening sea.

Clouds banded the deep blue at the horizon. There were three stars out, the same stars that he had looked at as a boy when his sunup to sundown work day had ended. Between hunger and hunger there had been some times when you could look at the stars and wonder, as there were now between times of work and work.

The controls were set. There was nothing to do but wait for land to rise up over the edge of the world.

At the end of the metal ribbon was a transparent crystal sphere, fifteen feet in diameter, which hovered above the receiving stage. A dozen small tetron units sat around the room. By one ornate window a bank of forty-nine scarlet knobbed switches pointed to off. Two men stood on the metal catwalk that ran above the receiving stage, one young man with black hair, the other a dark giant with a triplex of scars down the left side of his face.

In another room, the corpses of the elders of Telphar sat stiff and decomposed on green velvet seats.

It was evening in the solarium on top of the General Medical building. The patients were about to be herded from their deck chairs and game tables under the glass roof back to their wards, when a woman screamed. Then there was the sound of breaking glass. More people screamed.

Alter heard the roar of helicopter blades. People were running around her. Suddenly the crowd of bathrobed patients broke from in front of her. He touched the cast that covered her left shoulder and arm. People cried out. Then she saw.

The glass dome had been shattered at the edge, and the flexible metal ramp ran a dark ribbon from the copter to the edge of the solarium. The men that marched across had the insignia of the royal guards. She clamped her jaws together and moved behind the nurse. The men marched in, fire-blades high, among the overturned deck chairs. There were three stars visible, she noted irrelevently, through the bubble dome.

Good lord! They were coming toward her!

The moment the guards recognized her, she realized the only way to get out was to cross the suddenly immense span of metal flooring to the stairwell. She ducked her head, broke from the crowd of patients and ran, wondering why she had been fool enough to wait this long. The guard tackled her and she heard screams again.

She fell to the hard floor and felt pain explode along the inside of her cast. The guard tried to lift her, and with her good arm she struck at his face. Then she held her palm straight and brought the edge down on the side of his neck.

He staggered and she felt herself slip to the floor. Then someone grabbed a handful of her hair and her head was yanked back. At first she closed her eyes. Then she had to open them. Night was moving above her through the dome of the solarium. Then the cracked edge of the glass passed over her, and it was colder, and the blur and roar of helicopter blades was above.

"On course?"

"Dead on course," said Tomar back into the microphone. Below, the rim of land slipped back under them. The moon bleached the edges of the varicolored darknesses beneath them; then went down.

"What are you thinking about, Major?" came the voice from the speaker again.

"Not thinking about anything," Tomar said. "Just thinking about waiting. It's funny that's most of what you do in this army: wait. You wait to go out and fight. And once you go out, then you start waiting to turn around and come back."

"Wonder what it'll be like."

"A few bombs over that generator, then we'll have had active combat, and everyone will be happy."

A laugh, mechanical, through the speaker. "Suppose they 'active' back?"

"If they cripple our planes like they've done before, we'll make it to the island again."

"I had to leave a hot cup of coffee back at the hangar, Major. I wish it was light so we could see what we were doing."

"Stop bitching."

"Hey, Major."

"What?"

"I've invented a new kind of dice."

"You would."

"What you do is take fifteen centiunit pieces and arrange them in a four-by-four square with one corner missing. Then you take a sixteenth one and shoot it within forty-five degrees either way of the diagonal into the missing corner. It works out that no matter how you do it, if all the coins in the square are touching, two coins will fly off of the far edge. Each of those has a number and the two numbers that fly off are like the two numbers that come up on the dice. It's better than regular dice because the chances are up on some combinations. And there's a certain amount of skill involved too. The guys call it Randomax. That's for *random numbers* and *matrix*."

"I'll play you a game someday," Tomar said. "You know, if you used a smaller coin than a centiunit for the one you fire into the missing corner, say a deciunit, the chances that it would hit both corner coins would go up, that is your randomness.

"Really?"

"Sure," Tomar said. "My girl friend's a mathematician, and she was telling me all about probability a few weeks ago. I bet she'd be interested in the game."

"You know what, Major?"

"What?"

"I think you're the best officer in the damn army."

Such was the conversation before the first battle of the war.

Such was the conversation Jon Koshar monitored in the laboratory tower of the Palace of the Stars in Telphar. "Oh damn," he said. "Come on, Arkor. We'd better get going. If the Duchess doesn't get here with Geryn soon... Well, let's not think about it." He scribbled a note, set it in front of one visiphone and dialed the number of another that was on a stand in front of the receiving platform of the transit ribbon.

"There," he said. "That's got instructions to follow us as soon as she gets here. And she better not miss it." They went down the metal steps to a double doorway that opened onto a road.

Two mechanical vehicles stood there, both with pre-controls set for similar destinations. Jon and Arkor climbed into one, pushed the ignition button, and the car shot forward along the elevated roadway. White mercury lights flooded the elevated strip as it wound through the city. The road dipped and houses got wider and lower on each side. The horizon glowed purple and above that, deep yellow clouds dropped into late evening. There was a sound of planes overhead.

As the car halted at the barren limit of the last suburb of Telphar, a sudden white streak speared from the horizon. "Uh-oh," said Jon. "That's what I was afraid of."

Something caught fire in the air, twisted wildly through the sky, and then began to circle down, flaming.

"Major! Major! What happened to D-42?"

"Something got him. Pull over. Pull over everybody!"

"We can't spot it. Where'd it come from?"

"All right, everybody. Break formation. Break formation, I said!"

"Major, I'm going to drop a bomb. Maybe we can see where that came from in the light. I thought you said cripple."

"Never mind what I said. Drop it."

"Major Tomar. This is B-6. We've been—" (Unintelligible static.)

Someone else gave a slow whistle through the microphone.

"Break formation, I said. Damn it, break formation."

Over the plain, a sheet of red fire flapped up, and Jon and Arkor pulled back from the railing that edged the road. Another white streak left the horizon, and for a moment, in the glare, their shadows on the pavement were doubled in white and red.

The sound of the explosion reached them a moment later, as broken rocks leapt into visibility like a rotted jaw swung up through red fire.

Another sound behind them made them turn. The lighted roadways of Telphar looped the city like strands of pearls on skeletal fingers. A car came toward them.

Another wailing missile took the sky, and a moment later a screaming plane answered, tearing down the night. This one suddenly turned as its flaming motors caught once more and careened above their heads so close that they ducked and disappeared among the city towers: an explosion, then falling flame drooled the side of a building. "I hope that's nowhere near the Palace of the Stars," a voice said next to Jon. "We'll have a great time getting back if it is."

Jon whirled. The Duchess had gotten out of the car. The red light flared a moment in her hair, then died.

"No. That was nowhere near it," Jon said. "Am I glad to see you."

Tel and Alter, still in her cast and hospital robe, followed the Duchess out of the car.

"Well," he said, "you brought the kids too."

"It was better than leaving them back in Toron, Jon, Geryn is dead. I asked what to do, but I didn't get any answer. So we lugged his body along just in case. But what do we do now?"

From the railing Arkor laughed.

"It's not funny," Jon said.

The Duchess looked overhead as another missile exploded.

"I had hoped this wouldn't happen. This means a war, Jon. A real one, and unstoppable."

Another plane crashed, too close this time, and they ducked behind the cars. "Gee," breathed Alter, which was the only thing anybody said.

Then Arkor cried, "Come on."

"Where to?" asked Jon.

"Follow me," Arkor repeated. "Everyone."

"What about Geryn?"

"Leave that corpse behind," Arkor told them. "He can't help."

"Look, do you know what's going on?" Jon demanded.

"More than Geryn ever did," the giant returned. "Now let's get going." They sprinted out along the road, then ducked under the railing and made their way across the rocky waste.

"Where are we going?" Tel whispered.

Jon called back over his shoulder, "That's a very good question."

The plane got tipped, and for seven seconds, while the needles swung, he didn't know where he was going, east or west, up or down. When the needles stopped, he saw that it hadn't been any of the first three. Suddenly the green detector light flashed in the half darkness of the cabin. The generator! The radiation generator was right below him. Then he was blinded by a white flare outside the windshield. Oh damn!

He felt the jerk and the air suddenly rushed in cold behind him. There was a hell of a lot of noise and the needle quietly swung... He was going down!

Land lit up outside the front window; a small blockhouse set in the wrecked earth. There were three whirling antennae on the roof. That must be it! That must!

It happened in his arms and fingers, not in his head. Because suddenly he pushed the stick forward, and the plane, what was left of it, turned over and he was staring straight down, straight ahead, straight, straight below him. And coming closer.

It must have been his arms, because his head was thinking wildly about a time when a girl with pearls in her black hair had asked him what he had wanted, and he had said, 'Nothing...nothing...' and realized he had been wrong because suddenly he wanted very much to... (The blockhouse came up and hit him.) ...Nothing.

Tel and the Duchess screamed. The rest just drew breath quickly and staggered back. "He's in there," Arkor said. "That's where your Lord of the Flames is."

The landscape glowed with the encroaching light of the flaming torch, and they saw the blockhouse now with its whirling antennae on the roof. Before the plane hit, a darkness opened in the side of the blockhouse and three figures emerged and sprinted among the rocks.

"The middle one," said Arkor. "That's him, face him, concentrate on him..."

"What do you...?" Tel began.

"You ride along with me, kids," Arkor said, only he didn't move. Two of the figures had fallen now, but the middle one was running toward them. The torch hit, and his shadow was suddenly flung across the broken earth to meet them...

CHAPTER ELEVEN

THE GREEN of beetles' wings...the red of polished car-buncle...a web of silver fire, and through the drifting blue smoke Jon hurled across the sky.

Then blackness, intense and cold. The horizon was tiny, jagged, maybe ten feet away. He reached a metal out and crawled expertly (not clumsily. Expertly!) across a crevice, but slowly, very slowly. The sky was sharp with stars, though the sun was dim to his light-sensitive rind. Like a sliding cyst, he edged over the chunk of rock that spun somewhere between Mars and Jupiter. Now he reached out with his mind to touch a second creature on another rock. *Petra*, he called. *Where is he?*

His orbit should take him between the three of us in a minute and a half.

Fine.

Jon, who is the third one? I still don't understand.

Another mind joined them. *You don't understand yet? I was the third, I always was. I was the one who directed Geryn to make the plan in the first place for the kidnapping. What made you think that he was in contact with the triple beings?*

I don't know, Jon said. *Some misunderstanding.*

There was the laughter of children. Then Tel said, *Hey, everybody, we're with Arkor.*

Shhh, said Alter. *The misunderstanding was my fault, Jon. I told you that Geryn talked to himself, and that made you think it was him.*

Get ready, Petra said. *Here he comes.*

Jon saw, or rather sensed the approach of another spinning asteroid, whirling toward them through the blackness. But it was inhabited. Yes! The three of them threw their thoughts across the rush of space.

There…

Roaring steam swirled above him. He raised his eyestalks another twenty feet and looked toward the top of the cataract some four miles up. Then he lowered his siphon into the edge of the pool of pale green liquid methane and drank deeply. Far away in a beryl green sky, three suns rushed madly about one another and gave a little heat to this farthest of their six planets.

Now Jon flapped his slitherers down and began to glide away from the methane falls and up the nearly vertical mountain slope. Someone was coming toward him, with shiny red eye-stalks waving in greeting. "Greetings to the new colony," the eye-stalks signaled.

Jon started to signal back. But suddenly he recognized (a feeling way at the back of his slitherers) who this was. He leaped forward and flung the double flaps of leathery flesh across his opponent and began to scramble back up the rocks. Jon had him tight, but was wondering where the hell were…

Suddenly his eye-stalk caught the great form that he knew must be Arkor coming down over the rocks (with Alter and Tel. Yes, definitely; because the creature suddenly did a flying leap between two crags that could have only been under the girl-acrobat's control), and a moment later Petra arrived at the other shore of the methane river. Using her slitherers for paddles, she struck out across the foaming current.

Think at him, concentrate...*There*...

The air was water-clear. The desert was still, and he lay in the warm sand, under the light of the crescent moon. He was growing, adding facets; he let the pale illumination seep into his transparent body, decreasing his polarization cross-frequencies. The light was beautiful, too beautiful—dangerous! He began to tingle, to glow red-hot. His base burned with white heat and another layer of sand beneath him melted, fused, ran, and became part of his crystalline body.

He stepped up the polarization, his body clouded, and cooled once more. Music sang through him, and his huge upper facet reflected the stars.

Once more he lessened his polarization, and the light crept further and further into his being. His temperature rose. Vibrations suffused his transparency and the pulsing music made the three dust particles that had settled on his coaxial face seven hundred and thirty years ago dance above him. He felt their reflection deep in his prismatic center.

He felt it coming, suddenly, and tried to stop it. But the polarization index suddenly broke down completely. For one terrific moment of ecstasy the light of the moon and the stars poured completely through him. Chord after chord rang out in the desert night. Back and forth along his axis, colliding, shaking his substance, jarring him, pommeling him, came the vibrations. For one instant he was completely transparent. The next, he was white-hot. Before he could melt, he felt the crack start.

It shot the length of his forty-two mile, super-heated body.

He was in two pieces! The radio disturbance alone covered a third of a galaxy. Twelve pieces fell away. The chord crashed again, and the crack whipped back and forth vivisecting him. Already he was nearly thirty-six thousand individual crystals, all of which had to grow again, thirty-six thousand minds. He was no more.

Jon, the voice sang through drumbled silicate.

Right over here, Petra, he hummed back. (The note was a perfect quarter tone below A-flat. Perfect! Not clumsy. Perfect!)

Where's Arkor?

To their left the triple notes of an E-flat minor chord (Arkor, Tel, and Alter) sounded: *Right here.*

Just as they had made contact, before the music stopped (and once more their thoughts would become separate, individual, and they would lose awareness of each other and of the hundreds of other crystals that layover the desert, under the clear perpetual night)—just then a strident dissonance pierced among them.

There, sang Petra.

There, hummed Jon.

There, came the triad in E-flat minor. They concentrated, tuned, turned their thoughts against the dissonance. *There...*

Jon rolled over and pushed the silk from his white shoulders and stretched. Through the blue pillars, the evening sky was yellow. Music, very light and fast, was coming from below the balcony. Suddenly a voice sounded beside him: "Your Majesty, your Majesty! You shouldn't be resting now. They're waiting for you downstairs. Tltltrlte will be furious if you're late."

"What do I care?" Jon responded. "Where's my robe?"

The serving maid hastened away and returned with a sheer, shimmering robe, netted through with threads of royal black. The drape covered Jon's shoulders, draped across his breasts, and fell to his thighs.

"My mirror," said Jon.

The serving maid brought the mirror and Jon looked. Long, slightly oriental eyes sat wide-spaced in the ivory face over high cheekbones. Full breasts pushed tautly beneath the translucent material, and the slender waist spread to sensual, generous hips. Jon almost whistled at his reflection.

The maid slipped clear plastic slippers on his feet, and Jon rose and walked toward the stairs. In the lobby, the throng hissed appreciatively as he descended. On one column hung a birdcage in which a three-headed cockatoo was singing to beat the band. Which was difficult to do, because the band was composed of fourteen copper-headed drums. (Fourteen was the royal number.)

Across the lobby wind instruments wailed, and Jon paused on the stairs. "Don't worry," the maid said, "I'm right behind you."

Jon felt the terror rise. *Hey,* he called out mentally, *is that you, Petra?*

Like I said, right behind you.

Incidentally, how did I come up with this body?

I don't know, dear, but you look devastating.

Gee, thanks, he said, projecting a mental sneer. *Where's Arkor and Company?*

The music had stopped. There was only the sound of the three-headed bird.

There they are.

The winds screeched again, and at the entrance of the lobby, the people fell away from the door. There was Tltltrlte. He was tall, and dark, in a cloak in which there were many more black threads than in Jon's. He unsheathed a sword, and began to come forward. "Your reign is through, Daughter of the Sun," he announced. "It is time for a new cycle."

"Very well," said Jon.

As Tltltrlte advanced, the throng that crowded the lobby clapped their hands in terror and moved back further. Jon stood very straight.

As Tltltrlte came forward, his shoulders narrowed. He

pushed back the hood of his cloak and a mass of ebony hair cascaded down his shoulders. With each step, his hips broadened and his waist narrowed. A very definite bulge of mammary glands now pushed up beneath his black silk tunic. As Tltltrlte reached the bottom of the steps, she raised her sword.

Think at him, came Arkor from the bird cage.

Think at him, came from Petra.

Jon saw the blade flash forward and then felt it slide into his abdomen. *At her,* he corrected.

At her, they answered.

As Jon toppled down the steps, dying, he asked, *What the hell is this anyway?*

We're inhabiting a very advanced species of moss, Arkor explained, with the calmness that only a telepath can muster in certain confusing situations. *Each individual starts off male, but eventually changes to female at the desired time.*

Moss? asked Jon as he hit his head on the bottom step and died.

There…

The wave came again and thundered on the beach. He staggered backwards, just as the froth spumed up the sand. The sky was blue-black. He raised his fingers to his lips (seven long tines webbed together) and whined into the night. He lifted his transparent eyelids from his huge, luminous eyes to see if there wasn't some faint trace of the boat. Spray fell on them, stung the rims, and he snapped all three lids over them, one after another. He whined again, and once more the wave grew before him.

He opened the two opaque lids, and this time thought he saw them far off through the greenish spray. The pentagonal sail rode above a billow—blue, wet, and full. It dipped, rose, and he pulled back his transparent eyelid again, this time when the wave was down, and thought he saw figures on the fibrous hammock of the boat. On the blue sail was the white circle of a Master

Fisherman's boat. His parent was a Master Fisherman. Yes, it was his parent coming to get him.

Another billow exploded and he crouched in the froth, digging his hind feet deep into the pebbly beach.

The crosshatch of planking scudded onto the shore, and they swarmed off. One wore a chain around his neck with the Master Fisherman's seal. Another carried a seven-pronged fork. The two others were just boat-hands and wore identifying black belts of Kelpod shells.

"My offspring," said the one with the seal. "My fins have smarted for you. I thought we would never swim together again." He reached down and lifted Jon into his arms. Jon put his head against his parent's chest and watched water beading down the pentagonal scales.

"I was frightened," Jon said.

His parent laughed. "I was frightened too. Why did you swim out so far?"

"I wanted to see the island. But when I was swimming, I saw…"

"What?"

Jon closed his eyelids.

His parent smiled again. "You're sleepy. Come." Now Jon felt himself carried to the water and into the waves. The spray fell warmly on his face now, and unafraid, he relaxed his gill slits as water fell across him and they climbed onto the boat.

Wind caught the sail, and the open-work of planking listed into the sea. Long clouds swung rapidly across the twin moons like the tines of the fishing forks the fisherman saluted the sacred phosphor fires with when they returned from their expeditions. He dreamed of his, a little, in the swell and drop. His parent had tied him to the boat, and so he floated at the end of a few feet of slack. Water rolled down his shoulders, slipped beneath his limp dorsal fin, and tickled. Then he dreamed of something else, the thing he had seen, glowing first beneath the water, then rising… He whined suddenly, and shook his head.

He heard the others on the boat, their webbed feet slipping

on the wet planks. He opened his eyes and looked up. The two boat-hands were holding onto stays and pointing off into the water. Now his parent had come up to them; holding a fishing spear, and they were joined by the Second Fisherman.

Jon scrambled from the water onto the plank. His parent put an arm around him and drew him closer. (*Here he comes*, Arkor said.) His other hand went to the seal of authority around his neck, as though it gave him some sort of protection.

"There it is," Jon suddenly cried. "That's what I saw. That's why I was afraid to swim back." (*There it is*, Jon said.)

A phosphorescent disk was shimmering under the surface of the water. The Second Fisherman raised his spear higher. "What is it?" he asked. (*What is it this time?* Petra wanted to know.)

Indistinct, yet nearly the size of the ship, it hovered almost three breaststrokes from them, glowing beneath the surface.

(*I'll have a look*, said Petra.) The Second Fisherman suddenly dove forward and disappeared. Still holding to the frame of the boat, Jon and his parent went under the water where they could see better.

One of Jon's eyelids, the transparent one, was actually an envelope of tissue which he could flood with vitreous solution when he was submerged to form a correcting lens over his pupil.

Through the water he saw the Second Fisherman bubbling through the water toward the immense, translucent hemisphere that dangled ahead of them. The Second Fisherman stopped with an underwater double-reverse and hovered near the thing. (*It's a huge jellyfish*, Petra told them.) "Can't figure out what it is," the Second Fisherman signaled back. Then he extended his fork and jabbed at the membrane. The seven tines went in, came out.

The jellyfish moved, fast.

The tentacles hanging from the bottom of the bag raveled upward like snagged threads. The body bloated and surged sideways. Two tentacles wrapped around the Second Fisherman as he tried to swim away. (*Eep*, said Petra. *These things hurt.*)

Jon's parent was on top of deck again, shouting orders to the boat-hands. The ship swung toward the thing which was now heaving to the surface.

(*Look, let's finish this thing up for good. Concentrate.* That was Arkor. *There...*)

(From beneath the water they felt Petra reach her mind into the pulsing mass: *There...*)

(As the tentacles encased her and she jammed the spear home again and again through the leaking membrane, she felt Jon's mind join in: *There...*)

The boat rammed into the side of the jellyfish, the planks tearing away the membrane and the thick, stinging insides fountaining over them. Now it nearly turned over, and tentacles flapped from the water in wet, fleshy ropes. The Second Fisherman was caught in one of the snarls.

Their green faces were lighted from beneath by the milky glow.

(*There...*) Suddenly it tore away from the planks, going down beneath the water. (*There...*) The Second Fisherman's head bobbed to the surface, shook the green fin that crested his skull, and laughed. (*There...*)

3 to 6, 3 to 6, (Jon's frequency oscillated from 3 to 6 as he drifted through clouds of super-heated gas) 3 to 6, 3 to 6—7 to 10! (Someone was coming.) U to 10, 7 to 10, (It was getting closer; suddenly:) 10 to 16! (Then:) 3 to 6, 7 to 10, 3 to 6, 7 to 10, (they had passed through each other. *Hi*, Petra said. *Have you any idea where we are?*)

(*The temperature is somewhere near three-quarters of a million degrees. Any ideas?*)

9 to 27, 9 to 27, 9 to 27 (came puttering along and passed through both Jon and Petra;) 12 to 35, 10 to 37, (and then, again) 3 to 6, 7 to 10, 9 to 27, 9 to 27, 9 to 27 (*We are halfway between the surface and the center of a star not unlike our sun*, said Arkor. *Note all the strange elements around.*) 9 to 27, 9 to 27, 9 to

27.

7 to 10, 7 to 10, 7 to 10 (*They keep on turning into one another,* Petra said.) 7 to 10, 7 to 10, 7 to 10.

3 to 6, 3 to 6, 3 to 6 (*At this temperature you would too if you were atomic,* Jon told her.) 3 to 6, 3 to 6, 3 to 6.

9 to 27, 9 to 27, 9 to 27 (*Where's our friend?* Arkor wanted to know.) pi to e, pi to 2e, 2pi to 4e, 4pi to 8e, 8pi to 16e, 16pi to 32e.

(*Speak of the…*Jon started. *Hey, we've got to do something about that. Not only is it transcendental, it's increasing so fast he'll eventually shake this star apart.*) 3 to 6, 3 to 6, 3 to 6.

(*So that's what causes novas,* said Petra.) 7 to 10, 7 to 10, 7 to 10.

(At the next oscillation, Arkor, acting as a side-coefficient, passed through the intruder.) 32^2pi to 64e (Arkor got out before the second extremity was reached. The wave cycle shuttered, having been reversed end on end.) 642pi to 32e (It tried to right itself and couldn't because Jon spun through the lower end divisibility) 642pi to 16/9e (then Arkor jumped in, tail first it recovered and it resolved into:) 642pi to 4/3e, 642pi to 4/3e, 642pi to 4/3e (it quivered, its range no longer geometric)

(*Watch this,* said Petra. *About face…* She gave it a sort of nudge, not passing through it, so that when it whirled to catch her, she was gone, and it was going the other way:)

4/3pi to 642e, 4/3pi to 642e, 4/3pi to 642e.

(*I hope no one ever does that to me,* said Petra. *Look, the poor thing is contracting.*)

4/3 to 640e, 4/3pi to 622, 4/3pi to 560, 4/3pi to 499,

(Somehow the *e* component chanced to slip through 125. Jon moved in like a shower of anti-theta-mazons and extracted a painless cube so fast that the intruder oscillated on it three times before it knew what had happened to it:)

4/3pi to 5^3e, 4/3pi to 5^3e, 4/3pi to 5^3e under high gravity—very high, that is, two to three million times that of earth, such as inside a star—in such warped space there is a subtle difference between 5^3 and 125, though they represent the same number. (It's like the notes E-sharp and F, which are technically the same, but are distinguished between when played by a good violinist with a fine ear. When the root came loose, therefore, the variation threw the wave-length all off balance:) $4/3$pi to 5e, $4/3$pi to 5e, $4/3$pi to 5e...

(All right, everybody, concentrate—
There, there, there...)

For one moment, the intruding oscillation turned, ducked, tried to escape, and couldn't. It contracted into a small ball with a volume of $4/3$pie^3, and disappeared.

There...

Jon Koshar shook his head, staggered forward, and went down on his knees in white sand. He blinked. He looked up. There were two shadows in front of him. Then he saw the city.

It was Telphar, stuck on a desert, under a double sun. The transit ribbon started across the desert, got the length of twelve pylons, and then crumpled.

As he stood up, something caught in the corner of his eye.

His eyes moved, and he saw a woman about twenty feet away from him. Her red hair fell straight to her shoulders in the dry heat. He blinked as she approached. She wore a straight skirt and had a notebook under her arm. "Petra?" he said, frowning. It was Petra, but Petra different.

"Jon," she answered. "What happened to you?"

He looked down at himself. He was wearing a torn, dirty uniform. A prison uniform. His prison uniform!

"Arkor," said Petra, suddenly. (Her voice was higher, less sure.)

They turned. Arkor stood in the sand, his feet wide over the white hillocks. The triple scars down his face welled bright blood in the hot light.

They came together now. What's going on?" Jon asked.

Arkor shrugged.

"What about the kids?" Asked Petra.

"They're still right here," Arkor said, pointing to his head and grinning. Then his finger touched the opened scars. When he drew it away, he saw the blood and frowned. Then he looked at the City. The sun caught on the towers and slipped like bright liquid along the looping highways. "Hey," Jon said to Petra. (Now, he realized; it was Petra with a handful of years lopped off.) "What's the notebook?"

She looked down at it, surprised to find it in her hands. Then she looked at her dress. Suddenly she laughed, and began to flip through the pages of the notebook. "Why, this is the book in which I finished my article on shelter architecture among the forest people. In fact this is what I was wearing the day I finished my article."

"And you?" Jon asked Arkor.

Arkor looked at the blood on his finger. "My mark is bleeding, like the night the priest put it there." He paused. "That was the night that I became Arkor, really. That was the time that I realized how the world was, the confusion, the stupidity, the fear. It was the night I decided to leave the forest." Now he looked up at Jon. "That was the uniform you were wearing when you escaped from prison."

"Yes," said Jon. "I guess it was what I was wearing when I became me, too. That was the time when freedom seemed most bright." He paused. "I was going to find it no matter what. Only somehow I felt I'd gotten sideswiped. I wonder whether I have or not."

"Have you?" asked Petra. She glanced at the City. "I guess when I finished that essay, that's when I really became myself, too. I remember I went through a whole sudden series of revelations about myself, and about society, and about how I felt about society, about being an aristocrat, even, what it meant and what it *didn't* mean. And I suppose that's why I'm here now." She looked at the City again. "There he is," she nodded.

"That's right," said Jon.

They started across the sand, now, making toward the shadow of the ruined transit ribbon. They reached it quicker than they thought, for the horizon was very close. The double shadows, one a bit lighter than the other, lay like two inked brush strokes over the page of the desert. "But how come we're in our own bodies," the Duchess asked, as they reached the shadow of the first pylon. "Shouldn't we be inhabiting the forms of…" Suddenly there was a sound, the shadow moved. Jon looked up at the ribbon above them and cried out.

As the metal tore away, they jumped back, and a moment later a length of the ribbon splashed down into the sand, where they had stood. They were still for a handful of breaths.

"You're darn right he's there," Jon said. "Come on."

They started again. Petra shook white grains from her note-book cover and they moved along the loose sand. A road seeped from under the desert, now, and began to rise toward Telphar. They mounted it and followed it toward the looming city. Before them the towers were dark streaks on the rich blue sky.

"You know, Petra's question is a good one," Arkor said a few minutes later.

"Yeah," said Jon. "I've been thinking about it too. We seem to be in our own bodies, only they're different. Different as our bodies were at the most important moments of our lives. Maybe, somehow, we've come to a planet in some corner of the universe, where three beings almost identical to us, only different in that way, are doing, for some reason we'll never know, almost exactly what we're doing now."

"It's possible," Arkor said. "With all the myriad possibilities of worlds, it's conceivable that one might be like that, or like this."

"Even to the point of talking about talking about it?" asked Petra. She answered herself. "Yes, I guess it could. But saying all this for reasons we don't understand, and saying, 'Saying all this for reasons we don't understand…'" She shuttered. "It's not supposed to be that way. It gives me the creeps."

There was another sound, and they froze. It was the low sound of some structure tumbling, but they couldn't see anything.

Another fifty feet, when the road had risen ten feet off the ground and the first tower was beside them, they heard a cracking noise again. The road swayed beneath them. "Uh-oh," Arkor said.

Then the road fell. They cried out, they scrambled; suddenly there was cracked concrete around them, and they had fallen. Above them was a jagged width of blue sky between the remaining edges of the road.

"My foot's caught," Petra cried out.

Arkor was beside her, tugging on the concrete slab that held her.

"Hold on a second," Jon said. He grabbed a free metal strut that still vibrated in the rubble, and jammed it between the slab and the beam it lay on. Using the wreck of an I-beam for a fulcrum, he pried it up. "There, slip your foot out."

Petra rolled away. "Is the bone broken?" he asked. "I got a friend of mine out of a mine accident that way, once." He let the slab fall again. (And for a moment he stopped, thinking, I knew what to do. I wasn't clumsy, I knew…)

Petra rubbed her ankle. "No," she said. "I just got my ankle wedged in that crevice, and the concrete fell on top." She stood up, now, picking up the notebook. "Ow," she said. "That hurts."

Arkor held her arm. "Can you walk?"

"With difficulty," Petra said, taking another step and clamping her teeth.

"Alter says to stand on your other foot and shake your injured one around to get the circulation back," Arkor told her.

Petra gritted teeth, and stepped again. "A little better," she said. "I'm scared. This really hurts. This may be a body that looks like mine, but it hurts, and it hurts like mine." Suddenly she looked off into the city. "Oh hell," she said. "He's in there. Let's go."

They went forward again, this time under the road. The sidewalks, deserted and graying, slipped past. They passed a shopping section; teeth of broken glass gaped in the frames of store windows. Above, two roads veered and crossed, making a black, extended swastika on a patch of white clouds.

Then a sudden rumbling.

Silence.

They stopped.

Now a crash, thunderous and protracted. An odor of dust reached them. "He's there," Arkor said.

"Yes," said Jon.

"I can..."

Then the City exploded. There was one instant of very real agony for Jon as the pavement beneath his feet shot up at him, and he reached his mind out as a shard of concrete knocked in his face (all the time crying, *No, no, I've just become Jon Koshar, I'm not supposed to*...as a lost Prince had cried out half a year and half a universe away) and at the same time, *There...*

Petra got a chance to see the face of the building beside them rip off a foot before the air blast tore the notebook from her hands, and at the same time she welled her thoughts from behind the bone confines of her skull. *There...*

And Arkor's thoughts (he never saw the explosion because he blinked just then) tore out through his eyelids as fragmented steel tore into them, *There...*

It was cold, it was black. For a moment they saw with a spectrum that reached from the star-wide waves of novas to the micro-micron skittering of neutrinos. And it was black, and completely cold. A rarefied breeze of ionized hydrogen (approximately two particles per cubic rod) floated over half a light year. Once, a herd of pale photons dashed through them from a deflected glare on some dying sun a trillion eons past. Other than that, there was silence, save for the hum of one lone galaxy, eternities away. They hovered, frozen, staring into nothing, above, below, behind, contemplating what they had seen.

Then, the green of beetles' wings, and they flailed into the blood of sensation from the blackness, whirled into red flame the color of polished carbuncle, smoothly through the nerves and into the brain; then, before the blue smoke, burning blue through the lightning seared axion of their corporate organisms, they were snared within the heat and electric imminency of a web of silver fire.

CHAPTER TWELVE

IN THE laboratory tower of Toron, the transparent bubble above the receiving stage brightened. In shimmering haze on the platform, the transparent figures solidified. Then Alter and Tel slipped beneath the rail on the stage and dropped down to the floor (Alter still wore the hospital robe and the cast on her left arm) while Arkor, Jon, and Petra used the metal stairway to descend. A battery of relays snapped somewhere and the scarlet heads of forty-nine switches by the window snapped to off. The globe faded.

"A bit more explanation," Petra was saying. "Hey, kids, keep quiet."

"Well, as far as the Lord of the Flames goes, on Earth anyway, it's more or less trivial and irrelevant," said Arkor. "You're still right. This war is in Toromon, not outside it."

"My curiosity is still peaked," Jon said. "So give."

"From what I gathered while I saw scanning the minds of those two who came out of the generator building with the Lord of the Flames (I should say the host of the Lord of the Flames), there's a tribe behind the barrier which resembles more or less what man might have been forty or fifty thousand years ago. Physically they're squat, thick-boned, and have the elements of a social system. Mentally they're pretty thick and squat too. The Lord of the Flames got into one of them just about when he was at age four. Then he gave the kid about sixty thousand years worth of technical information. So he began building all sorts of goodies, forcing his people to help him, using some equipment from a ruined city that dates from pre-Great Fire times behind the barrier. That's how the generators and the anti-aircraft guns got constructed."

"Our war is still going on," Jon said.

"Well, the Lord of the Flames is no longer with us," said Petra. "We've chased it to the other end of the universe. Now that we've removed what external reason there was for the war, we've got to think about the internal ones."

"What are you going to do immediately about the kids?" Jon asked.

"I think the best thing for them to do is to go off to my estate for a little while," Petra said.

"It's on an island, isn't it?" Tel asked.

"That's right," Petra said.

"Gee, Alter. Now I can teach you how to fish, and we'll be right by the sea."

"What about Uske?" Arkor asked. "You can either walk into his room and interrupt an obscene dream he's having, and present your case and be arrested for treason, or you can leave well enough alone at this point and wait till the opportunity comes to do something constructive."

Suddenly Jon grinned. "Hey, you say he's asleep?" He turned and bounded for the door.

"What are you going to do?" Petra called.

Jon looked at Arkor. "Read my mind," he said.

Then Arkor laughed.

In his bedroom, Uske rolled over through a silken rustle, opened one eye, and thought he heard a sound.

"Hey, stupid," someone whispered.

Uske reached out of bed and pressed the night light. A dim orange glow did not quite fill half the room.

"Now don't get panicky," continued the voice. "You're dreaming."

"Huh?" Uske leaned on one elbow, blinked, and scratched his head with his other hand.

A shadow approached him, then stopped, naked, faceless, transparent, half in and half out of the light. "See," came the voice. "A figment of your imagination."

"Oh, I remember you," Uske said.

"Fine," said the shadow. "Do you know what I've been doing since the last time you saw me?"

"I couldn't be less interested," Uske said, turning over and looking the other way.

"I've been trying to stop the war. Do you believe me?"

"Look, figment, it's three o'clock in the morning. I'll believe it, but what's it to you."

"Just that I think I've succeeded."

"I'll give you two minutes before I pinch myself and wake up." Uske turned back over.

"Look, what do you think is behind the radiation barrier?"

"I think very little about it, figgy. It doesn't have very much to do with me."

"It's a primitive race that can't possibly harm us, especially now that its—its generators have been knocked out. All of its artillery it got from a source that is now defunct. Look, Uske, I'm your guilty conscience. Wouldn't it be fun to really be king for a while and stop the war? You declared war. Now declare peace. Then start examining the country and doing something about it."

"Mother would never hear of it. Neither would Chargill. Besides, all this information is only a dream."

"Exactly, Uske. You're dreaming about what you really want. So how does this sound: make a deal with me as your guilty conscience and representative of yourself; if this dream turns out to be correct, then you declare peace. It's the only logical thing. Come on: stand up for yourself, be a king. You'll go down in history as having started a war. Wouldn't you like to go down as having stopped it too?"

"You don't understand…"

"Yes, I know. A war is a bigger thing that the desires of one man, even if he is a king. But if you get things started on the right foot, you'll have history on your side."

"Your two minutes have been cut down to one; and it's up."

"I'm going; I'm going. But think about it, Uske."

Uske switched off the light and the ghost went out. A few minutes later Jon crawled through the laboratory tower window, buttoning his shirt. Arkor shook his head, smiling. "Well," he said. "Good try. Here's, hoping it does some good."

Jon shrugged.

In the morning, Rara got up early to sweep off the front steps of the inn (windows boarded, kitchen raided, but deserted now save for her; and she had the key); she swept to the left, looking right, then swept to the right, looked left, and said, "Dear Lord, you can't stay there like that. Come on, now. Get on, be on your way."

"Oh, I'm sorry."

"For pity's sake, woman, you can't go around cluttering up the steps of an honest woman's boarding house. We're reopening this week, soon as we get the broken windows repaired. Vandals didn't leave a one, after the old owner died. Just got my license, so it's all legal. Soon as we get the window, so you just move on."

"I just got here, this morning… They didn't tell us where to go, they just turned us off the ship. And it was so dark, and I was tired… I didn't know the City was so big. I'm looking for my son—not so big! We used to be fishermen back on the mainland. I did a little weaving."

"And your son ran off to the City and you ran off after him. Good luck in the New Land; welcome to the island of Opportunity. But just get up and move on."

"But my son…"

"There are more fishermen's sons down here in the Devil's Pot than you can shake a stick at—fishermen's sons, farmers' sons, blacksmiths' sons, sons' sons. And all of their mothers were weavers or water carriers, or chicken raisers. I must have talked to all of them at one time or another. I won't even tell you to go down to the launch where they take the workers out to the aquariums and the hydroponic's gardens. That's what most of the young people do when they get here…if they can get a job. I won't even tell you to go there, because there're so many people that work there, you might miss him a dozen days running."

"But the war—I thought he might have joined…"

"Somewhere in this ridiculous mess," interrupted Rara, her birthmark deepening in color, "I have misplaced a niece who was as close to me as any daughter or son ever was to any mother or father. All reports say that she's dead. So you just be happy that you don't know about yours. You be very happy, do you hear me!"

The woman was standing up now. "You say the launches to the factory? Which way are they?"

"I'm telling you not to go. They're that way, down two streets, and to your left until you hit the docks. Don't go."

"Thank you," the woman was saying, already off down the street. "Thank you." As she reached the middle of the block, someone rounded the corner a moment later, sprinting. He brushed past the woman and ran toward the door of the inn.

"Tel," whispered Rara. "Tel!"

"Hi, Rara." He stopped, panting.

"Well, come in," she said. "Come inside." They stepped into the lobby of the inn. "Tel, do you know anything about what happened to Alter? I got a weird story from General Medical. And then you disappeared. My lord, I feel like a crazy fool opening this place. But if somehow she wanted to get to me, where would she go if I wasn't here? And then, what am I to do anyway. I mean I have to eat, and—"

"Rara," he said, and he said it so that she stopped talking. "Look I know where Alter is. And she's safe. As far as you know, you don't know where she is, if she's alive or dead. But you suspect she isn't alive. I'll be going to her, but you don't know that either. I just came to check on some things."

"I've got all her things together right here. They gave me her clothes at the hospital, and I put them all into a bundle in case we had to make a quick getaway. We had to do that once when we were working in a carnival where the manager suddenly took a liking to her and made himself a pest. She was twelve. He was a beast. Maybe you should take—"

"The fewer things I take the better," Tel said. Then he saw the bundle on the table by the door. On top was a leather thong to which a few chips of colored shell still clung. "Maybe this," he said, picking it up. "What shape is Geryn's room in?"

"The place has been ransacked since they took him away," she said. "Everybody and his brother has been picking at the place. What about Geryn, how is he?"

"Dead," Tel said. "What I really came about was to burn his plans for the kidnapping."

"Dead?" Rara asked. "Well, I'm not surprised. Oh, the plans! Why I burned those myself the minute I got back into his room. They were all over the table; why they didn't take them all up right then, I'll never—"

"Did you burn every last scrap?"

"And crumbled the ashes, and disposed of them one handful at a time over a period of three days by the docks. Every last scrap."

"Then I guess there's nothing for me to do," he said. "You may not see me or Alter for a long time. I'll give her your love."

Rara bent down and kissed him on the cheek. "For Alter," she said. Then she asked, "Tel?"

"What?"

"That woman you brushed by in the street when I saw you running up the block…"

"Yes?"

"Did you ever see her before?"

"I didn't look at her very carefully. I'm not sure. Why?"

"Never mind," Rara said. "You just get on out of here before… Well, just get."

"So long, Rara." He got.

Not so high as the towers of the Royal Palace of Toron, the green tile balcony outside Clea's window caught the breeze like the hem of an emerald woman passing the sea. There was water beyond the other houses, deeper blue than the sky, and still. She leaned over the balcony railing. On the white marble table were her notebook, a book on matter transmission, and her slide rule.

"Clea."

She whirled at the voice, her black hair leaping across her shoulder in the low sun.

"Thanks for getting my message through."

"This is you," she said slowly. "In person now."

"Uh-huh."

"I'm not quite sure what to say," she said, blinking. "Except I'm glad."

"I've got some bad news," he said.

"How do you mean?"

"Very bad news. It'll hurt you."

She looked puzzled, her head going to the side.

"Tomar's dead."

The head straightened, the black eyebrows pulled together, and her lower lip tautened across her teeth until her jaw muscles quivered. She nodded once, quickly, and said, "Yes." Then, as quickly, she looked down and up at him. Her eyes were closed. "That...that hurts so much."

He waited a few moments, and then said, "Here, let me show you something."

"What?"

"Come over to the table. Here." He took a handful of copper centiunit pieces from his pocket, moved her books and slide rule over, and arranged the coins in a square, four by four, only with one corner missing. Now he took a smaller, silver deciunit and put it on the table about a foot from the missing corner. "Shoot it into the gap there," he said.

She put her forefinger on the silver disk, was still, and then snapped her finger. The silver circle shot across the foot of white marble, hit the corner, and two pieces of copper bounced away from the other side of the square. She looked at him, questioningly.

"It's a gambling game, called Randomax. It's getting sort of popular in the army."

"Random for random numbers, max for matrix?"

"You've heard of it?"

"Just guessing."

"Tomar wanted you to know about it. He said you might be interested in some of its aspects."

"Tomar?"

"Just like I monitored your phone calls, I overheard him talking to another soldier about it before he—before the crash. He just thought you'd be interested."

"Oh," she said. She moved the silver circle away from the others, put the dislocated copper coins back in the square again, and flipped the smaller coin once more. Two different coins jumped away. "Damn," Clea said, softly.

"Huh?" He looked up. Tears were running down her face.

"Damn," she said. "It hurts." She blinked and looked up again. "What about you? You still haven't told me all that's happened to you. Wait a moment." She reached for her notebook, took a pencil up, and made a note.

"An idea?" he asked.

"From the game," she told him. "Something I hadn't thought of before."

He smiled. "Does that solve all your problems on—what were they—sub-trigonometric functions?"

"Inverse sub-trigonometric functions," she said. "No. It doesn't go that simply. Did you stop your war?"

"I tried," he said. "It doesn't go that simply."

"Are, you free?"

"Yes.

"I'm glad. How did it come about?"

"I used to be a very hardheaded, head-strong, sort of stupid kid, who was always doing things to get me into more trouble than it would get the people I did it to. That was about my only criterion for doing anything. Unfortunately I didn't do it very well. So now, still headstrong, maybe not quite so stupid, I've at least picked up a little skill. I had to do something where the main point wasn't whether it hurt me or not. They just had to be done. I had to go a long way, see a lot of things, and I guess it sort of widened my horizons, gave me some room to move around—some more freedom."

"Childhood and a prison mine doesn't give you very much, does it?"

"No."

"What about the war, Jon?"

"Let's put it this way. As far as what's on the other side of the radiation barrier, which is pretty much out of commission now, there's no need for a war. None whatsoever. If that gets seen and understood by the people who have to see and understand it, then fine. If not, well then, it isn't that simple. Look, Clea, I just came by for a few minutes. I want to get out of the house before Dad sees me. Keep on talking to him. I'll be disappearing for a while, so you'll have to do it. Just don't bother to tell him I'm alive."

"Jon..."

He smiled. "I mean I want to do it myself when I come back."

She looked down a moment, and when she looked up he was going back into the house. She started to say good-bye, but bit back the words.

Instead, she sat down at the table; she opened the notebook; she cried a little bit. Then she started writing again.

THE END